SO-AXX-035

The Chippendale Factor

The Chippendale Factor

JOHN MALCOLM

First published in Great Britain in 2008 by
Allison & Busby Limited
13 Charlotte Mews
London W1T 4EJ
www.allisonandbusby.com

Copyright © 2008 by JOHN MALCOLM

The moral right of the author has been asserted.

A CIP catalogue record for this book is available from
the British Library.

10 9 8 7 6 5 4 3 2 1

13-ISBN 978-0-7490-7950-5

Typeset in 11/16 pt Sabon by Joseph Brown

Printed and bound in Great Britain by
MPG Books Ltd, Bodmin, Cornwall

JOHN MALCOLM is the author of sixteen crime novels, including the Tim Simpson mysteries, as well as a number of reference books on antique furniture, written under the John Andrews authorship. He is managing editor of *Antique Collecting* magazine and was Chairman of the Crime Writers' Association in 1994–5. He originally comes from Manchester but spent part of his boyhood in Uruguay before returning to England. He and his wife live in Sussex.

Chapter One

Spikey Yelland used to be a punk, with pinned clothes and hair like a sparsely prickled porcupine, but all that was gone now. His head was fashionably close-cropped. He dressed better than most runners, occasionally wore a tie or sported a tweed jacket and cords not unlike some of mine, sometimes wore creaky old leather shoes. One day he was going to have his own shop. Or be big at fairs. He'd be a silver specialist. Quite a few of today's respectable, plummy-spoken dealers started like him. You'd be surprised. The hawking of gear from shop to shop could rub big knowledge off on runners if they were sharp. Silver was supposed to be in the doldrums but Spikey seemed to manage.

I was packing up some creamware Ellen Stanton had admired when the doorbell rang and he burst into the shop.

For a moment I thought he was going to dig a special treasure out of his big coat pocket. He did a good line in small, silver, elephant- and pig-shaped pincushions with date-marks around 1910, Art Deco inkwells, tinkling clocks, toast racks and mustard pots, things like that. I usually bought them on the spot. You have to have small things – smalls, as the trade call them – for your bread and butter. For cash, if possible.

But he didn't produce anything except a newspaper, *The Times* in tabloid it was, and he brandished it.

'Seen the news about Justin Harrington?' he demanded, a bit out of breath.

'News? Justin Harrington? What news?'

'Dead. He's bloody dead, Bill. Didn't listen to the radio this morning so I saw it when I opened my paper in Stanley's. Gave me quite a turn.'

Spikey had a habit of taking a break in Stanley's Café near Godstone around nine-thirty in the morning. Coffee and a sausage roll. You could always tell when he'd been there because small flakes of pastry adhered to his frontage. They did now.

I put down the creamware jug I was holding, slowly, hearing crinkling movements from its bubble wrap.

'Dead?'

'Sounds like suicide. They found his car near a flooded quarry in Yorkshire.'

'Yorkshire?'

'A quarry. Or a flooded sand pit. Or gravel. Middle of nowhere, anyway. The implication is that he jumped in. The body was recovered the day before yesterday. Here, read for yourself.'

Spikey handed over his crumpled copy of *The Times* with a suppressed air of triumph. I took it off him. My own copy was still in the kitchen, unread, patiently waiting for me to brew coffee. I don't watch breakfast TV.

'Seems like the car had been there for a day or two. Someone local phoned the fuzz. Not often that folks leave a swish BMW estate around on its lonely ownsome in those parts.'

'Good God.'

'I wonder what it was about. Maybe the quacks gave him the old hopeless red light. You never know. Bit overweight, wasn't he? Last time I saw him on the box he looked puffy to me.'

'Good God.'

'Shock, ain't it? It happened two days ago, they reckon. His wife was somewhere on holiday. The Continent. They had to find her before publishing the news, I suppose.'

'Elizabeth? Away, was she?'

Spikey put on a look of surprise. 'Didn't know you knew the Harringtons, Bill. Not your sort, I'd have thought. Flash bugger: I did that programme for him just once, then he dropped me like a stone. Used a cheap girl researcher from then on. Typical of TV. We're all bodies under a juggernaut for them. He wasn't exactly the trade's favourite person, was he? Owed a lot of favours. All that pontificating. Those duff knowing tips about all sorts of gear. And the prices! I should get so lucky. Fancied himself as a sort of sharp Arthur Negus, didn't he, with a bit of Dickinson thrown in?'

'No,' I said, 'not Dickinson. And certainly not Arthur Negus. He was much too long ago.'

'Maybe not. Tailored by Connock and Lockie, though, wasn't he? Best cutters in London. Very smart. The books were mostly rubbish. All tips and tits. Chinese meal principle. And he still traded all over. Through "associates" as he called them. Very dodgy.'

I smiled at the tailoring talk. It was one of Spikey's enthusiasms. I'm not sure when he abandoned the *Daily Mirror* in favour of *The Times* but it was probably not long after the punk spikes were cropped off. Both events raised eyebrows at Stanley's. Spikey was once a roadie with a punk rock band and had a reputation for smashing up pirate tape recorders along with their owners. Hard to imagine now but, as Justin used to say, ex-mistresses make the most moral pillars of society.

I left the creamware in its cardboard box and moved to the shop window, watching a lorry go by on its way into Westerham and on towards Redhill. Justin Harrington was dead. Good grief. Justin Harrington was dead, taking Baz Stevens with him. Which part of his rolling kaleidoscope could have caught up with him, I wondered, which bit of his complex, evasive but entertaining performance came round too fast? The numb sensation that a close death brings came back to me, deadening my hearing like a damp blanket.

'Is life a boon?' I could hear him quoting, his Gilbertian sense of humour still holding out. 'If so, it must befall, that Death, whene'er he call, must call too soon.'

Well, Death had called. Much too soon.

A voice broke through my muffled senses.

'Did you know Harrington and his wife quite well, then, Bill?'

Spikey Yelland was good at small silver but had no conversational finesse, never had.

I pulled myself together just for a moment.

'Oh yes,' I said. 'I knew both of them. Quite well.'

Chapter Two

Spikey had not long left on his cheerfully morbid run to spread the news to the trade and chat about it when the telephone rang. I picked it up, still feeling numb, starting to consider what had happened. There was a void like a lost tooth before the anaesthetic wears off.

'Mr Franklin?' An efficient, secretarial voice came down the line.

'Yes?'

'Leggatt's Finance here. I have Tony Fitzsimmonds for you.'

'Oh?'

Surprise, surprise: I hadn't heard from Tony Fitzsimmonds for a long time.

A slight pause, then the well-spoken tones I remembered came down the line. Tony usually avoided any hearty mock-Irishness despite occasional Gallic constructions; he emulated the guise of a cool, educated City man rather than a Dublin entrepreneur.

'Bill? Tony here. How are you?'

I produced a mental vision of him: in his City office, chalk-stripe or charcoal jacket hung up to reveal waistcoat and shirtsleeves, broad green braces prominent, at his big desk with view towards the Thames from the glazed wall down one side. A large painting of a shiny brown horse on an inner wall. A secretary or colleague across the desk from him, knee and ear cocked.

'I'm well, thank you, Tony. You?'

'Pretty good. But this is sad news we're reading today.'

'About Justin, you mean. Yes, I'm afraid so.'

De mortuis nil nisi bonum is the line to take on these occasions. Better safe than sorry.

'You knew him very well, didn't you?'

'Yes I did. I'm afraid I hadn't seen too much of him lately, though.'

'Had you not? Well, he was a busy man of course. The TV programme was wildly successful.'

'It was indeed.' Was I being too noncommittal? Should more regret tinge my tones?

'Bill, we were very grateful to you for your help over that Blackham Leasing proposal and the inherent fraud.'

'My pleasure, Tony. Señor Carrasco was a shocker.'

Long ago, I used to be in the machinery business, with Latin America a speciality. Some five years earlier, through Justin, I had been asked to look at some invoices submitted by an egregious scoundrel who called himself Carrasco. The fact that he had chosen Montevideo's airport name, as an Englishman might call himself Heathrow or Gatwick, did not inspire confidence. He was expecting Blackham, a leasing subsidiary of Leggatt's, to advance him a vast sum for a moribund production line whose invoice description was a load of creative invention.

'But you've now been in the antiques business for a few years?'

'I have, Tony. I decided to stop circling the world.'

'How's it going?'

'Very well, thanks.'

'I seem to remember you were a whizz on Arts and Crafts? According to Justin.'

'One of my many talents, yes, Tony.'

'Never be modest with a City man, Justin used to say. They bray, most of them. It's what they understand. Always bray if you don't want to be a bit suspect. Or condescended to.'

He chuckled. 'I'm sure. What about mid-Georgian mahogany?'

'Not a very hot topic these days, Tony. But I have done quite a bit on it in my time.'

'The market's quiet, sure, Bill. Which means there may be opportunities.'

'As always, fortune favours the brave. And the top-quality stuff always does well.'

'Well spoken. Look, this very sad and unfortunate demise has come at a very awkward time for us. Justin was advising us on matters that need to be concluded soon.'

'Oh dear.'

'Yes, Bill. I wondered if there might be scope for you to help us in his place? Might you be interested?'

No, my first thought shot into my head, no, no. City bloodsucking is not for me. But tides were obviously turning and curiosity prevailed. Trade wasn't booming. I temporised.

'I'm flattered, Tony. What sort of thing had you in mind?'

'If you're interested, perhaps we could meet for lunch? Discuss it then.'

Lunch, I thought weakly. No one has offered me a business lunch in years. No harm in finding out what he wants. Evidently something not to be discussed on the phone.

'That sounds very nice.'

'Good. Great. Time is of the essence. Tomorrow?'

My God, I thought, this is a bit quick.

'Yes,' I answered.

He named a restaurant in the West End, which was a relief. To me, the City is a place where they make money, not lunch. The West End is where they spend it. I agreed.

There was another pause. Then, just a bit too casually, he said, 'You and Justin went quite a long way back, didn't you?'

'Yes,' I answered, because it was the easiest answer, 'quite a long way.'

For some reason, this seemed to satisfy him.

'See you tomorrow, then,' he said.

'See you tomorrow, Tony,' I replied. And I remember thinking straight away: now what did I do that for?

I went back to the cardboard box and finished wrapping the creamware carefully, almost in automatic mode. I still wasn't sure whether I now felt numb or stimulated. It was as though I'd developed a temperature and gone slightly deaf at the same time.

Leaving the packing, I went into the kitchen and looked at the paper. It wasn't front page news, but it wasn't far inside. *TV Presenter Found Dead* went the headline. Then there was a simple report to say that Justin Harrington of the TV antiques programmes had been found dead near a flooded gravel pit or quarry near a village on the Ouse to the north-west of York. He was alone and police were investigating. His wife, who had been away on the Continent, had returned but was too upset to speak to reporters. It was not clear what he was doing in the area nor whether the circumstances were suspicious. Condolences were pouring in from many fans of his programme. An executive of the TV company made a cautious statement. There was a picture of him.

'Die? It's the last thing I shall do.'

Suicide seemed so unlikely. I shook my head as I picked up a roll of packing tape and returned to the shop to finish off the cardboard box. Baz Stevens: Justin Harrington. How did he really manage it? Start as one person and end up as another? Cope with a change of name? Become somebody else? Was that what had got him in the end? Life as a palimpsest, one story written over another, obliterating the original?

The thought was silly. I had known Baz a lot better than that. Too well, in fact. Change name? I knew when and why he said he did it. Lots of people do it. Women do it all the time. They cope with it easily. A Mary Smith can become Mary Farquarson on marriage, get used to it and then, if Farquarson goes up the spout or gets the chop, become Mary Morelli or Mary Peterson-Hendriksson. Or go back to being Mary Smith. No one thinks twice about it. They – women – change personalities frequently. They put on a new persona in the morning, decide to act a different part, make up as villain or victim depending on the day to come. They dye their hair, alter their shape, put on a different camouflage. What they see in the mirror today may bear no relation to what they saw yesterday. Roll on stockings or tights and your legs are different. Roll on fishnets with a suspender belt and you're a vamp with that inviting naked bit between stocking top and knickers. Clamp on a long straight covering and you're a frigid schoolmarm. It's a perpetual stage performance.

Baz Stevens was like that, once he became Justin Harrington. His clothes were a careful statement. There was a feline streak to him. There often is in compulsive womanisers. Something empathetic, something women recognise. In his case, it wasn't marriage that pushed the change. It was more powerful: a family rejection combined with a practice to deceive.

What's in a name, anyway? So many names are recent inventions, a move from one pigeon-hole to another. It's not difficult. Many people change the label on life's suitcase. Immigrants, escapees, inheritors, aspirants. Those marrying into better families than their own, criminals, politicians.

Men in show business do it all the time. Actors. Authors. Playwrights. Television presenters.

Ah yes, television presenters.

Baz Stevens: Justin Harrington.

Reality: appearance.

He was Basil, really, but no one at school called him that. Just Baz. Or Stevens. Not such a bad name but evidently not one suited to his selected path. He chose the new combination with care. Astounding, really, that something so fundamental can be so ephemeral.

Harrington: it sounded old, long-term English, possibly even slightly aristocratic. The sort of name immigrant Americans would go for. He said it was from cousins on his mother's side. Most likely an invention, a lie amongst many lies.

Justin: softer, upper-echelon, even artistic. If you were from Yorkshire, it might seem soft. Just in; a new innings, a new beginning. The day he set foot back in England after his disastrous time in Lille.

That had all come long before the public persona. It was part of a deliberate escape, a shedding of skin, like a snake. Or like one of those pond-originated insects: a dragonfly that leaves a transparent version of itself hanging from a sticky reed as its solidity departs. It flies off over the teeming watery surface, wings humming, eyes bulging, thorax curved as though about to sting, away to dry land and flowers. It leaves the reed and the empty skin-shaped version behind in the belief that time and weather will make them disappear. Only the denizens of the pond remember the previous form the departed took.

The newspaper mentioned a village on the Ouse to the north-west of York?

'Ousedon Overwood Hall,' I remember him trumpeting. Something about the name made him resonate. 'Deserted in the early Thirties. The Slump. Bulldozed in the Forties. A council house estate built on the site. Who knows what happened to its Chippendale furniture?'

'If it had any.'

'It had some all right. Probably shipped to America and lost for ever.'

'No documentary evidence is there, though? Just local stories.'

He'd pull a face at that. He published a book on vanished country houses and always seemed to have a copy nearby. The lost gardens at Grimston and similar tales inspired a nostalgia in him. He saw nothing inconsistent in the way he mocked it in other people.

Then there was the burning ambition to hoodwink experts. Like the painter Tom Keating, it wasn't the money; it was a form of rebellion.

'The Royston Room. A model for us all to follow. There never was a Royston Hall. Read Cescinsky's *Gentle Art of Faking Furniture*, Bill. Reader, do not thou likewise.'

I put down the tape. While I was thinking, mind far away, I'd done with the creamware. Thoughts dominated actions.

My stock of antiques watched me, waiting for developments.

Chapter Three

Later on, bubble wrap neatly taped, I left the shop and went round to Crockham Hill.

'Steve's in the garage,' Ellen said, giving me a knowing look from the front doorway before she pecked my cheek. 'Home for a few days' holiday.' She nodded at the carton that was separating us. 'You can leave that pottery in the kitchen if you like.'

'Thanks.'

I carried the cardboard box of creamware carefully past the polished mahogany hall table. You wouldn't want to scratch the immaculate surface of a reeded leg, Regency card table in the manner of Gillows if you could help it, not under the eye of Ellen Stanton. Her pink sweatshirt top and dark blue trousers were spotless. She'd taken care about her appearance that morning; she must be going out.

She still swelled in the right places.

'How did your trip go?' I asked.

'Leeds is still Leeds,' she answered. 'For two whole days. But I saw Steve's tutor, which was good. Steve is a real problem right now. He's not working.'

'Have you heard about Justin Harrington?'

'Yes,' said Ellen. 'I've heard.'

I followed her into the wider part of the hall with its green japanned longcase clock by Kipling, then down the passage at the side of the wide, balustraded staircase. This half-panelled passage led to the back of the house and into what were once the servants' working spaces. The kitchen had a long French farmhouse table made of fruitwood in the centre and I put the box down on that, swerving to avoid the hooped back of one of six yew-wood Yorkshire Windsor chairs ranged around it.

The table and chairs came from me, too. The late Fred Stanton paid for those.

'A quarry in some unknown bit of Yorkshire,' Ellen said. 'I can't think why he went there to do it.'

'Extraordinary. But that's where he came from, originally.'

'We'll find out why in due course. I'm sure it'll all come out.'

'It?'

'Yes.' Her face clouded. 'I imagine there'll be a lot of it, Bill.' Her mouth crooked slightly at one corner as she gave me a straight stare, then it flickered into a knowing smile, like a Buenos Aires society hostess hearing mention of a scandal.

'I thought perhaps he might have been ill.'

Now she put on a blank look. 'I suppose he might have. And done himself in for that reason, you think?'

'It's a possibility.'

'Doesn't sound like Justin Harrington to me.' She looked aside and gestured at the box. 'I did pay you for this, didn't I?'

'Oh yes, thank you, ma'am.'

'As I say, Steve's in the garage. Rocker box trouble again, he says.' She rolled her eyes upward in an expression of amused intolerance. 'That and noisy camshaft gears or something.

Just like his father. The trips around Leeds were one long rattle to me.'

'I'll go and see him. How is he?'

'Fine, I think. We haven't talked about things properly yet. His future, I mean. The college think that he's taking a long time to grow up. It's a problem.' She picked up a bag. 'I'm off to Waitrose. Will you talk to him?'

'Sure. But I can't stay long.'

She nodded and walked briskly past me back to the hall. Smart figure, still a good shape. Her new Mini Cooper was parked outside and she didn't look back. There wasn't a chance to get a remark in sideways, not while she was feigning indifference. And she was worried about Steve.

Quite apart from our own complications, she knew that I knew. Always did. Amongst many other things. She told me herself, probably because she knew that I knew anyway. Hence the knowing smile.

I walked round the farm table, past the Aga and out via the scullery door into what was once a stable yard. Across its paved surface the double doors of a coach house were open and a small pre-war Riley saloon warmed its chrome radiator in the rising morning sun. The centrally hinged bonnet had one louvred side folded back and a young man in shirtsleeves was stooping with his head close to the revealed engine. He leant over the black mudguard in a supple curve.

'Morning, Steve.'

The young man straightened up and smiled at me. 'Bill! Hi. Just the chap.'

'I've put your mother's creamware on the kitchen table.'

'Good. Just look at the oil coming out of these bloody rocker boxes.'

He had taken off the nearer of the two aluminium rocker boxes that covered the engine's overhead camshafts. Working mechanisms with coiled springs were revealed. I peered at the result. In the centre space between the rocker boxes the four sparking plug sockets were filled with little pools of dark oil. A smell of warm lubricant and hot metal pricked my nostrils.

'The bloody gaskets never seal properly. If you tighten the rocker boxes down too hard you strip the thread on the long studs. Or snap something else. It pisses me off.'

'It's a marvellous little engine, though.'

'Course it is. But it has its foibles. Camshaft drive gears are bloody noisy. In the Fifties they put Tufnol phenolic resin gears in to cut down the racket. Just as you told me. Amongst other things. But Freddy Dixon used to do wonders with Riley engines.'

I knew all this and Steve Stanton knew I knew it, but it was all part of a Riley man's automatic patter. It was pleasant to have something in common with Ellen's son. But Steve was distrait this morning; his light brown hair was unusually rumpled.

'Heard about Harrington?' I asked.

'Yes. Mother told me. Read it out from the newspaper at breakfast. Very fishy. Definitely rum.'

'There was a suggestion he might have been ill.'

He looked at me sharply. 'Suggestion? Who from? Funny way to top yourself if you're frightened of dying of cancer or something. Jump into a quarry? It'd be an exhaust pipe job for me. Can you see Judicious Justin jumping into a quarry rather than onto a sympathetic nurse? I can't.'

'It doesn't seem his style, I agree.'

'Course it doesn't. Why there? That bit of Yorkshire? And by the way, if you read your paper carefully, it doesn't say they found him in the water. It says that "his body was recovered". Might have been in the car – that's more the way to go, bit of hose from the exhaust – but it doesn't say that, either. Very canny. Police are keeping their blue serge cards close to their blue serge chests.'

Like his late father, Steve Stanton always liked mysteries and conspiracies. Life's blood to old Fred, razor instincts honed in all those boardroom battles he'd made his money from before he got tired and retired, then a stroke shook him up, then one tragic day his heart stopped. Leaving Steve bereft.

'I – I suppose I naturally assumed—'

'So did Mother, until she thought about it. She knew what he was like. Women always saw through that man.'

'True.' No they didn't, I thought, as I replied automatically, a lot of them didn't. Your mother certainly took her long and pleasant time to see through him if it wasn't straight away.

'Mother's gone shopping, I suppose.' Steve Stanton interrupted my thoughts as he wiped his hands on a rag. 'We'll have to make our own coffee. Let's go and see that creamware, Bill. Leeds, is it?'

'Probably,' I answered. 'They made a lot of it.'

'How appropriate.'

I smiled at him. He had all sorts of enthusiasms, taken from both parents, and he was doing business studies at Leeds, or was supposed to be.

'Fine,' I said. 'Let's have coffee while I tell you about Leeds creamware.'

His eyes fixed on mine. 'You haven't bought a Riley yet?'

'No, I haven't.'

'You should. You know your Rileys. Although you'd probably upstage me by getting a Kestrel Sprite.' He grinned as he gestured at his father's Kestrel Nine. 'Turn your nose up at one of these.'

I never quite understood why Fred Stanton, who had money, spent so much time reconstructing the motoring past in the form of a car which, for all its charm, was a lesser version of a more famous one. There was something endearing, something doggedly quixotic about it, which appealed to me. A love of underdogs, perhaps. Everyone has their oddities and Fred had passed his on to his son. The lad seemed almost more enthusiastic about it than his father. All over the country, people were reconstructing the past in an idealised, perfected form, using modern technology in order to recreate an illusion. Like Morgan cars, for instance. Most car freaks chose outstanding objects, icons of pride like Jags or Astons, and made efforts to improve them as though the past was somehow perfectible.

'Emotional shell shock,' Baz-Justin would say. 'The whole country's terrified of looking ahead. So much safer to reconstruct an idealised past whilst clinging to its own apron strings. Utterly atavistic.'

'So much for the antiques trade, then,' I once answered. 'Or programmes about it. Not living off the past?'

He bared his teeth back at me.

Steve seemed content to continue his father's nostalgic game in minor key. Why? Just parental loyalty, when he could have replaced it with something new of his own? Was it an heirloom, to be passed on perpetually with the family silver? At times it must have been emotionally painful for Steve to get in that car.

'I can't afford a Kestrel Sprite,' I answered defensively to his waiting expression. 'And right now, I haven't time, anyway.'

'Nonsense. You need a Riley, you do. Even if it isn't a Sprite.'
Young Steve Stanton gave me a penetrating look. 'You should
get one. A Nine, like me. Or another Falcon Twelve, like you
once had.' He grinned. 'That or another wife. Or maybe that
and a wife.' He turned his look to cautious, in case he had
gone too far with someone his senior. 'You need a wife.' Then
he grinned again disarmingly. 'An old Riley would be cheaper,
though. And much less hassle.'

Chapter Four

The next day, on the train going up to London, I saw that *The Times* had courageously ventured an obituary under a showbiz photograph:

Justin Harrington
Chartered Accountant who turned publisher,
antiques expert and broadcaster

Justin Harrington, who has been found dead in mysterious circumstances, was an accomplished and engaging man of the world whose abilities enabled him to follow more than one profession. He combined wide connoisseurship with forthright personality, leaving a promising career as an accountant and management consultant to become a publisher specialising in art and antique reference books before embarking on yet another career as a television presenter. A fellow broadcaster described him as deeply iconoclastic and highly original, having a talent for humour combined with biting irony. His programme, How Old Is It? *had a wide following.*

Justin Basil Harrington was born Basil Stevens in Leeds, Yorkshire, in 1940. He was educated as a boarder at the Midland School, his mother having died when he was young. His father, Ralph Stevens, travelled widely in the wool textile business but settled in Lille with a new French wife after a business failure. A brief try at life in Lille sparked his son's change of name to Harrington, relatives on his late mother's side, and a return to England to take articles with a London firm of accountants. He was soon involved in management consultancy, which had passed through its early stages and was expanding rapidly. His assignments took him all over the country.

I sat back for a moment, looking out of the train window at the passing suburbs. Management consultancy?

This department, he wrote in his first report, on a public utility's administration, is managed by three people. A spastic, a lunatic and an alcoholic.

That was how he always was. Rebarbative. A journalist and publisher, seeking the bubble reputation with a cannon mouth. But at the time I met him, or rather re-met him one Sunday morning in Vallance Road, he was a management consultant, as his obituary stated, working for a firm of chartered accountants and auditors. Being the Justin he had become, he belonged to its consultancy branch rather than anything to do with balance sheets. This was an activity into which the firm placed its mavericks, ex-army officers and Aussie con men, those who could strut the swagger and bray the jargon. They could also, in Justin's case, moonlight extensively.

Even in those days, before political correctness blunted the cutting edge of our abundantly irreverent language, his superiors required his first fractious analysis to be rewritten. He was sent for his next assignment to a northern factory producing sanitary fireclay products – urinals, to be precise – where his natural iconoclasm and Yorkshire irony could be given full sway.

'Marcel Duchamp would have loved it here,' he told me on the phone. 'We make urinals by the thousand. Invert them and you have modern art in mass production.'

I went back to the obituary:

He had always been an avid collector, starting with stamps, coins and records. During this time, however, he became a connoisseur of antiques, with a particular interest in walnut furniture of the late seventeenth and early eighteenth century before moving on to mid-eighteenth century Georgian mahogany of the heyday of Chippendale and Hepplewhite.

Observing that the antiques subjects which interested him were poorly covered in the books then available, in 1970 he set up the publishing firm of Harrington and Beckland together with Celia Beckland, who he had met on one of his assignments in the publishing industry. She provided the editorial and publishing knowledge to supplement his flair for commissioning and promoting original titles, which broke new ground in their field. The firm also reprinted facsimile editions of the works of Chippendale, Hepplewhite, Sheraton and the designers of the nineteenth century. Their partnership was successful and though not large, the firm is still acknowledged as a leader in the specialised field of art and antiques reference.

In 1990 a chance conversation at dinner with the television producer Rupert Barford led him to make a proposal for a new programme dealing with antiques. Harrington felt that existing coverage had become stereotyped and that a more analytical and challenging approach would cast an original light on this very wide subject. The programme How Old Is It? *became established rapidly and Harrington's ebullient style, in which no respect was shown to pieces he deplored, soon attracted a wide following. His pungently expressed opinions gave rise to offence in some quarters but he was unrepentant, saying that it was the duty of his kind of journalism to question accepted tastes. The opening shot of the first programme was marked by his dramatic quotation from Frank Arnau:* 'During his lifetime, the French painter Corot produced two thousand paintings. Of these, five thousand are in the United States of America.' *To audiences used to the rather hushed reverence with which many antiques were presented, his scepticism was refreshing. Quotations such as* 'To satisfy the present demand for antique furniture with antique furniture is beyond the bounds of possibility' *earned him few friends in the trade, but he often acted as a consultant on authenticity. He was working on a new programme at the time of his death.*

He was an enthusiastic bon viveur, fond of good food and wine, and was in demand on several television programmes dealing with the pleasures of cellar and table. Always impeccably dressed, his presence added a colourful cachet to such programmes even if their presenters might find his views alarmingly controversial. He did not suffer fools gladly.

He married Elizabeth Williams of Muswell Hill, London in 1965, with whom he had one son, Robert in 1966 and a daughter Rosalind in 1970. They survive him.

Not bad, I suppose. A bit dry and concise, perhaps. Not a full page by any means. He would be miffed that it wasn't nearly as long as, say, the gentleman-dealer Alistair Sampson's but then Justin had a dodgy relationship with what you might call the Establishment. I liked the euphemisms. The so-called stamp collecting and the disaster at Lille, for instance. He told me, one long wine-fuelled evening, that the Lille wife had been his father's mistress for years, was the reason why his mother died. Like father, like son: he had a long affair with Celia Beckland, of course. She left her job to set up the publishing firm with him. Theirs wouldn't be the only publishing venture created so that two people could screw each other. 'Man of the world' is of course code for a womaniser in the same way that 'Did not suffer fools gladly' is generally code for a rude bastard. At least they didn't say 'he did not wear his heart on his sleeve', which is code for a cold-hearted swine. Justin wore his heart on his sleeve all too well.

The quotations or adaptations from Frank Arnau's book *3000 Years of Deception in Art and Antiques* were a bit hoary but most of Justin's own would have been unprintable.

Like most obituaries it was pretty tactful.

It's what's left out that matters.

The London restaurant was modern but not sparse. It had the regulation polished board floor of fashion but at least the chairs looked more comfortable than those Arne Jacobsen 'Ant' style things so favoured at present. I wasn't grumbling; I hadn't been up to London for a buckshee lunch for a long time. A life of solitary trading doesn't present them very often. Although generally I agree with what Ronald Reagan said about free lunches – there ain't no such thing.

'Bill.' Tony Fitzsimmonds rose from behind the table that he must have occupied a few minutes before I arrived. 'It's good to see you.' He held out his hand and we shook. 'You're looking well.'

Someone observed long ago that once you pass a certain age, people do not ask you how you are any more. They observe that you're looking well, as though this is exceptional, if not just surprising.

Tony Fitzsimmonds was looking pretty well himself even though his characteristically thick Irish hair was nearly white. It wasn't an old white though, more a vigorous white, as though it should be white, had been blancoed, or bleached by an expensive process, rather than what it once was. Below the hair his face had a clean tanned colour, the sort of costly hue that is obtained by exposure to golf courses and horse races. He was impeccably dressed in financial charcoal, with a striped shirt and silk tie. Sitting at the same table was another man in sober, subfusc financial raiment, who rose deferentially after Fitzsimmonds waved towards him.

'Bill, I hope you don't mind, I asked Jim Macallister to join us. Jim, this is Bill Franklin. Bill, Jim Macallister. Jim has been working with Justin Harrington on the structure of potential projects we hope to finalise very soon.'

I shook hands with Macallister, who was a studious-looking bespectacled man I put down almost immediately as an accountant. Men like Tony Fitzsimmonds always have a number cruncher on hand to pour cold water on the fervid presentations of those hoping to extract money from them. Macallister, after one had taken in the rather prominent spectacles, was a wiry sort of man who might be a squash or tennis player when not sitting in front of a glowing spreadsheet.

We ordered lunch, which included a bottle of wine, and Tony Fitzsimmonds smiled at me as we sat back after the decision making. 'I've told Jim how you saved us from a disaster over Señor Carrasco,' he said.

I shrugged modestly. 'It wasn't too difficult if you knew the equipment involved.'

'He got three years for attempted fraud,' Tony Fitzsimmonds said, with grim satisfaction, 'but I expect he was out in less than half of that.'

'Very likely.'

Macallister looked at me curiously. 'But now you're an antiques dealer?' he queried.

'I am.'

'I'm told that times are tough at present.'

'They are, if you're trying to stay in the middle or lower end of the market. That's in severe doldrums. The top end is demanding but business is still there to be had.'

They exchanged glances, ones that seemed positive. Fitzsimmonds approved the wine after one sip and spoke carefully. 'We were talking to Justin about an investment project, a fund a bit like some of those proposed in America, with pretty big sums going into art and antiques for a medium-term return.'

'The American ones are about art rather than antiques.'

'I know. Justin was clear about that, too.'

'Was he going to advise you on content?'

'He was, along with a few other experts. In limited fields. From the project's point of view he could provide a high profile as front man.' Tony Fitzsimmonds smiled slightly. 'His name was well known in view of the TV.'

Whereas mine isn't, I thought, but waited. There was a convenient break while our first courses were served. When in doubt, say nothing. Then bray.

'We were working on a suitable strategy with him.' Jim Macallister took up the story. 'There are not many examples for comparison, are there?'

'The British Rail Pension Fund is the classic case always cited,' I answered.

'But recently doubts have been expressed about the success of that.'

'Not by the people who ran it.' It was time to start braying. 'There was a letter in the ATG recently refuting some poor report on the Fund and saying that its blend of art and antiques made £170 million from an investment of £40 million.'

'ATG?'

'The *Antiques Trade Gazette*.'

'Ah. But the rate of return wasn't so great, was it?'

'They started in 1974 and earned eleven per cent a year over the investment period, beating inflation by about four per cent. One analyst – James Goodwin – has pointed out that if they'd waited another five years before selling off the bulk of the collection they might have got a twenty per cent return. As in the theatre, timing is everything.'

Tony Fitzsimmonds smiled. 'As in the theatre and the Stock Exchange? You've obviously studied the case.'

'I have.'

He looked at me directly. 'Would you be interested in advising us about our project?'

I put down my fork. 'This is an investment project on art and antiques, is it?'

'It is.'

'What would you want me to do?'

'Bring your knowledge to bear on the content and your proven intuition about fraud to shield us from chisellers. I'm sure I don't have to tell you how prone this field is to deception. It could be good fun as well as challenging. Interested?'

'I'm interested.'

'Wonderful. In that case, rather than embarrass you here at table, I'll send you a proposed contractual agreement. I think you'll find our fees generous but you'll decide for yourself. I won't say more until you've signed the agreement because confidentiality is a key part of it. I've no doubt that you are the soul of discretion but we have to have our confidentiality clause signed and sealed before we can reveal much more to you.'

'Fair enough.'

'That's splendid. I wish all my lunches were as positive as this. Let's enjoy the rest of it. Call it a memorial lunch to Justin, who liked a good lunch. And who was perceptive enough to introduce you to us.' He suddenly looked thoughtful. 'Maybe you can tell us about a side of Justin we don't know. I first met him at a book launch. How about you?'

Chapter Five

My old photographs bring on a detachment that disconcerts me. I am reminded of men who talk about themselves in the third person; something a doctor might describe as a form of schizophrenia. Perhaps mine is a visual version of the malady. Even the name I recall, for the early ones, belongs to a remote arrangement. William Franklin Gonzalez is the full Spanish-matronymic mode set out on my birth certificate, but he has long gone. I do not think of him now. I am simply Bill Franklin.

Old images only distract me.

Mine are kept in an ancient school trunk floored in the spare bedroom. They picture a scatter of locations and the foreign years that have promoted my separation. It is a battered trunk, scarred by time, and its contents could be part of an auction lot at a country sale, acquired almost accidentally. But they are mine. They lie dormant, withholding their emotional bite until the odd moment of exposure. Being brought up conventionally, I worry about pillars of salt, so mostly they stay undisturbed.

But every now and then, at the risk of petrifaction, I get them out.

Packs of old photographs fill the trunk's neglected interior. The annual School House assemblies, recorded by shiny black and white ranks of set expressions and rigid stances relict of the late nineteenth century, are quite large. They are separate from the rest. If you were to draw out the stiffly mounted pictures, fifty unblinking faces would stare back at you. Five congregations span five years, some ten faces gone from each successive assembly. Like lucky escapees from a wartime *stalag*, you know that those missing made home runs, away to the lesser dangers of real life. The remaining and the replacements shuffle onwards, filling the ranks to the remorseless tread of time, growing older with each tableau.

They still look absurdly young.

If you looked at the first one of the series you would be staring at a shiny rectangular assembly of about fifty boys in four banked rows in the garden of a large redbrick Victorian house. Cross-legged juniors in shorts sit on the grass at the front. Seniors and staff sit squarely on chairs. The middle orders stand upright behind them. The back rank rises above the assembly by standing on benches brought out from the dining hall for the occasion. It looks remote and old-fashioned, like a print in a history book used for exams. Or perhaps an illustration paged into a dated literary biography. As though someone else must have been there, not me. The photographic event was something of an ordeal every year, a break in routine requiring sartorial care on pain of corporal punishment, somehow tense, so that the few smiles are on edge. The photo celebrates no victory except that of time, another year gone by, thank God, another hurdle survived somehow, the relieved mind yearning ahead towards a distant, permanent, unimaginable release. Those were the days, my friend? We thought they'd never end.

This is a picture of School House boarders, more than forty years ago. There I am, among them, still relatively fresh from Uruguay. Involuntarily, I shiver at the thought.

In the photograph Baz Stevens is in the centre, standing in the third rank. His dark hair is brushed straight off the forehead, already giving his face a high-domed look. Even then, when he was perhaps only fifteen, his eyes were deep set. The Suburban Svengali, some wag once called him, once he became Justin Harrington.

'Crap,' I could hear him saying yet again. 'It was all crap. A bunch of duds called masters peddling an ethos that was redundant ninety years ago to boys who were second-rate wankers. That includes me. A minor public school; Jesus! Twilight of the dinosaurs.'

'Not true,' I would have replied. 'Academically it was very good. And some of the boys have done well.'

The building behind the faces is set like a brick Stonehenge. The house stood towards the edge of town, on the corner of a busy crossroads and a long residential avenue. The main school building was in the town centre. The avenue was started some time in the 1890s but it gradually becomes more modern as you journey further out, steadily deteriorating into Thirties semi-detached uniformity before reaching the inevitable railway line. At its opening end the houses were once solidly Victorian. Sailing over assembled ranks of imprisoned boys in dark blue suits are walls punctuated by windows with white sashes, dominating a rather bleak garden, which was always out of bounds except for joyful end-of-term blanket beating and this one, summertime occasion. Big Midland gables with heavy barge boards soar thickly over smaller, upper windows where dormitories and studies were lined along brown linoleumed corridors. Yet the ugly hard-walled building, seemingly forever durable, was knocked down long ago. An old folks' block or two, sheltered flats or something, stand in its place. Old age edging youth out of space; how appropriate.

'The geriatric ascendant over the adolescent,' Justin would probably growl. 'This country in a nutshell.'

The second row in the photograph, seated with mostly folded arms, exudes expressions of power. There is Roland Minor, for instance, jaw jutting a little, expression stern. He is about to leave for his military service. The uniform blue suit makes him look different; he turned into a striped City peacock once he'd left the army and become Henry.

In the centre of that row, grey-suited, stiff-collared and waistcoated, sits the dominating figure of old Welshie Williams, MA, Cantab, his big hook nose and horn-rimmed spectacles prominent. Despite a small grudging smile on the thick twisted lips he is a fearful, congested sight, like a purple version of the actor Hugh Griffith playing a bad-tempered housemaster addicted to wielding a cane. Next to him his wife Mabel, bulky-busted but otherwise small, briefly holds a rather simpering Queen Mother expression. They are flanked by Matron on one side, in white uniform with a starchy flapped cap that only just contained her abundant Irish hair, and the house tutor on the other. He was a black-haired man with a harelip who only lasted four terms.

What was his name? Strang, that was it. Sticker Strang, addicted to pasting newspaper cuttings into a scrap book when he wasn't marking maths prep.

It was my ex-wife, Marian, who found, years back, that the albums once containing the photos had clear plastic retainers made of a compound that was damaging the surfaces. She disassembled them all, threw the albums away and put the separate photos into this old school trunk. There she left them, in miscellaneous envelopes or piles, so that my school, college and bachelor snaps are jumbled together with a few joint images of married life. Poignant portraits of her lie alongside a fading view of my father in an absurd striped poncho, posing beside a huge Chilean cactus. There is a tiny view of my Gonzalez mother, with me on the promenade at Pocitos, with the beach and the muddy River Plate, full of floating little jellyfish and condoms, behind. Here is one of me standing outside Montevideo's old British School in the side road behind the Ombú on an Avenida España clangorous with ancient trams. It is in the happy, pre-Tupamaro days before idealistic socialism brought the inflation that generated the world's first middle-class urban guerrillas. Beside me are my friends, Luis del Castillo and the portly Obis Otero. In the background the boxer Tomás Puig, nose already broken, lounges with a sardonic grin beside the smooth-haired Irureta Goyena. How old are we? Twelve, maybe going on thirteen. Soon my father's peregrinations will take him to Trinidad, to the dismay of my mother, and I will be sent to England to boarding school.

It is an odd mixture, this potential stew of disparate pictorial histories, piled like uncooked ingredients into an expectant culinary container. It would take long days to rearrange and blend them satisfactorily, if they could be blended.

Into what?

In the middle rank the eye catches the prominently ill-fitting and irregular grey suit of Roland Minor's younger brother Tertius below a broad squinting face – he had incurably bad eyesight from a trembling retina. In the evening, promptly at seven-thirty, after first prep and before the juniors went to bed, we were served a half-slice of bread and margarine with a cup of burnt Camp coffee or thin cocoa. When in frustrated mood Tersh had an occasional habit of placing his bread slice between the pages of an improving book from the junior library shelved along the hall wall. He would then compress the soft crusted rectangle by closing the pages and standing on the book before replacing it, to outside appearances unaltered by its squashed organic marker. A book I vividly remember, entitled *Mountaineering in the Land of the Midnight Sun* contained several, of various vintages. When, on rainy days, a book battle took place, the library being divided between opposing sides at each end of the hall and hurled with great vigour, it was not unusual for one of the mouldering organic relics to fly out and score a quite different form of hit on its intended victim.

Some years after leaving, quite by accident, I bumped into Roland Minor in a bookshop in Guildford. Separated by the yawning gap of nearly five years' distance at school, unknowing of our future involvement, we exchanged a few polite enquiries. At that time, the sartorially conscious Minor was commodity broking in the City. He had changed. His news was encouraging and apposite. The visually hampered Tertius was running a mushroom farm.

Behind me, the last time Marian looked, there had been a click of tongue, disapproving, and what I knew was a compressed look was directed at the carefully posed images from the redundant past.

Here was the prelude to everything; this was where we all started. I am not Lot's wife, nor was this Sodom and Gomorrah. Its sights will not turn me to stone. They are too distant to explain to Tony Fitzsimmonds except to say, as I did that day – very simply,

'We were at school together.'

Chapter Six

The following afternoon there was another shock. Roland Minor came in to the shop. This was very unusual. I hadn't seen him for a long time. In this unbuttoned afterlife he had become Henry. Tersh was called Olly. I used to be Monty, for Montevideo, but I left him behind. I saw Minor-Henry very occasionally in the way of trade and Tertius-Olly, now deep in mushrooms rather than squished books, not at all.

'Good afternoon, Bill,' Henry Roland said, smiling rather briefly in concessionary fashion.

'Good afternoon, Henry,' I answered politely. 'This is a surprise.'

At school people rarely spoke about how their fathers gained a living. It had come as a strange revelation to find that Henry Roland, after his spell of commodity dealing in the City, had taken over his father's substantial antiques business near Basingstoke. This was due to the premature death of his eldest brother, Major, in a car accident. I had never, in the five years I was a boarder, heard Minor or Tersh speak about their father's occupation. Major had already left school by the time I arrived, gone to the khaki-clad discipline of military service, which was rather like boarding school only the food was better and you didn't get caned. He was the one who had been destined to take over the family business. It astounded me to find, years later, that the Rolands I knew at school were the Rolands of Basingstoke. The prestigious Roland business was long-established, carried the cachet of BADA membership, even employed its own restorers. It was sited in a large country mansion called Buckton House, of Georgian façade and grandiose rooms but little land in an accessible village on the old A30 road to the east of the town. The Rolands did not live in Buckton House, over the shop, so to speak. At one time all its rooms were given over to antiques, elegantly downstairs and in reducing quality as one ascended staircases to what were once bedrooms off spacious landings, narrowing up into attics.

The Rolands' father was a big man of daunting ebullience and reputation, whose intensely territorial outlook frightened lesser trade fry. He was an old-fashioned dealer belonging to the time when trade barons dominated the scene, before the auctioneers moved in. He was used to big margins, as befitting the king of the local ring. Roland senior's clients were country gentry, Americans, and top London dealers prepared to pay high prices for his encyclopaedic knowledge. I would never have dreamt of buying off Roland senior.

I had bought off Henry Roland, though. These days Henry liked to pretend that he was in direct lineage, had been born to his family business and schooled by his daunting father. That wasn't true; it was all intended for Major. Sweet are the uses of adversity.

'Heard about Justin Harrington?' He still affected a rather brisk City manner, narrowing his eyes significantly for emphasis as he spoke. He wore pinstriped suits and highly coloured silk ties knotted tight up against shirts of Bengal stripe with white cutaway collars. His black leather shoes were brightly polished, relict of his military service. Spikey Yelland called him The Pride of Jermyn Street. This was mildly derisive but not entirely without envy. There's an old Jewish saying: what you resist, you become. Shot of his punk hairdo, Spikey Yelland was heading down the same sartorial path.

Up to now, though, Henry Roland had not ascended to the heights of Connock and Lockie.

'Indeed I have,' I answered. 'Quite a shock.'

'Shock? I should say so. Just been to Dorking; they're all agog there.'

Henry Roland was getting on in years, like all of us, but still traded sporadically with the Dorking antiques crowd, not that he thought of them as equals.

'Money, I expect?'

'You bet. Did he owe you, too?'

'Nope. Haven't seen him for some time.'

'Lucky for you. Bloody Baz Stevens. He was my fag once, you know.'

'So was I, in my first term.'

Henry Roland smiled wolfishly. 'Don't I remember. You were lousy at making toast, too. Small world, ain't it?'

'Very. Did Harrington owe you?'

Roland twisted his expression. 'I should say so. More than I like to tell anyone. Via his "associates" as he called them, but basically it was Harrington. A whole shipment to New York.'

'Oh dear.'

'Due this week. Payment, I mean.'

'I'm sure you'll get it in due course.'

'Wish I could share your confidence. When these things happen, everything freezes solid. All lawyers and trustees, it becomes, slicing their fees off the top. Agreements made in trust go out of the window. Gentlemen's agreements aren't worth a damn these days.'

The Roland business, traditional, conservative, based on a firm belief in the taste of the eighteenth century and good Georgian furniture, was not prospering. It no longer employed restorers. Like me, it used self-employed craftsmen when necessary. There were rumours that the large Georgian property was up for sale to developers. I didn't like to enquire. Over a few years the extensive showrooms had been reduced: first the attics, then the upper floors being shut off. Now there were only four downstairs rooms in use for display. All the traditional furniture trade has had a bad time for the last few years, ever since 9/11. You have to be quick on your feet and Henry Roland wasn't; he was shuffling along, waiting for the old days to come back again. It was essentially an eye problem; his eye was quite good for eighteenth-century work, but it flinched when more recent pieces came into focus. Henry was like his father and all those encrusted old BADA men who believed that the Regency was a vulgar disaster and everything that followed it a catastrophe.

'All that brown furniture,' Spikey Yelland said on one of his visits, thumbing back the lid on a silver mustard pot with a dodgy liner. 'Dead in the water, Bill. Gone.'

He didn't look round my shop as he spoke.

'Oh yes, dead,' I riposted. 'Dead like Christie's just sold the Kedleston bookcase for a million and a half. And dead like two hundred and thirty thousand for a pair of Beckford's benches. Mahogany's dead all right.'

'That's not brown furniture,' Spikey said, defensive, 'that's country house provenance. Museum stuff. Expensive from the start; the raw material – good mahogany – all had to be imported. Didn't just grow on trees, you know.'

'Very funny. You think all the town stuff's dead then, do you? Have you tried buying a good bit of town eighteenth-century mahogany lately?'

'Sorry. But all the lads say brown mahogany's dead.'

'All the lads, the lads you talk to, think that late nineteenth-century repro is Georgian brown furniture. Or that duffed-up Victorian wardrobes made into so-called Georgian bookcases are antiques. They can't help it, I suppose. They've never seen the real thing. Spend their time watching junk being sold on the telly and thinking people like Justin Harrington are kosher.'

'Ooh, I say, steady on. Touched a nerve, has he?'

I didn't answer. I knew that Henry Roland might have to wait a long time before the old days came back again. In our trade they always used to come back but in antiques, as in the theatre, timing is everything. We might all be bankrupt by then. Or dead. If they ever did come back.

'There'll be probate and so on,' I agreed. 'That takes time.'

'Time?' Henry snorted. 'Time? Time means nothing to those legal villains. With suspicious circumstances like these, it will be years.'

'I've only read what's in the newspaper today. It does all seem odd.'

'Odd? Odd? You're in very understated vein today. It's not just odd; it screams criminal action.' His mouth twisted. 'You mark my words: someone's done that bugger in. Never do it himself, no guts for that. Remember how he always dropped out of the school steeplechase with some spurious injury? No stamina. Then there was rugger. He couldn't take that. Too much pain. Yellow, he was. Never could understand how he got anywhere. Remember his postage stamp fiddle?'

'Um, I don't think I remember the details—'

'Rooking the juniors by using Stanley Gibbons Stamp Catalogue prices to unload duff stamps on them. Everyone knows the stamps aren't worth those prices. He put false postmarks on them, too. Or Harris did. I threatened to have him flayed – six of the best – if he didn't give them their money back.'

'I'd forgotten about that.'

'Probably just before your time. He was a year ahead of you, wasn't he?' The eyes narrowed again, like those of a pith-helmeted subaltern studying the flicker of a distant heliograph. 'You got to know him quite well, though, didn't you? From after school as well, I mean.'

'For a while I did, yes. But that was some time ago. I haven't seen him for ages.'

'Very wise.' Roland glanced round, assessing. 'You've done well, you know. Some saleable stock here. Best to avoid Harrington's sort. That cabinet looks like an Ashbee.'

'It is.'

'Thought so. Not my style, but didn't Harrington's firm publish something of yours on the Arts and Crafts Movement?'

'It did.'

'How did it do?'

'It made them money. Not me.'

'Still in print?'

'Good God, no. It sank like a stone long ago.'

'I seem to remember it was rather good. Ahead of its time. Not that I can stand Arts and Crafts. Socialist humbug.'

'Thank you, Henry. Would you like a cup of tea?'

My unexpected visitor looked slightly startled at this offer, as though such an invitation caught him off balance. 'Well. That's very kind. If it's no— I mean, if you're making one yourself, I could certainly – it's not been my day.'

'It's about my normal time for it. It's no trouble at all.'

'Thank you.'

'Come through to the kitchen. I'll hear the bell if anyone comes in.'

Roland nodded and followed me briskly, seeming to recover a little. 'Odd, ain't it? Strange, I mean, how things work out. After school, that is. Over forty years ago now. For me, anyway.'

I switched on a kettle. 'I never knew, then, that your family was in this business. No idea. I know we've discussed it before, but it still seems strange, as you say.'

'And you – Olly always said you'd go off to be an engineer. Somewhere abroad. Back to South America, wasn't it?'

I took two mugs off a dresser. 'I meant to, certainly. That was the idea. For a while I almost did. I didn't reckon on this country losing all its industry, though.' I got out a jug of milk. 'Tell me: why do you think someone did Harrington in?'

He blinked, then looked round carefully, as though sensing for eavesdroppers. 'You really did know him, didn't you? After school, I mean. He was too young for me at school. Snotty-nosed junior, even if he did fag for me for one term. A backslider, always scrimshanking. Full of clever chat, like a barrack-room lawyer, even at that age. Gift of the gab. Crooked, too. The stamps for instance. There were other frauds; something to do with gramophone records.'

'But you've been dealing with him. Now, I mean.'

He pulled a wry face. 'No choice. Needs must, these days. But you got on with the bastard, didn't you?'

His persistence was disconcerting. Henry Roland was a

daunting, muscular figure when at school, tending to arrogance and peremptory treatment of juniors. He left to go into the army for his national service and became a second lieutenant in an infantry regiment stationed in the Middle East, where the incautious or unlucky British soldier was grabbed, kidnapped, tortured horribly and ended up with his testicles cut off and sewn into his mouth. Henry Roland might be stiff, authoritarian and brisk but he was practical, courageous and had an engagingly grim sense of humour. He was reliably old-fashioned. I found that an agreement with him would be honoured even if, like his father, he was commercially rapacious. His stated contempt for Harrington's school career and character hadn't prevented him from dealing with the present TV celebrity.

'Very well, for a while,' I answered. 'The problems came after Baz went into publishing.'

'Publishing! The bastard learnt from Stanley Gibbons all right. Picking other people's brains. Blowing the gaff, too.'

I ignored his implication, reflecting that a book on Arts and Crafts furniture would not constitute a threat to this visitor. 'Yes. I agree. That's not necessarily a reason for killing him, though.'

Henry Roland waved a hand dismissively. 'Of course not. Publishing types are too feeble to do that kind of thing. Money's the key. Money. Harrington was hand in glove with some very big money men. Not nice money men. Very sinister.'

'In the City?'

He paused cautiously before replying. 'There are one or two with a City presence, yes. But most are from what are euphemistically called offshore funds these days. The sort of thing Leggatt's get involved with.'

Taken aback, I kept my face steady and my mouth shut. Tony Fitzsimmonds was an aggressive *éminence grise* to the old, conservative trade. The idea of outside finance sweeping change through the art and antiques business, of money lent to buyers to fund spectacular, record-breaking investments in art was still regarded with understandable suspicion. Once I'd digested the remark, I made appropriate noises.

'Oh dear. I wonder why he needed them.'

'Publishing gobbles up money. So does setting up dot.com ventures. A lot of cash went down the drain when the first launches took place, remember? That roadshow chap's site came a cropper but Harrington trousered a mint. Then there's the export trade. He goes, or rather went, in for big hitters. Big prices, trading on his TV name and those ridiculous estimates they always give in those shows. Needs finance. Risk capital. Hefty stock in hand. You must know all this.'

'I heard on the grapevine that he was behind all the publicity about the Fauville cabinet last year. Bert Higgins was just the front man.'

'I should say so. Got old Higgins to write a book on Goderoy as an *ébéniste*. Neglected master of the Louis Sixteenth period, out of the Georges Jacob stable, and all that malarkey. What rubbish. I pulled Higgins's leg hard about it at the BADA Fair. Harrington's firm published the book and then they sprung the cabinet at the right New York auction. The Yanks love French furniture with a plate of scholarship on the side. A classic ramp. As neat a million as anyone ever swiped. Goderoy is a minor cabinetmaker. Couldn't touch Jacob. You mark my words; he's overdone it this time. Just like his last term at school. Or the lack of it.'

'Oh?'

'Don't you remember? You were there. I heard it on the grapevine. He got expelled for some swindle or another.

Something to do with printing. They gave him the chop in the Easter holidays along with Harris.'

'I thought they said – and he always told me – he had to leave because of some family problem. The family moved away somewhere abroad. France, wasn't it?'

Henry Roland snorted. 'Not what I heard. I knew the house tutor, old Sticker Strang, quite well. He was in the Territorials. Met him at a Colchester weekend training camp. He'd long left School House but he kept his ear in. The new house tutor told him that Stevens was sacked. One swindle too many.'

'I'd completely forgotten he missed his last term. We were told he had to go to France with his family. His father's job was moved to Lille. I remember now that he told me the same. He spoke French quite fluently, so it all fitted in.'

'I'm not surprised.'

In the midst of this disturbing exchange for some strange reason a random thought occurred to me.

'Your father was very good on that French stuff, wasn't he? Furniture, I mean. I've never got a proper grip on it. To me the real thing and the later repros look the same under all that gilt or chalky paint. He'd have sussed out the Goderoy quality instantly.'

Henry Roland tightened his grip on his mug of tea. 'The old man was brilliant at detecting the real thing. Wish I could say the same of myself. The old man really reckoned French furniture. Loved it. Thomas Chippendale imported it, he used to say, and he knew what he was doing.'

'Did he?'

'He did. Nothing chauvinistic about the old man.' He took a swig, planked the empty mug down and stood up abruptly. 'Well, Harrington's gone, and what's gone has gone. Good riddance to bad rubbish. Doubtless much unpleasantness will come out. Doubtless everyone will try to swipe my money. Must be on my way. Thanks for the tea. My turn next time. Do drop in when you're passing.'

Mildly surprised at both the invitation and the abrupt ending of our talk, I stood up as well. 'My pleasure. Give my best to Tersh – I mean Olly – when you next see him.'

'I will. You should drop in on him, you know. Over in Frimley, covered in compost. He'd be pleased to see you.'

'Next time I'm passing, perhaps. Please keep me posted on anything you hear about Harrington, won't you?'

'You likewise.' The eyes narrowed at me again. 'You'll be more likely to get news than me. You hadn't dealt with him at all recently?'

For a moment I was so surprised that I didn't reply. I wasn't quite sure what he meant. Then I pulled myself together.

'Certainly not,' I said.

He nodded. 'Sorry to press it. Must be off.'

And he left, stopping to watch a motorbike go by before getting into his car.

I sat still, bemused. Some turn in the conversation had not been to Henry Roland's liking. Something to do with France and French furniture, and his father. And maybe me.

And the late Justin Harrington, of course.

Henry Roland's white Land Rover Discovery had not long rolled off towards Westerham on its high-sprung, enquiring journey when, out of the corner of my eye, I saw the silver bullet nose of a new Mini Cooper poke into my little parking area. My heart began an irregular tripping beat for the three minutes that elapsed before Ellen Stanton came briskly into the shop.

'He got his rocker boxes fixed,' she announced, standing for a moment in the doorway. 'And he drove off to Redhill to help George Baker with some preselector problem or another on George's Sprite. Or Imp. Or Gamecock. Or something. George has got several.'

Then she closed the door, making the little bell ring in glad anticipation.

She was still wearing the pink sweatshirt top and dark blue trousers. She still swelled in the right places.

She walked across to the left hand side of the shop and stared at a green stained cabinet on green stained cupboard, top and bottom inlaid with floral motifs, the prominent hinges carefully pierced.

'What is this?' she demanded.

'It is an Arts and Crafts cabinet. By a man called Ashbee and the Guild of Handicrafts.'

'It's quite pretty as well as chunky. I thought all Arts and Crafts stuff was dreadfully dull oak with hearts cut out of it.'

'That's Voysey you're thinking of. Dull oak is a good description. This is Ashbee.'

'I like it. Is it very expensive?'

'Very. When it was made it cost a fortune.'

'Oh, dear. When you say that, it means it really is very expensive. Who else has this sort of stuff?'

'Paul Reeves. Martin Levy of Blairman's in Mount Street. One or two others.'

'My. You are keeping high company.'

'Nothing but the best.' I was looking at her. I hadn't known her for very long.

She smiled slightly and looked round carefully, seeming to assess. Her dyed blonde hair was carefully brushed and she poised herself on her small feet as though about to do a pirouette. She might not be young but she was a very good-looking woman, cool and self-assured.

'Steve says he's going to finish at college and then go into business on his own. Vintage cars. It's a hell of a relief. I thought he was going to chuck college in. I think he'll turn out just like his father after all.'

She frowned as she said this and looked down for a moment.

'He's a very nice young man. I like him. I'm sure he'll do well, especially with a business studies course behind him. Would you like a tea or a coffee?' I asked. 'Or maybe a drink?'

I was standing in the doorway that opened into a little hall, off which the stairs went up to the bedrooms on the left and another door, straight through, led to the living room with its French windows opening onto the garden. The door was open and you could see right across the living room, which was tidy and light, to the neat plants beyond.

She shook her head without speaking and walked straight up to me, close, so that I involuntarily took a step back into the hall, thinking she wanted to pass towards the garden. She didn't. She put an arm what seemed right round my waist and drew me to the bottom of the stairs.

Close to, she was warm and soft.

She kissed me. Then she drew back just a little, cocking her head so as to focus properly on my face.

'No ghosts?' she asked.

'No. No ghosts,' I answered.

'Now then, Bill,' she said. Her breath was sweet but it was damp, hot and urgent. 'Now, *now.*'

Chapter Seven

She turned on her side towards me and put an arm across my chest. A knee gently pushed itself between my thighs. Her face, close by, was not quite in focus but I could see its relaxed, slightly swollen surface, fair and clean, with just a line here and there to remind me of its maturity. Her blue eyes looked at me thoughtfully from under a tousled tumble of hair.

'I wonder,' she said, snuggling down, 'just how long it will be before the solids hit the fan.'

'Eh? Solids? What solids?'

'Oh, you know perfectly well what I mean. Justin and solids go together. We can't avoid the subject any longer. There are bound to be some really nasty things come out now that he's dead. In Yorkshire, of all places.'

'You think? I thought that *de mortuis nil nisi bonum* should be the rule. And he came from Yorkshire, remember?'

'Bill, stop pretending. I don't care where he came from. He was bloody dangerous. There'll be all sorts of nastiness in the air. You should know: you knew him better than I did. I've told you that I had an affair with him and I'm not particularly proud of it, but I never really got to know him. He didn't let his women in too close, ever. For good reason. I've talked to one or two of the others, you see – we do that – and he told each of them a different story.' She frowned slightly. 'It was a strange thing with him, like inventing stories to tell children at bedtime. Each version had a different concept, as though he was conducting a narrative experiment. Each ending would have to be unique.'

I thought of Henry Roland's recent reminder about Baz's expulsion, and his own version of it, and grunted.

Ellen ignored the grunt. 'I think he was seeing how far he could get and how many stories he could keep on the go before the whole construction started to totter. It was fun for him. He was easily bored.'

'But he was never boring.'

'No, he was never boring. Like destruction is never boring. Excitement has to have fear close by somewhere.' She tightened her arm on me slightly. 'Don't get yourself hung up on that, or try to emulate it, Bill. For a while it's like a drug but there's always a morning after. Creative people leave a trail in their wake. A trail of smashed people and things. Well, I don't have to tell you.'

I suddenly thought of a story by John Fowles – *The Ebony Tower* – that hinges on a worthy artist and reviewer interviewing an egotistical, acerbic old painter who lives with two young girls and has always snapped his fingers at life's conventions. The interviewer is left devastated by the knowledge that he is a decent chap but that his decency makes him second rate compared with the unscrupulous, vibrant, immoral old man. It wasn't a comforting thought.

I don't know why it is that sex brings out the literary in me. Not always with reassuring results. It brings irrelevancies to mind.

Ellen nudged me. 'Well, say something, Bill. Talk to me. I'm not here just for the fucking, you know.'

I rallied myself; women always set such store by words. 'I think it's all about risk. People who take risks are always more exciting than those who don't. And those who don't get it in the neck just the same, only in a more boring fashion. Baz thought you might as well go for broke. Given a choice, he'd try for high stakes, burn the candle at both ends. That was his attraction, I would say. He let you in on a risk of some sort, didn't he? An adventure. Made it seem personal, as though it was just for you, but in fact it was for him. Something that your life and his – which meant Elizabeth and his children – wouldn't know about, something secret. Although in fact Elizabeth usually did.'

She hardly seemed to hear me. 'The excitement may be powerful but the aftermath is usually awful. I hurt poor Fred terribly at a time when he was having to adjust to his illness. I didn't know, then, that his illness had certain effects.'

'There are remedies for that.'

'Viagra? It wasn't an option. And he hated the idea of it anyway. The deliberation of it.'

'I can understand that,' I said. But I thought: life is never ideal, it's always full of compromise. Preparation wins over spontaneity, like ant over grasshopper, tortoise over hare.

'You liked him, didn't you?'

'Fred? Yes of course. I'm sorry I didn't know him for long.'

'Thank God he didn't put money into Justin's investment fund.'

'No.' That made me think of Henry Roland, waiting for payment on a container gone to New York. Why call on me now? What did he really want?

Why did talk of French furniture upset him?

'We very nearly did invest. Something held Fred back at the last moment. I think he'd already started to suspect things about me. It stopped him. Justin wasn't having his money as well as his wife. The fund's situation was all explained away so smoothly when it lost money, but there were some angry people about. Very angry. Justin had his lavish management fees but they'd paid for them.'

'A lot of those tax-relief investment schemes were duds. The idea of investing in art and antiques, like the British Rail Pension Fund, is a light to a lot of moths tired of the Stock Exchange. It's like the dot.com boom; after the field gets massacred, the survivors don't do badly. Baz survived.'

'He was a shit.'

'Women go for shits. Worthy men are boring.'

'Stop it. Fred wasn't boring. I don't find you boring. Mind you, I don't think you're so worthy. A bit of a hypocrite but I can take that. We all are.'

'Me? A hypocrite? Why?'

'I think you've got history. Don't tell me you're pure as the driven snow.'

'I never have.'

'All that travel. All those years. Why on earth did you do it?'

'It was my job. What I did.'

'But how boring.'

'It wasn't boring. It was challenging. It needed skill and technical and marketing knowledge. HG Wells said that the life of the average commercial traveller is far more exciting than that of the creative writer. He was right. I gave it up because my time had come. Nowadays I deal strictly with the past.'

'True.' She pushed the knee a bit further. Her hand on my chest slid downwards. 'That's enough of Justin. I think that your history needs further exploration.'

Right then, with keen timing, the telephone by the bed rang. Compulsively, I slid sideways and grabbed it with a curse.

'Hello?'

'Bill?' The voice was clipped. 'Henry here.'

I nearly asked who's Henry, then recognised Henry Roland's voice.

'Hello, Henry.' He couldn't be home yet, surely? 'Where are you?'

'Still driving. On my mobile, so I'll be brief.'

'Fire away.'

'Harrington. I've had a call. Would you believe it? Police.'

'Oh? What do they want?'

'They want to see me. About Harrington.'

'Really? Why?'

'Don't know. But I told you, didn't I? It must be suspicious. Someone's done him in.'

Ellen smiled wickedly. Her hand slid further downwards.

'Get rid of it,' she hissed in my ear. 'You shouldn't have answered.'

What was that joke of Alan Bennett's about a camp antiques dealer? *Sorry about my hands – I've just been stripping a tallboy.*

'You think?' I said to Henry.

'I'm certain. Bloody suspicious. Why would they want to see me otherwise?'

'When?'

'Soon as I get back. Now. No messing. Must be serious. Some chap from the Fraud Squad.'

The hand took on major distracting activity. I wriggled desperately.

'Bill? Are you there?'

'Yes, Henry, sorry. Fraud Squad?'

'That's what he said. Listen: anything you hear, anything at all, for God's sake tell me, will you?'

'I promise.'

'I need any information I can get. You knew him.'

'But—'

'Christ, there's a bloody police car coming up behind me. I'll have to stop talking. Call you later.'

'Tell me how you get on, Henry.'

But he'd gone.

'Very rude,' Ellen said, doing even more distracting things. 'It's not good of you, Bill, to put business in front of my needs. Rude. Don't answer that phone again or I'll be cross. I don't expect to be sidelined. You're keeping a lady waiting.'

I nearly said: I thought you said you weren't here just for the fucking. But I didn't. It might have upset her at a critical moment. She might have taken umbrage and stopped what she was doing. I was intrigued by Henry and my thoughts but they could wait. I do have a sense of priorities. I said nothing because it was much safer. Women set such store by words.

Henry never called back.

Chapter Eight

The first of Ellen's conceptual solids arrived the next morning, at about ten-thirty. There were two of them. Their car was a nondescript saloon, not old but not remarkable either, not particularly clean, just functional. As they got out I saw that one was thin and wiry, medium height, dressed in a grey suit. The other was bulkier but not much taller. He was the driver. His grey trousers were rumpled but he was in shirtsleeves. He put on his jacket, a brown tweed one, when he got out of the car. They both wore ties. I watched them pause and exchange some remarks before they came to the door of the shop. The bell tinkled as they came in.

I stood in the centre of the shop and faced them.

'Mr Franklin?' The thin wiry one tugged at a pocket as he looked at me.

'That's me.'

He held up a card he managed to extract from his jacket. 'I am DS Walters, Hampshire Police. This is DC Green.'

He gestured at the bulkier one, who nodded whilst managing to look round my shop, slowly assessing.

'Sergeant. What can I do for you?'

Theft, I thought at first, they're on some theft job or another. Well, I haven't bought anything dodgy. But the police think that all antiques dealers are crooks.

The thin one's face was impassive as he stuffed his card away. 'Do you know an antiques dealer called Henry Roland, Mr Franklin?'

I must have blinked in surprise. 'Indeed I do.'

'Have you seen him recently?'

'He was here yesterday.'

Were they from the Fraud Squad, perhaps?

'What time was that?'

'Has something happened to Henry?'

'If you could just answer the question, sir.'

'It was about teatime. Between four and five o'clock. Is he all right?'

'You say between four and five. You're sure of that?'

'Certain.'

'And was that the last contact you had with him?' The sergeant's face was still set. His detective constable peered at me over his shoulder.

'No it wasn't. He called me on his mobile a bit later.' I nearly said that he called whilst driving his car, but thought better of it. Henry might be in trouble – in a driving, rather than a commercial sense.

'What time would that be, sir?'

'About six, maybe a bit after. I think he was on his way home.'

A perceptible expression relaxed the sergeant's face. His constable almost moved his head in a faint nod. The mobile, I thought, they've checked calls made on the mobile. They know I'm telling them the truth. Christ, what has happened to Henry? Did they nick him for using a mobile whilst driving? Not a detective matter though, surely, that.

'May I ask what your conversations were about?'

I bit back a retort. I think I managed to sound calm in reply. 'Look, what has happened? Is Henry all right?'

'Please bear with me for a moment, sir. Did you do business with Henry Roland? Was that it?'

'Not now. I have in the past, quite a while ago, but I hadn't seen him for some time. He came here a bit out of the blue.'

'Why was that?'

'It was about the death of Baz – Justin Harrington. We were at school together, you see. A long time ago.'

Now the sergeant blinked.

'Justin Harrington?'

'Yes. In Yorkshire somewhere. It was in the papers. And then on TV, too. *The Times* had an obituary the next morning.'

The constable, Green, nodded briskly. 'I saw that on telly. The wife always watched his programmes.'

His sergeant took over again. 'Why did he come to see you about that?'

'Henry was concerned about money Harrington owed him.'

'How much?'

'I've no idea.'

'But he thought you could help him?'

'Yes. I couldn't.'

'Oh? But he actually came to see you about his problem?'

'In a roundabout way, yes. He needed to talk to someone. I think he was upset about the debt and was looking for any information he could find.'

'And he thought you might be a source?'

'Yes.' I shortened my voice. 'He was mistaken. He suspected that there was a sinister side to the death.'

'Oh? Why?'

'I've no idea. What is this all about?'

'And then he called you after his visit?'

'Yes.' He's dead, I thought, he's bloody dead. Now I know it.

'What was the call about?'

'One of your lot called him about Harrington.'

'Our lot?'

'Yes, a policeman. From the Fraud Squad. He said that he was going to meet him as soon as he got back to his shop.'

Henry wouldn't like that, I thought, no one ever called Buckton House a shop. Much too grand.

'Let me get this straight.' Sergeant Walters actually looked surprised. 'You say he called you to say that a member of the Fraud Squad was going to meet him at his premises? On his return some time after, say, six o'clock yesterday?'

'Yes.'

'To discuss something to do with Justin Harrington?'

'Yes.' I felt my face muscles sag. 'He's dead, isn't he?'

Sergeant Walters' face creased. 'Now why do you think that, sir?'

Suddenly I went cautious. These people were looking for suspects, culprits, someone to blame.

'Because of the cast of your inquiries. You referred to my "last contact" and you are speaking of him in the past tense. You asked did I do business with him, not do I do business with him. He's dead, isn't he?'

'I'm afraid he is, sir.'

I sat down heavily on a nearby country Chippendale chair.

'Christ. Poor old Henry. Dead? Jesus.'

Another ghost, I thought, to add to the list.

Walters looked down at me. 'Sorry about that, sir. We do have procedures, you see.'

My legs felt weak. 'That means he hasn't died of natural causes. You'd have told me, sent a policewoman or something.'

'Indeed.'

'How did he die?'

'He was shot in his car on arrival at his premises. We believe the assassin was waiting for him.'

'Dear God. *Shot? Shot?* Henry Roland?'

'Yes. One bullet, in the head.'

'*Henry Roland?*' I heard the pitch of my voice rise. 'Shot in the head? I can't believe it.' A sudden image came to me of Henry, still just Roland Minor, sitting arms folded, in his blue suit, jaw jutting a little, in that School House photograph, all that time ago. He couldn't have had any inkling, then, of how his life would end. Could he?

The policemen were standing looking at me.

'It's terrible,' I said. 'It sounds like a professional.'

'Why do you think that, sir?'

Caution returned. 'I – I don't know. It doesn't seem otherwise, does it? As cold-blooded as that?'

'Did Mr Roland have any enemies that you know of?'

'No. I mean, not that I know of. I'm not familiar with his life. We met very seldom.'

'But you were at school with him?'

'Yes. Partly. He was older than me.'

'May I ask where you were between six and nine o'clock yesterday evening, sir?'

That irritated me.

'You may.' I didn't like being treated as a suspect.

He flinched just once at my testily pedantic reaction but he wasn't put out in any way. 'So where were you?'

'Here.'

'Can anyone verify that?'

'Yes. I had a visitor. Mrs Stanton. She's both a friend and a client. She arrived at about five-thirty or so – after Henry left – and stayed for a light supper. She left about eight-thirty to nine to go home. She lives over at Crockham Hill.'

'I'd like to check that.'

'Of course.'

'Do you own a gun of any sort?'

'No, I do not!'

'Was Mrs Stanton here when Mr Roland phoned you?'

'Yes.'

I quickly blotted out, mentally, her activities during that call.

'And you say he said he was expecting a member of the Fraud Squad to see him when he got back to his premises?'

'That's what he said.'

'You've no idea why the Fraud Squad might be involved?'

'None. This is terrible. I didn't know Henry all that well but he was here, alive and well.'

'But worried about money? About a debt of Justin Harrington's?'

'Yes.'

'I'm sorry to persist this way, sir, but we have to check his movements the day before yesterday and you seem to be the last person he spoke to, you see. It is also important that you do not withhold any relevant information from us, otherwise you will be committing a serious offence.'

'Dear God. I'm not withholding any. You didn't know anything about the Fraud Squad man, did you? So don't get all pompous with me – Sergeant.'

Detective Constable Green cleared his throat. 'Can we brew you a cup of tea or something? It's been a shock, I'm sure. I'm afraid we'll need to go through a few things in some further detail, if you're all right.'

I rallied myself. The empty feeling, the numbness, was back in full spate. I needed diversion. Another face had gone from the School House photograph. First, Baz-Justin. Now, Henry. Tomorrow? I stood up, testing the legs to support me. They did.

'Come through to the kitchen,' I said. 'I'll make it.'

'Thank you, sir. If you're quite sure. This may take a little time, you see.'

'Yes. I mean, I see. Come through.'

I led the way through the door to the hallway with the living room and garden beyond. The staircase, up which Ellen and I had progressed in lustful anticipation so recently, was off to my left. Again I had the irrelevant thought that there was no need for these two to know the circumstances under which I'd taken Henry Roland's last call. My replies needed control.

I went into the kitchen followed by the two men and picked up the kettle. Detective Constable Green spoke, as though sudden death and assassins were all very well but somewhere in the manual it said that you had to keep the incidental talk flowing so as to reassure the witness or suspect in hand. That way he or she might make unguarded remarks.

He looked at a Detmold print of a pea-brained moorhen scurrying across the kitchen wall and spoke.

'Have you been in the antiques trade for long, Mr Franklin?'

Chapter Nine

After about an hour or so the two policemen left, saying they'd need a formal statement later. They were full of suspicions. I was reminded of Henry Roland's last blurted question about any recent dealings with Justin Harrington; they probed and probed about business until I had to snap at them.

'Take a look at my books if you want! You'll find no transactions with Henry or Justin in them.'

Sergeant Walters gave me a pained look, one that said that accounts mean nothing in your trade. But it slowed him up; he wasn't going to trudge through tedious trading sheets just then.

'And by the way,' I demanded, 'what will you do about your Fraud Squad man? If one really did call Henry.'

Sergeant Walters' lips tightened. 'We shall look into the matter.'

'It was on his mobile, so you must be able to trace it. Like you did me.'

'Possibly. It is not always easy. We'll check while we are proceeding with our inquiries.'

'You found my call easily enough. Why not his? You'd do better to proceed after the mobile phone company records for that call than to pester me.'

His lips tightened further. 'We'll call it a day for now,' he said. 'You won't be going anywhere far away, will you?'

I bit back a natural retort. 'I'll go where my business dictates,' I snarled.

They left for wherever theirs dictated, presumably back to Basingstoke. But they took my books with them. I went back into the kitchen and made a strong coffee. Images of Henry Roland kept coming to me, images I didn't want. The coffee didn't suppress them.

About half an hour later I heard the doorbell tinkle and went to see who it was. Keeping an antiques shop is a bit similar to what keeping a brothel must be like: you never know who's going to breeze in for a lustful bargain.

It was an American dealer called Chuck Vance.

'Hi, Bill,' he said, grinning and sticking his hand out for a shake. 'How are you?'

'Good grief,' was all I could reply as I took the hand in a firm grip. I was still more than a bit shell-shocked over Henry Roland, though I'd simmered down whilst sipping the coffee and thinking about the phone call.

Chuck Vance was from New York. He was short and thickset, overweight, energetic and very shrewd. He was a good dealer with fine contacts in the museum and public gallery line but, more important, some wealthy private clients. The economic gap between the top and the rest keeps opening up in America; you need rich clients and they demand the best. Chuck wore casual clothes that cost a great deal of money. They kept him relaxed amongst affluent people.

Normally, when he was coming, he warned me in advance. He'd never arrived unexpectedly before.

'You look kind of surprised,' he said.

'Surprised? My flabber is gasted. When did you get in?'

'A day or three back. I was going to call you but I just didn't. Don't know why. I came over for the Christie's 20th century sale yesterday and now I'm on the road. How are you doing? You look bemused to me.'

'I am. Have you heard about Justin Harrington?'

'Sure, I heard. Can't say I'm upset though. I always thought he was kind of nasty. Sorry about that; you knew him, of course.'

'I did. It's not only that. Henry Roland called here the day before yesterday.'

'Roland? The Rolands of Basingstoke?' Chuck shook his head. 'I never could do business with them. Never. The old man was just plain damn arrogant and the son, Henry – he dresses like a dummy – always wants too much money. I told him that his routine mahogany was way off but he didn't listen; just got on a high horse about it.'

'Well, he's dead. I've just had the police here. Someone shot him.'

That made him stare. 'Someone shot Henry Roland? *Shot* him? Right here in England?'

'Yes. One shot to the head. In his car. As he arrived back at Buckton House in the evening.'

'Jesus. Who did it? A husband? A pillaged mahogany freak? His tailor? His bank?'

'I've no idea. The thing is, he was here that same afternoon. I seem to have been the last person to speak to him. According to the police. He called me on his mobile after he left and they tracked me. Come in, anyway.'

Chuck came further in and stood in the middle of the shop. He grinned at me again, knowingly. 'So you're the cops' prime suspect?'

'Almost. I'm polishing up my alibi, though.'

'Keep polishing, Bill. Keep buffing away. Stay loose. Gee, how terrible. Last man in? That's always a tough position to play, right? But I didn't know you did business with Roland.'

'I don't. Didn't. Not for a long time. He was traditional Georgian and I bought some later stuff off him, years ago, when he didn't reckon it.'

Chuck's eyes strayed to my Ashbee cabinet. 'Then he got wise?'

'Maybe. He still stayed with Georgian, though.'

'Clinging to the wreckage, huh? So why did he come to see you yesterday?'

'It was to do with Justin Harrington. We were both at school with him. Henry had shipped a container-load of some sort to your side of the pond and Harrington owed him. He was worried about his money, I think. Or just wanted to talk. Tap my brains. Harrington's death was suspicious, he said.'

Chuck's eyes widened. 'Really? Everything else about Harrington was suspicious, I guess, so why not his death too?'

'You think?'

Chuck put a finger to his nose. 'He was a showman. He ran a circus, like Barnum. More than one circus. Circuses. I heard some rumours. Nothing solid. Ours is a small world but there's big money in fine art these days and it's overheating things. So some people are looking at antiques.'

'That, in New York, usually means French furniture.' Like Goderoy's Fauville cabinet, I suddenly thought.

'It did. Things are changing. I heard that Harrington was

involved in some schemes. Leggatt's have been mentioned in that connection.'

I must have blinked but I kept my voice innocently curious. 'Why would that kill him?'

Chuck Vance shrugged. 'Big money brings big problems. I avoid people like Tony Fitzsimmonds.' He walked slowly across to the cabinet. 'People like him get serious over big money. Very serious. They take offence and get heavy. This is by Ashbee, right?'

'Right first time,' I answered, fielding the change of subject.

'I read your book, time ago. He was a big cheese in the Arts and Crafts over here.'

'He was.'

'Messed around with Frank Lloyd Wright in Chicago?'

'Amongst other things, after founding the Guild of Handicraft, yes.'

'An idealistic pioneer and socialist, right?'

'Yes.'

Chuck made a dismissive gesture. 'I've been to Chipping Camden. Those guys left the East End of London, where real furniture was made, to live in the country and go broke.'

'They did.'

'Frank Lloyd Wright used machinery. Became a modernist. These guys didn't. Ashbee ignored Frank Lloyd Wright. He and his crew all went out of business.'

'True.'

He opened one of the cabinet doors and looked inside at the pale holly surfaces of small drawers inlaid with flowers. 'The work of atavistic perfectionists,' he said, almost to himself. 'For rich people to buy. How much?'

I named a substantial five-figure sum and he winced. 'Negotiable?'

'Not much. You don't find these every day.'

He scratched his jaw and I waited. Chuck had bought off me quite steadily but nothing as important as the Ashbee cabinet.

'Your book was all about this stuff, hey?'

'It was.'

'Did it make money?'

'No.'

'Why did you write it?'

I chuckled for the first time since the detectives arrived. 'You want the two-day course or the ten-thousand-word précis?'

'Spare me. Just the executive one-page summary will do.'

'The movement attracted me because it has a history rich in paradox. It was dominated by architects who admired buildings not designed by architects. They preferred barns, cottages and stables to the discipline of formal design. They cherished asymmetry, wanting to give the false impression that their houses had grown over many years. They designed from the inside out, imposing their view of life on the spaces and furnishing of the interior. They tried to control what people lived with.'

'That makes them crazy.'

'A lot of architects were and are that crazy. They were dedicated socialists who put suites of rooms for servants in their houses. They provided workers with better homes and evening-class institutional culture whilst paying cabinetmakers eightpence halfpenny an hour.'

'About fourteen or fifteen cents? Wasn't that good?'

'No, it wasn't. Skilled female embroiderers could earn from four to ten pence an hour in the 1880s. You didn't live well on eightpence halfpenny an hour.'

'Never give a sucker an even break, huh?'

'Many of the key figures had private means and were comfortably off. Few of them succeeded commercially. The garden city developments they produced in emulation of rural villages, but without pubs of course because drink was a curse, needed the strong modern industries they despised to sustain them. They weren't modernists. They liked the past as much as do Quinlan Terry and Prince Charles. But they led the way to a lot of modernist principles. I said paradox and I meant it. End of executive summary.'

I didn't say that Justin Harrington hated it, but he did. Something about the Arts and Crafts paradox was too close to home for Justin Harrington; he and Baz Stevens lurked within similar contradictions. But he published the book.

'You didn't say *why* you wrote the book,' Chuck said.

'I was flattered. I liked the idea of being an author. A published author. Englishmen still think books are prestigious.'

'Uh-huh. Like a moth to the flame. Harrington asked you to do it?'

'He did.'

'You weren't trading then.'

'Nope.' I didn't mention my unpublished book on Georgian Revival furniture for Justin and all the fruitless work still lying in a drawer. There seemed no point in admitting to any more weaknesses.

He looked around carefully, then back at the cabinet. 'You just do furniture?' he asked.

'Mostly. The Arts and Crafts Movement produced glorious silver, metalwork, ceramics, textiles, lighting, wallpaper, stained glass, jewellery and printed matter. I have sold some of it, but not much. It may seem odd to concentrate on its furniture. Yet it was in the furniture that paradox was most evident, the effect of principle most revealed. For some reason, perhaps rooted in religion, the heart shape and the flat-capped upright met with their approval, particularly Voysey.'

'I think his stuff is kind of miserable.'

'He was a rural Yorkshire vicar's son. Evangelical. Plain oak surfaces and rush seating are nearer to God than buttoned chintz. But he fetches a lot of money. People go mad for his stuff.'

'Yorkshire? Ain't that where they found Harrington?'

'Yes. That's a thought. But Harrington hated Voysey's work.'

'Money is money.'

'Harrington was from Yorkshire but he couldn't stand Voysey. The whole Arts and Crafts thing was anathema to him. He had to publish to fill his list, but he hated it. Chippendale was his kind of Yorkshireman.'

I remembered one of his outbursts.

'Arts and Farts. Expensive indulgence for the champagne socialist. The painstaking preservation of traditional rural skills, with an output too expensive for ordinary working people. Fine cabinet work, inlaid and decorated pieces for the better off, the professional classes and landowners who believed the movement needed support. It was a load of shit. Look at Morris and Gimson and those terribly expensive country chairs. Rush seats for fat arses. Hypocrisy run riot.'

I said: 'You are right, Chuck. In America, where the machine was no enemy and social perceptions were different, the movement had a much wider impact. Modern thinking about work's rewards approves William Morris's beliefs entirely.' I grinned. 'The drudgery has been passed on to third world countries.'

'How paradoxical.' His voice had gone dry.

'Homily's over. Are you interested? Or have I put you off?'

He stopped scratching his jaw.

'Market's real tough right now, Bill.'

'Not the top end. This is top end. Museum fodder.'

'Provenance?'

'Impeccable. Ashbee retired to Kent and this came from Kent. A friend of his bought it fresh from Chipping Campden. I have the invoice.'

'You've got it all cut and dried, huh?'

'It's what's wanted nowadays. Assurance. And generally speaking there aren't bogus Arts and Crafts pieces around the way there is other period furniture. It makes life easier.'

He nodded sagely. 'How come you didn't punt it through Harrington, if you knew him?'

'I don't need an intermediary. I can sell this myself.' I wasn't going to tell him the real reason.

'From what I hear, he might have got a hell of a price for it, using Leggatt's.'

I thought: so you really do know something about Baz. And Yorkshire. And Leggatt's. What is this impromptu visit really about?

'Nothing solid, of course,' he went on, as though reading my thoughts. 'Just rumours.'

'Rumours?'

'Sure. You've heard about these new fine art funds?'

'I've heard that American investment bankers are poised to move into the art market in a big way, yes. Some big banking banana predicted in April that thirty billion dollars of private equity would move into art funds in the next ten years. Three billion a year?'

'You're well informed, Bill. *Business Week* says that there are already plans to launch six new art investment funds this year. Six new funds in one year? This means that people who couldn't give shit for art are going to cream off the top of the market and use it to make a whole heap of money. Most will never see the paintings and things that they buy. How's that for paradox? What would the original painters and craftsmen think of that?'

'Is there really that much art available?'

He shook his head. 'Nope. Or rather, there isn't now but there will be.'

'Supply and demand? Like Corot?'

During his lifetime Corot produced some two thousand paintings. Of these, five thousand are in the United States of America.

'You've got it.'

'It will all end in tears. But that's art, not antiques.'

'Of course. But some smart guys are thinking about antiques. Like top of the range furniture.' He gestured at the cabinet. 'Some of them are taking my advice to buy things now, before a furniture fund is set up by some smart-ass banker and prices take off.'

'All they have to do is give me a cheque.'

He smiled. 'What else have you got?'

'Top of the range? Designer stuff?'

'Yup.'

'An Eastlake chiffonier, straight from *Hints on Household Taste*? 1865? That do you? You lot in the States were keen on Eastlake furniture, weren't you?'

'You're not kidding?'

'This is designed by Blomfield. The architect in whose office

Thomas Hardy worked. Oak. Hinges in the form of flesh, fish and fowl. Stencilled decoration by Clement Heaton. It was illustrated in the first couple of editions and then dropped.'

'I know it. Jesus, I know it. I've already seen it.'

'There were just two or three made. I've only seen one other and it isn't as good as this one. It's the one you've seen too, probably: it doesn't have the Heaton stencilling, I bet.'

'Where is this marvel? '

'In the living room. You want to see it?'

'Lead me to it.'

I led him through the hall to it. He slavered over it. First he blanched at the price, then he didn't.

'We are talking unique here,' he said. 'I've got a first edition of *Hints on Household Taste*. It was a landmark book in America. This is in it, all right.'

'We are talking unique, as you say.'

'Provenance?'

I shook my head. 'I bought this from an early oak dealer who hated it. He said he bought it in a south London sale. It's unmistakable, though.'

Chuck pressed his hands together. 'We might do a deal for this and the Ashbee together. You got photographs?'

'I have.'

'Listen, I've got a client who wants to set up a real collection. I can't buy these on spec because I don't know this bit of the market well enough. I'm going back Saturday. Email me the images. Let me show him and talk it through. I'll call you as soon as I can.'

'OK, Chuck. I'll try not to sell them before then.'

He peered at me. 'I'm glad I stopped by. You've kept real quiet about these.'

'I'm going to the Midlands Antiques Fair next month. I won't be keeping quiet then.'

His eyes were still peering. 'You very upset about these guys? Harrington and Roland?'

'It's a shock. I was at school with them.'

'He really called you? Roland? His last telephone call?'

'I think so.'

'Jesus. No wonder you're fazed. What did he say?'

'That a man from the Fraud Squad phoned, wanting to see him about Harrington.'

'Really? The Fraud Squad were on to Harrington? For what? What were he and Roland up to?'

'I've no idea.'

He grinned. 'You mean you weren't in on the deal?'

'Certainly not!'

'No shit? You've really got no notion of what the scam was?'

'None.'

'But the Fraud Squad were on to it?'

I hesitated. 'The police who called here seemed surprised about the Fraud Squad. Perhaps it was a hoax. It might have been a ploy to get him to go to Buckton House rather than home. Then they waited for him.'

'Wow.' He eyed me appraisingly. 'You're kind of in the limelight, ain't you?'

'It was a bizarre day. Both Harrington and Roland: I knew them but they were out of the past. Times gone by.'

'But Roland was right here, the day before yesterday.'

'That's the past now,' I said. 'Even if the past has teeth. And, talking of the past, could you please find out something for me?'

'Sure, if I can. What?'

'They said that the Fauville cabinet was bought by a private buyer?'

'They did.'

'Can you find out who it was? And where the cabinet is now?'

His stare became more penetrating as he smiled a wider smile. 'You really do want to live dangerously, don't you?'

It was after Chuck Vance left that I heard the soft burble of a motorbike on the road outside. It went past steadily, without the urgency I always associate with motorbikes, and its note died away softly but didn't entirely vanish.

For some reason, it caught my attention.

I thought about Chuck, who had gone off in his hire car, a Ford Focus, and the thing about inviting danger. I didn't think about danger seriously; I suddenly needed to know who bought that Fauville cabinet. French furniture was important. I didn't think why but information about it had become necessary.

Then I heard a motorbike coming back again, the same one by the sound of it.

I went into the shop and stood at the left-hand long window, next to a bookcase of Gothic design I'd bought at auction. My position gave me a view of the road and my car parking area at the side of the building.

The motorbike came into view and, as it approached, I saw that it was a big green one, powerful, with two men on it. They were wearing those spherical helmets that make motorcyclists look like space explorers, with tinted visors so that their faces are invisible. They also wore smart leather outfits, close fitting, with streamlined colour styling in green that was identical for both, so that they looked like anonymous beings created just for machine control purposes.

As it approached, the bike slowed down.

It isn't anyone I know, I thought, as it came nearer, there are one or two bike freaks I know in the trade but they have vintage machines and that's a new one.

I thought about Henry Roland, stopping to watch a motorbike pass before getting into his Discovery. Had that one been green, too? I'd been watching Henry, not the bike, so I had no memory of what colour it was. I thought there were two people on it, but I might be wrong.

The green bike was dawdling now, almost stopping in front of my shop. I moved sharply round the bookcase to get a better look. As I did so, the pillion passenger moved his or her head forward, closer to the front person, as though to say something. I saw the front one's elbow move as the nearby glove slid to twist the handle grip. The bike, without any hurry, moved at gathering speed away from my frontage and disappeared in the direction of Westerham. Its powerful burble died away.

What, I wondered, was all that about?

Chapter Ten

'Dead as a fucking doornail,' Spikey Yelland said, sipping his mug of coffee. 'Shot straight in the head. Still sitting at the wheel of his motor. No sign of who did it. He was a stuffy old bastard but I wouldn't wish that on anyone. Mind you, at least it was quick.'

'Indeed,' I agreed, putting down my own coffee.

We were sitting in my kitchen. Spikey had missed out on his Godstone café, Stanley's, and his sausage roll, having rushed in to see me all agog. Business was still business, mark you; on the table, in addition to my coffee pot, was a small 1907 silver elephant pincushion for which we had not yet agreed a price.

'They do say,' Spikey gave me a sly glance, 'that he'd been over to see you, the same sort of time. Or not long before.'

'Oh do they? Who might "they" be?'

'The Dorking boys. Who else? Henry Roland called on them too, before coming to see you. Looks like he was trying to find out if any of them were owed by Justin Harrington, the way he was.'

'And were they?'

Spikey shook his head. 'Don't know of anyone. Mind you, there might be. They keep pretty schtum about their dealings, most of them.'

'When you say "owed the way he was" do you know how much Henry Roland was owed?'

'Not a clue. Thought you might know a bit about that.'

Ho, ho, I thought, Spikey's on a fishing trip, keeping himself in the know so that he can chat to the trade in confidential gossip mode. It all adds to a runner's credibility. That, or someone has put him up to probing me.

'I'm afraid not,' I answered him.

'But it's quite a coincidence, that, isn't it?'

'What is?'

'You knowing Harrington and Roland like that, I mean, just about the time they've both snuffed it? In dodgy circs? Especially just after Hooray Henry consulted you about his container.'

'*Et tu, Brute?* First the Hampshire police and now you. It just so happens that we were at school together years ago. And our paths crossed after. Pure coincidence. I hadn't been much involved with either for a long time. I don't do drugs and nor did Henry, but they seemed to think this was like a drug pattern murder. I hadn't seen Henry for yonks so some sort of trade in that can be ruled out. They had to admit there was no evidence of drugs, anyway.'

'But all the same, Henry Roland told someone in Dorking he was off to see you, like Mohammed to the mountain. Got them all stirred up about you.'

'Nosy bastards.'

'Oh, don't take it personal, Bill. You know what the trade's like: full of that sharden-whatsitsname—'

'*Schadenfreude*. A malicious enjoyment of others' misfortunes.'

'That's it. Well, they were all enjoying the way the great Rolands of Basingstoke were having to shorten sail if not man the bloody lifeboat. Rolands were always such arrogant buggers, particularly the old man. Trod on everybody, he did. Recently Henry's been pretty civil for a change, quite polite, suffering like the rest and having to eat humble pie. Then he goes off for a bit, they say to France, and comes back his old opprobrious self, all toffee nose and cavalry twill trousers. Got up their hackles just like he always did, apparently. Like a dog with two whatsits, he was. Then he comes back again, this time all flustered – for him flustered is like ice cool for normal folk – about Justin Harrington having croaked in dodgy circumstances whilst owing the Pride of Jermyn Street for a container-load of kit. The Dorking crowd are only human. They enjoyed that. It wasn't like Henry Roland to confide in them but he was upset enough to let drop this info. And that he was off to see you. As though you'd have all the answers.'

'Ha!' I said.

'Well, I must admit it surprised me. All due respect but quite the dark horse these days, aren't you, Bill? I didn't know you knew Handsome Justin Harrington and his wife until the day before yesterday. Kept that well under your hat, you did.'

'Hats were not involved. There was no need to mention it, Spikey.' I heard my voice shorten its tone. 'No call at all. My business has, or rather had, nothing to do with Harrington. And precious little with Henry Roland. We traded in different fields.'

'No offence meant, Bill. No offence. You know how people talk. Not me, of course. But they're bound to speculate. Others,

I mean. Maybe that you and them – Roland and Harrington – had some big deal going.'

So that's it, I thought. The trade think I was in cahoots with those two. So, too, probably, do the policemen. I'm in a hot seat here.

'We didn't.' My voice was still short. 'I've told you already.'

'No, no, I understand that. Message received. Didn't mean to upset you.'

'I'm not upset!'

'No, no, course not. Course not.' He gestured at the article on the table. 'How about the elephant, then? A hundred quid do for you? That should leave plenty in it for you.'

My baleful gaze fell on the small silver elephant pincushion on the table, the object of a quick change of subject. If Spikey didn't believe me, who would?

'The back leg's bent,' I snarled. 'And it needs a new velvet cover.'

'Eighty-five, then?'

'Done,' I said.

'Phew.' Spikey put on a relieved expression. 'I'm glad that's OK, then.'

He got up, wandered over to the wall on which Detmold's brainless moorhen still ran on scaly legs, and peered at two cartoon figures in an old grubby frame next to it.

'What are these?' he asked.

'They're two cartoon characters from an Argentine magazine called *Patoruzú*. One is fat and lazy, called Bólido. The other's called Fúlmine. He brings bad luck. If he wishes you well, disaster occurs. The Trinidadians call it goat's-mouthing. They say everything a goat breathes on dies. "Don't goat's-mouth me" means don't wish me luck as I go on stage, say break a leg.

In the cartoons, Fúlmine always goat's-mouths everyone. Just nostalgia: the cartoons date from my youth.'

'Let's hope this doesn't make me a Fúlmine, then.'

'What?'

He grinned and started rummaging about his second-hand jacket. He was wearing a baggy tweed one, rather long, with big poacher's inside pockets in an old-fashioned country style. It was good quality but it made me think of Oxfam shops. 'I'm glad I showed you the elephant first. You might not have been so keen if I'd taken this out ahead of it.'

He flourished an article he heaved out of the jacket with some triumph. It had a domed circular silver-lipped top with a velvet cover about three inches across in total, but otherwise was made of silver, especially the central handle under the dome, a balustered shaft which ended in a flat circular base.

'I've seen one of these in silver before,' he said. 'Another sewing accessory, it is.'

'I can see that,' I said.

'Like it? You can use it to mend holes in your socks or as a pincushion.'

'I don't mend socks. But I agree that it's a mushroom,' I answered, thinking, but not of price. 'And I'll have it.'

Chapter Eleven

I found the farm on the outskirts of Frimley, at the end of a shabby industrial estate that ran out into flat fields of unkempt appearance. Sheep might be grazed on them but they weren't right now, so the grass was tufted and lumpy. The hedges surrounding the fields were unenthusiastic about their function, growing sparsely, with gaps filled by sagging wire fencing. Bits of horned machinery rotted in one corner. Damp air breezed across my face as I got out of my car, adding to an impression of raw neglect and economic deterioration.

The mushroom-growing premises were three big long sheds like those used for chicken batteries only taller. In front of them was a large mobile cabin used as an office. Weeds grew under it and ivy was trying to get up one side. An old blue Mercedes estate car was parked outside along with a white Ford Transit van. The big littered yard between the cabin and the sheds was concreted over but there were potholes here and there. A bellowing forklift truck, driven by a mad lad in a baseball cap, bumped and bucked as it careered about carrying a pallet with a big wooden tray on it.

The divided inside of the cabin-office was full of papers and smelt musty. Well, it smelt of mushrooms, I suppose, but the aroma was somehow frowstier, combining mushroom with dank flooring and dusty documents. A middle-aged woman behind a congested desk stared at me expectantly as I came through the door. She wore glasses and sat in front of a monitor screen that flickered fit to give you a blinding headache, let alone make cataracts form in sheer self-defence.

This was local industry in Blair's Britain.

'I'm looking for Oliver Roland,' I said, by way of answering her stare.

'He's out in the sheds.' She was well spoken. 'The middle one, probably. Are you on business? Is he expecting you? You can wait here if you like.'

'No thanks. I'm an unexpected old friend. I'll find him.'

She opened a desk drawer. 'You should have a security pass.'

'Don't worry. I know all about factories. I promise not to get run over by the forklift or steal the stock.'

She smiled thinly and closed the drawer. I said thanks once again and sortied out across the yard to the middle shed, passing through big trailing plastic or rubber doors that would let the forklift through on a central, scruffy channel painted on the floor. Inside there was a free, reasonably lit passage down the middle but huge racks lined the sides, kept gloomy by sliding screens. There was a smell of compost.

'Keep 'em in the dark and spread shit on 'em.' I murmured the old management joke to myself.

Halfway down the passage a stocky figure in a long brown coat was holding something to his nose and sniffing hard, like someone really needing a snort.

'Tersh?' I spoke out loud as I walked up to him. 'How are you?'

His head came up from his cupped hand and bent back, nostrils flaring, as the half-closed eyes struggled to focus. He wore a tie under the brown coat but it was skew to the check shirt collar, which wasn't buttoned at the top. He'd put on weight. He didn't recognise me in the poor light.

'It's me. Bill Franklin. Henry told me you were here. How are you?'

He squinted unbelievingly for a moment and then half-smiled, making his broad face crease into a puckish expression.

'Monty Franklin.' He came up close to me and peered harder, face close enough for me to see his pupils trembling. 'Is it really you?'

His hand came up to shake mine.

'It's me.' I shook the firm hand and nodded at the mushroom in his other one. 'Want a library book to keep that in? *Mountaineering in the Land of the Midnight Sun?*'

He smiled fully for a moment. 'I might have known you'd not forget that.' Then his face went serious again.

'Look, I'm very sorry to hear about Henry. It's terrible news.'

He nodded without replying, the eyes seeming to steady a bit as he stared at me curiously. I wondered if he'd tried some sort of laser treatment for them; they're supposed to have a cure for trembling retinas these days.

'He came to see me, you know, the same day,' I said, waiting for him to say something.

'Did he?' It seemed like news to him. 'You and he didn't do business though, did you?'

'No. He seemed upset about Baz Stevens. Justin Harrington, you know.'

'I know. Fat cat bastard. Friend of yours, wasn't he?'

'Yes, once. A while ago. But Henry did business with him, didn't he?'

The forklift bashed through the rubber doors with a bellow of diesel engine and a chill draught, still carrying a heavy wooden tray. The speed the mad lad was going, nobody stood a chance if they happened to be in the wrong place.

Tersh scowled, but he didn't remonstrate with the mad lad. 'Come to the office,' he said, his voice neutral. 'It's no good here.'

I followed him back through the doors, across the yard and into the cabin. The middle-aged woman didn't look up as we went through her office but he spoke to her.

'Sylvia, this is Monty Franklin,' he said and put his head back to squint at her. 'He was at school with me. And knew the worst.'

'I used to be Monty,' I said to her, 'and he used to be Tersh, for Tertius. But I'm Bill now and he's Oliver, or Olly. It's what happens to you when you grow up.'

She returned a small smile as we left her to go through a dividing wall into a separate end office. He closed the door and gestured at a chair close up to what had to be his desk. It wasn't a clean office and it was congested. Packs of button mushrooms were stacked on things and packaging littered the floor. It wasn't a prosperous sight. I'd heard that mushroom growers were getting stiff competition from Eastern Europe, Poland or somewhere like that, where labour costs nothing, but I didn't like to enquire.

'They seem to think Stevens committed suicide,' he said abruptly. 'What do you think?'

'I've no idea. I can't think why.'

'He was a shady bastard, maybe that's why. Something caught up with him.'

'Henry didn't think he'd have the guts to kill himself.'

'No, I know. What do you think?'

'I don't think he'd commit suicide, no.' I made my voice gentle. 'Henry came to see me that day. What happened to him?'

His face twitched. 'Didn't anyone tell you? He was shot. In his car. The big Discovery.'

'Why on earth?'

He turned angry. 'How the hell should I know? I've never been part of the family business. Know nothing about antiques. Can't see, can't drive. My father deliberately kept me out. Minor – Henry – set me up in this place when he was working in the City. Long time ago; it was smaller. Then Major died in the car crash. Henry took over. Major, Minor, Tertius: I'm the only one left now. Neither had any children. Nor have I.'

'I'm sorry. I'm really sorry.'

'The business at Buckton House has been going down. Not Henry's fault. The old antiques trade is finished. There'll be nothing left of the Rolands of Basingstoke.'

'I never knew, at school, that that was your family business.'

'No call to mention it. We were in trade. Not gentlemen. And people always think the antiques trade is dodgy.' He gave me a squint-eyed, significant look. 'Anyway, it's all gone now.'

'You'll sell the antiques business up?'

'Not mine alone to sell. There's a trust. Complicated. Henry's widow – Janet – will be the main beneficiary. I'll have to soldier on here. Problem is, the lease will be up soon.'

'The property, Buckton House, must be valuable.'

He scowled. 'Why are you here? What do you want? After all this time?'

'I'm in a bind. I knew Henry. I knew Justin Harrington. Not well for some years, but they're suddenly both dead. People think I'm involved, somehow. I'm not, but I'll be blamed with something. I need help. Did Henry tell you what business he was doing with Harrington? What was in the last container, for example?'

He shook his head. 'I didn't ask much about the business. Too busy here. But it was something to do with his trip to France. He said things were picking up. Why should people think you were involved? Henry said he hardly ever saw you. You weren't really in the trade the way we were. On the fringe. Come to it late, haven't you?'

'That's true. But people jump to conclusions. Why France? Your family business was always Georgian mahogany.'

He shook his head. 'Not always. My father was good on French furniture. Before the business got so Georgian he used to handle quite a bit of French stuff. People at auctions here didn't know it the way he did. He said the best place to sell it was Paris. There was a firm near Saint-Germaine-en-Laye – Monsieur Dubois, my father always talked of him as Mr Woods, he came to see us a few times – they had a showroom on the Faubourg Saint Honoré and there was some business they did. I think Henry kept in touch. There was a son who took over.'

I nodded slowly. 'Henry said, the day he called, that your father was good on French furniture. He said that—'

'What was good enough for Chippendale was good enough for him,' Tersh interrupted, nodding. 'I remember Father saying that quite often. We used to groan when he said it.'

'Henry said it, too, the day he came. The day he was shot. I wondered if it had any significance.'

'Search me. I grow mushrooms. Henry didn't talk about the business much when he came here. Which wasn't often. He might have been doing something with the Dubois.'

'But why shoot him? Did he really have such enemies?'

'The police asked me that. One of them was rude enough to say that his death was typical of drug-related murders. Cheeky bastard; I put a flea in his ear, I can tell you.'

Well, I thought, it does smack of criminal activity. But I was suddenly thinking of something else.

'When Henry was in the City,' I asked, 'did he have any contact with Leggatt's at all?'

Tersh squinted at me. 'Why do you ask?'

'Just curious.'

'No. He didn't.' Tersh was looking heated. It was so obvious a lie that I registered it and moved on.

'I never used Fat Arthur for restoration, myself,' I said.

He paused just for a second at this apparent non sequitur. 'Henry hated him,' he said.

But used him, I thought.

I didn't say anything more. I was thinking about France, and Yorkshire. Sitting in that shabby office, amongst all that evidence of struggle and scrape, and packs of mushrooms, I was thinking of France, and Yorkshire again.

And Justin's love of Thomas Chippendale.

Chapter Twelve

If you set out to write a book on Georgian Revival furniture, you have to find out what is being revived. The fact that you get betrayed and the book lies fallow in a drawer doesn't erase the information from your memory.

Sweet are the uses of adversity.

Fact: Thomas Chippendale came from Yorkshire. From Otley, to be precise, on the Wharfe not far from Ilkley Moor. He was born in 1718, the son of a joiner and grandson of a carpenter. They spelt the name Chippindale. So did he, sometimes. Little is known about his early years or where he served his apprenticeship. Scholars differ. Ralph Edwards in his famous *Dictionary* suggested London, thinking that quality like Chippendale's could only be learnt in the capital. But we know now that in the eighteenth century good cabinet-makers were not confined to London. Christopher Gilbert, in his two-volume work on the famous man, suggested York, in the workshops of a cabinetmaker called Richard Wood. Gilbert's is a beguiling theory. If you travel from Otley eastwards to York, within five miles you pass Harewood House, where

Chippendale, later, did so much work for Edwin Lascelles, the Earl of Harewood. No one really knows where he learnt his trade when very young, but York is a good guess. When Chippendale published his famous *Director*, the highest concentration of subscribers outside London was in York. Richard Wood bought two copies. If you went north from Otley past Harrogate you'd come to Newby Hall, where there is more of his furniture. South to Leeds and you'd find Christopher Gilbert's Temple Newsam. A bit further south still, past Wakefield, you come to Nostell Priory, the most fully documented place. He got a lot of work from Yorkshire. Yorkshiremen tend to be clannish, like Scots.

'The Scots,' I can still hear Justin trumpet. 'Rannie and his grasping family. They financed Chippendale and then buggered the business by wanting their money back after Rannie croaked. All those commissions in Scotland; he bought them dear. Much too dear. Never get into the clutches of a Scotsman, Bill.'

'Haig tried to help,' I objected. 'He ran the business side.'

'An accountant. Rannie's stooge. Never let an accountant run your business. Especially not a Scottish accountant.'

Then he'd grin at this attack on his own profession.

Fact: by 1748 Chippendale was in London, getting married to Catherine Redshaw. They had nine children. The eldest was called Thomas and followed into his father's business in St Martin's Lane. Catherine died in 1772. Chippendale married again in 1777, to Elizabeth Davis, and had three more children.

'Not bad for a nearly sixty-year-old. Especially when you realise that he died in 1779. I won't have three children in my last three years, on a new wife. No chance.'

'You never know. Never give up, lad.'

Out of Chippendale's total of twelve, only four children survived beyond 1784. In the 1750s their father became a travelling man, like Justin and me. The idea of Chippendale chipping away at a bench is fanciful. He employed lots of men in several trades, designed lots of pieces, had to journey widely around the country to butter up the aristocrats who were his clients. The business needed organisation, control, and he touted for trade all over. It wasn't easy going up the Great North Road in those days. The aristocrats were bad payers, too.

'I am paid my rents once a year,' one landowner sniffed at Chippendale's plea for some cash against a huge bill, 'and that is when I shall pay you.'

Take it or leave it: tradesmen like tailors and cabinet-makers have always been treated disdainfully by aristocrats. Chippendale was no exception. He wasn't a royal supplier like his near neighbours Vile and Cobb, but even they had to grin and bear it when bills fell unpaid. Their swarms of craftsmen had to be paid weekly and there were huge bills for materials. Then Rannie's family wanted their money out of the business. It wasn't surprising that Chippendale took a few business short cuts. Not in the quality of his furniture; other kinds of short cuts.

To do with France, for instance.

The first London addresses for Chippendale start in Conduit Court, Long Acre, then in 1752 he rented Somerset Court, later renamed Northumberland Court. This was near the palatial residence of the Earl of Northumberland on the Strand. The Earl was created Duke in 1766 and was important as a patron. Chippendale rented a house in Northumberland Court in which he worked on the designs for his famous pattern book.

Many of the plates were engraved by Matthias Darly, who was possibly Chippendale's drawing tutor and who may have shared the house while the plates for *The Gentleman and Cabinet-Maker's Director* were being engraved.

The *Director* made Chippendale famous. It is a superb example of a pre-emptive competitive strike: a milestone in British publishing. It was a design reference book, a catalogue and a marketing tool.

'Brilliant. He left them all standing. The trade copied lots of the designs. They had to. Just think: until Chippendale published his *Director* in 1754, there wasn't a book of furniture designs available. There were a few pieces in architects' books of houses but nothing purely on furniture. You can argue whether Linnell or Vile and Cobb made better pieces – or Ince and Mayhew – or whether Lock was responsible for the designs, but the fact is that Chippendale did it. The first book of furniture designs for two hundred years.'

Justin Harrington had a thing, a compulsion about Chippendale. It propelled him into publishing. It gave him other ideas, too. About Yorkshire.

Fact: Chippendale moved to St Martin's Lane in antici-pation of big business once the *Director* was out. The Scotsman James Rannie financed him. The firm became a big furnishing supplier to the gentry, not just a cabinetmaking enterprise. Curtains, carpets, upholstery, coffins, you name it; they'd supply anything. French chairs, for instance. The 1754 *Director* shows designs that were based on the prevailing French taste, the Rococo and Gothic that was just starting to go out of fashion. Chippendale adapted these tastes to furniture with style and originality. His firm actually made a lot of the designs but not all of them. Some were made much later, by other people. He also bought furniture in France and supplied it to his clients. Thereby hangs a tale.

In 1769 Customs and Excise caught Chippendale dodging duty on the importation of sixty chairs from France. The dodge he was using was a common one at the time and probably since. The chair frames were supplied disassembled – what came to be known as CKD or 'components knocked down' condition. In the nineteenth century American Windsor chairs were imported this way. In this state Chippendale declared them as mere 'lumber' worth only eighteen pounds. Quite apart from the reduced value, lumber carried low duty as a raw material – wood – nothing like that of finished chairs. If successful, Chippendale would have reassembled and upholstered the chairs in his workshops. Customs, responding to London cabinetmakers' complaints, visited workshops to check on such practices and to seize smuggled goods. In this case the chair frames were seized on the Calais Packet, *John Gilby*, on arrival from Calais. Customs followed a simple form of justice in these cases: they paid the importer the declared value plus ten per cent and the duty paid. They then sold the goods at true market value, keeping the proceeds.

They also caught Chippendale with smuggled chintz fabrics for Mrs Garrick's bed furniture and other smuggled textiles like Gobelin tapestries used for covering French chairs. He was not alone in these guilty practices: other distinguished cabinet-makers and furnishers were cited in complaints to Parliament about such common proceedings. Imported mirror glass was also the subject of much smuggling. Since Chippendale was very active in supplying girandoles with carved frames, he probably used smuggled glass, too.

Christopher Gilbert recorded many of Chippendale's country house commissions, complete with documentary records and invoices. But not all of them. Much of the furniture Chippendale's workshops produced is unmarked, unlabelled, solid mahogany Georgian furniture. Not all his productions are to be found in the three editions of his *Director*. A lot of individual designs for particular clients lie unrecorded, especially those before the *Director* was published. Gilbert says that finding the early work would be pure treasure trove to historians.

Not fact, or at least not established fact: that, despite Justin's enthusiasm, Ousedon Overwood Hall was supplied with furniture by Chippendale. The house is not mentioned in Christopher Gilbert's book, which has details of all the documented work and supplies that have been established without doubt. Gilbert's is a scrupulous work of scholarship and he repeated that much of Chippendale's work remains to be found.

Ousedon Overwood Hall stood on the site of an original house of 1710 date, which was rebuilt in 1840 to the rather stolid sub-classical designs of the architect Decimus Burton. Like Grimston in North Yorkshire, where they also collaborated, the gardens were laid out by William Andrews Nesfield. Throughout the nineteenth century the house was owned by various members of a family called Thwaite, who made their money in wool, coal and shipping. In 1900 they were still relatively wealthy despite financial setbacks but, like many of the landed gentry, their fortunes went down quickly after 1918. Death duties and profligate expenditure brought about the abandonment of the house in 1932, its fabric having been neglected for nearly thirty years. Like Kenneth Clark's Sudbourne Hall, it was sold to a speculator who left it to fall into dangerously ruinous condition. In the late 1940s, under the Labour Government, it was compulsorily purchased for a nominal sum, demolished and a council house estate built on the site. The intention was to develop Ousedon Overwood as a satellite of York, but this was put into abeyance when the Conservatives returned to power.

Fact: Justin Harrington was found dead somewhere in the Ouse valley to the north-west of York. My guess was that it was near the village of Ousedon Overwood.

France, and Chippendale, and Yorkshire; it was all happening long before Henry Roland and Justin Harrington and somebody else thought up whatever it was that killed the two of them.

Chapter Thirteen

'Steve,' Ellen Stanton said, standing close to me in the hall in a way that made rational conversation difficult, 'has gone back to college.'

She had arrived out of the blue in her Mini Cooper and, after the bell on the shop door rang gladly at her entrance, she turned around and turned the key inside. Then, with door locked, she came across to stand close. Which made me lose concentration.

'To Leeds?'

'That is where he is at college, as you know.'

'In the car?'

'The car?' For a moment she looked puzzled. 'Oh, the Riley, you mean. Yes, he's taken it with him again. He took me in it last time even though he thinks it's much safer in the coach house at home. In any case, he and George Baker fixed the rocker boxes, or the timing gears, or whatever it was, and it gives him freedom up there.'

'Good lad.'

'I'm glad you get on well with him.'

'It's not difficult. As I've said, he's a very likeable young man.'

'I'm also glad that he's gone back. It means he can get on with his course and I can get on with you. Like this.'

This was the last thing she said before we progressed upstairs and urgent events took their vigorous course, events which gave rise to noises it would be ungallant to describe and which would have taxed a much younger man. There was a kind of determination with which she set about this particular coupling that was a bit alarming. It had a sense of purpose that suggested a hidden agenda intended to divert and yet determine something ulterior. It certainly made demands.

So that, when I was eventually asked what I had been doing since last time and whether the rumours she had heard were true, I recounted the happenings of the last two days lying flat on my back staring at the ceiling and pacing my breathing whilst talking.

I'm not sure that this was wise. In retrospect and in view of what followed, I should have adopted a more intimate approach than the sparse relating of events and their aftermath in the simple terms I produced. With perhaps just a touch of urbane objectivity about events that I couldn't resist. But I was knackered, and ulterior motives were far from my mind.

'I was going to complain of neglect,' she said eventually, turning on her side to face me, 'but I do understand now, with all this going on, that you have been somewhat preoccupied.'

She wrapped a length of sheet around herself as she spoke, indicating, as I understood it, that the noisy pleasures were over and this was to be a serious conversation undiverted by any distracting sight of the sources of those pleasures like, say, naked flesh. On the grounds, presumably, that sights of that kind might start things up again. Some chance; but I should have been on guard.

'Somewhat,' I agreed.

'Not one but two of your old school cronies have snuffed it. Or rather, have been snuffed. Henry Roland particularly. You've been involved with both of them in a business sense at one time or another. And you were at school together. My God, you're at centre stage. The police always look close to home. Apart from that, you may be in danger. What are you going to do?'

'I should leave the police to get on with it.'

'But you're not going to?' She leant forward with what I took to be curiosity. 'You're going to run around to the various *mises-en-scène?*'

'I don't think I can leave it to the police. They are probably jumping to the wrong conclusions. I think I may have to make inquiries of my own in sheer self-protection.'

'I had a fear you might say that.'

'Don't worry, I won't take any unnecessary risks.'

'I'm glad to hear it.' Her voice didn't seem to express much gladness or relief. She wound the sheet, if anything, a little tighter. 'I said I had a fear not because you might take unnecessary risks but because of an intuitive feeling I've had since we last had a little rendezvous and what you said then. About your running around.'

'Oh?'

'Yes. You see, he didn't say as much, out of macho pride I'm sure, but I'm pretty certain that Justin suspected, all that time ago, that someone was humping his wife. Some of the remarks he made gave me that feeling. A bit ironic for him to get wound up about it because he was humping anybody else's wife that was available. And the rest.'

'Just a minute—'

'No, don't interrupt. I seem to remember that you told me you were at school with Justin, then you ran into him again in the East End one Sunday morning. Brick Lane, wasn't it?'

'Yes.'

'And Elizabeth was with him?'

'Of course. In those days they were always together.'

'So that's when you first met her?'

'Well yes, but—'

'I thought so. When I think about it, and I have thought about it, somewhat at length, at the time I'm talking about the most likely candidate to have been humping Justin Harrington's wife would be you. You seem to know what she knew about his extramarital life. You knew her very well from early days and you know what they say: always look close to home and friends.'

'What? Ellen—'

'You see, if you're going to go off playing detective, you've every reason to visit, interrogate and console the grieving widow. Who won't be grieving much, by all accounts, and will be all too ready to be consoled. Is that what you intend to do? Because if you're going to start humping Elizabeth Harrington all over again, I'd just like to know, that's all.'

Chapter Fourteen

Ellen was right.

We used to get up before dark, shivering in the nose-nipping cold of an unheated Sunday morning. I didn't bother to shave. We drank a quick cup of tea in kitchen silence, listening vaguely to distant creaks in the old, much-divided house and stared at each other dumbly in the glaring artificial light. When the tea was finished we went out to the car, and performed its starting ritual: I switched on, set the ignition lever to retard and took the starting-handle out from under the driver's seat. At the bonnet I fumbled to insert the crank under the radiator and, when the engine turned over to the right point, pulled accurately once. The motor always fired immediately, despite a battery too flat to turn the heavy mass over on the self-starter. Sometimes, to save trouble, I parked on the slope facing the Archway Road and simply freewheeled away. More often there were other vehicles at the kerb that impeded a rolling start, so I had to use the handle.

No traffic disturbed the blank, watching windows. Only the soft burble of exhaust from the Riley Falcon echoed back occasionally as the car swept round a bend that curved past the chrome-capped bonnet. Sometimes Marian liked to stare sideways into big shop windows to watch the mirrored image of the car glinting in and out of glass as it sped down the empty streets like a fleeting black phantom. The sight always gave her a dramatic thrill, like seeing herself in a film or on a television screen. That's us, she would think, over there, rolling along in the dark like that, that's what we look like to the outside world: Bill and Marian Franklin, on their way, in their car; did you see them?

If we were a bit earlier than usual we'd park near the Public Baths in Cheshire Street, on the dog-leg between Brick Lane and Vallance Road. As we got out, the first stirrings of Bethnal Green heralded the hushed anticipation of those anxious to get into position. It was best to be there when the vans were opened or the wares first spread onto the rubble of cleared sites where heaps of splintered joists and unreclaimable timber were piled into dying bonfires amongst the piles of bricks. We would leave the car near Brick Lane and take the Cheshire Street turn for the south side of the blackened yellow brick of the railway viaduct into Vallance Road itself. There, terraced grids of tight-packed houses that might once have seen Jack the Ripper flitting by were being bulldozed down to hard core for an unknown infill, somewhere deep, where earthen pressure would blind those knowing windows. On this other railway-side, flaring with mantle-light, a pie stall would be open, surrounded by shabby, shivering dealers cupping their hands round mugs of milky, sugared tea drawn from a steaming urn that smelt of kerosene. These habitués were sometimes slightly hostile, sometimes unconcerned.

One Sunday a couple caught the corner of my eye as I turned to avoid a dealer's splattering cough. I registered them with a faint curiosity, finding it hard to see clearly. The man was about my own age, tall, high-haired in a vaguely familiar way, big, wearing a roughish Raglan overcoat and thick scarf, walking ahead of the young woman, who was pushing a pushchair with a kid in it. The kid was about two, or maybe a bit younger, bound up in a sort of brown siren-suit with a fur hood clamped round his head so that just the chubby face poked out. Little red wellingtons capped by brown sock-ends, turned down, covered his feet stuck on the chair's footrest. In the freezing half-dark, as they emerged from the dripping railway bridge that crossed Vallance Road just below Cheshire Street, they were caught in the glow of burning rafters on the collapsed pile of houses demolished along the first leg of the street. It looked like a bomb-site in an old newsreel. The cleared spaces were pitted with craters and puddles between which totters were setting up their booty: rags and clothes and books and household goods, for sale.

A Nativity family, I first thought, seeing the little unit picking its way through the rubbish, avoiding the pie stall, not coming close to the dealers but waiting for the grey dawning light to rise the few more lumens that would signal the scramble, the start of trading. Father, mother and child together; it'll be Christmas soon.

The young woman had an innocent air, with an excited stamp to the movement of her feet, like a child being hurried to a funfair in which it knows there will be excitements and disappointments, prizes won and lost, giddy experiences, colour, noise and brightness. This had something lurid, where adults got more excited than children. As she went by, across the road, I saw that she had light brown hair and was smooth-skinned, with a wide mouth above a pointed chin. The man had passed already, stopped and turned towards a totter with a pramload of leather-bound books, so I couldn't see his face.

'Amateurs. Harrington is the name.' Old Chess, near me, lifted his nose in a mock-snobbish expression as he spoke to Fat Arthur beside him. 'Justin Harrington, he's called. A writer. On antiques. Knows it all. Not that you'd've heard of him. Wouldn't buy our trash, would he?'

Fat Arthur pulled a face at him, half-concealing it. Fat Arthur was young then, still a green apprentice in a Hackney Road cabinetmaker's. His Portsmouth Road workshops were to come years later. He never liked old Chester Goldman; was a bit frightened of him. Not physically; old Chess was no physical match for anyone. But he looked like a masculine witch, a he-harpy, relict of legendary days at the long-gone Caledonian Market, the pre-war one that really was in the Caledonian Road. He might bring down a curse on you, tarnish your spoons, crack your crystal, flatten your impasto. There was something mystical about Chess, along with much, much knowledge. Fat Arthur was too frightened to sell to Chess and too frightened to buy from him. Either way he was sure he would lose, that Chess would know something he didn't, make a bloody fool of him so that all the other dealers would laugh. It really riled him; Chess was always telling him to go and learn something, denigrating him.

I had known Chess for a year. We had engineering in common. The old man had been a journeyman toolmaker back in the Twenties and he looked at metal with a boilersuited eye. Milling machines and lathes, grinders and polishers, castings and lost wax; we talked about those things when we first met, in the Portobello Road, arguing over a brass candlestick and a monkey-weight that was Benin. Chester Goldman was quite proprietorial about me now, had taken a shine to me, always greeted me with a twinkle and Marian with elaborate courtesy. Sometimes it was embarrassing. There were sides to this business, sides you took or didn't; if you were on Chess's side it cut you off from others. But I learnt from him.

A soft grey light suddenly made the girders above the viaduct more visible. There never was an actual signal. It was always an unannounced moment, when the dawn filtered a little more strongly across the sky to provide those few more precious yards of view, and the crowd around the pie stall would dissolve. It moved furtively in individual shuffles to tour the open vans, the stalls, the spread piles, the junk-piled prams wheeled by wheezing tramp-figures who emerged from hidden lairs to beckon with eldridge gestures or glare with defiant truculence.

Marian left on a navigation of her own. I downed my tea and moved towards a rusty Commer not far away, only to hear a protesting wheeze behind me.

''Ere!' Old Chess was indignant. 'Where're you orf in such an 'urry? Trying to shake me off, are yer?'

There was a kind of protocol, an etiquette amongst the trade, quickly learnt, that dictated the territorial behaviour of dealer towards dealer. You did not infringe the movements of the other or seem to pry into sources and prices paid.

'Going to Cutler Street, after?'

Cutler Street: like all those Jewish dealers, Chester Goldman loved small, bright things, coins and jewellery, opals and pearls, miniatures and icons. Things you could put in your pocket and run with. Things like sovereigns and Maria Theresa dollars, bracelets, diamonds in little velvet cases, figurines, porcelain medallions, art and life seen through microscopes, the tinier the better. It was bred in the bone. Sometimes he helped me with furniture, of course he did, but Sheraton chests had been thirty bob in Chess's day, walnut five quid, oak not much pricier. You couldn't carry that stuff far. He wasn't impressed by furniture. What he really liked would be there on the stalls at Cutler Street, glinting and glancing in the morning light.

I shook my head. 'Busy,' I said.

Goldman scowled. ' I suppose you're only young once. Can't work all the time, can yer?'

He produced another enormous wink and disappeared towards a stall loaded with trinkets. I headed for a big pantechnicon groaning with books. Sixpence for ordinary and ninepence for leather bindings; I needed to book-furnish some shelves for a bureau bookcase. It was almost fully light now and excited children's voices filled the air. Thickly clad adults bustled or stared intently, making quick shifts from activity to guarded reticence. Disinterest, casual enquiry, and an absence of interest in facial expression were carefully cultivated. Never let on, old Chess would have said, never let on what you're interested in or what you know. Never boast. Never tell anyone anything.

A Victorian buttonback armchair with cabriole legs, perched on the back of a light commercial lorry, caught my attention. How much, I asked the villainous-looking totter, a man with a cast in one eye and another that never saw you straight on.

'Two quid, same as allus; wot d'you ask for?' The eyes crossed over me. 'Don't think too long about it. The coppers are coming.'

This was true. At the bottom end of Vallance Road, police uniforms could be seen moving steadily towards us, pushing ahead of their black, silver-buttoned line a disgruntled detritus of dislodged illegal traders like rubble before a bulldozer. It was, clearly, a Sunday for a token show of the Law.

'Done.' I handed the two notes over. The chair might go on the back seat with a carton of books. Otherwise it would have to be the roof. I hadn't had a bad morning: the books, two candlesticks, a broken bird-in-cage automaton and the chair. Carrying the lot with what I hoped was an easily slung competence I strolled back under the railway bridge, whistling softly to myself.

In front of the Baths back in Cheshire Street, as I reached the car, I ran slap into him. It was inevitable. Another prelude, you might say, this time under the railway bridge between Cheshire Street and Vallance Road, where Cheshire Street becomes Dunbridge or something.

'Franklin! Monty Franklin!' The voice was deep, roughish, and I didn't recognise it at first. But I recognised the man.

'Baz,' I said, putting the chair down on the pavement. 'Baz Stevens.'

He grinned as he shook my hand and his head. 'Not any more. I'm Justin Harrington now.'

'Sorry?' I pretended not to know.

'I'm afraid I had to leave Baz Stevens behind. Family problems while we were in France. My stepmother and I found Lille too small for the two of us. When I came back I thought it best to make a clean break.' His voice dropped the roughish edge and sounded more sympathetic. 'So I changed my name completely. Baz Stevens is long gone. The Harringtons were remote cousins on my mother's side. Actually, since I left you're the first person I've met from the days in School House. Do you keep up with the old boys' club?'

'Absolutely not. You're the first person I've met, too. I avoid the people and try to forget the days. And I'm Bill now, by the way.'

He chuckled. 'Awful, wasn't it? But what a coincidence.'

'Yes. Amazing.'

I stood awkwardly for a moment, not quite knowing what to say. We had very little in common. He gestured at the chair. 'Is that for personal or for trade?'

'Oh, it's for trade. We sell them during the week, usually in the evenings.'

He raised his eyebrows in a characteristic way and nodded approvingly. 'Very enterprising. Victoriana, eh? The coming thing, I believe.'

I smiled. 'Is it? All I know is that it's easy to sell because it's cheap. I know that people who collect real antiques don't rate it.'

'I have to say I'm not keen. But you don't find much eighteenth-century stuff down here. Apart from the occasional ceramic bit.'

'True.'

'Justin?' A female voice broke into our exchange, a warm female voice that belonged to the young mother with brown hair and springy step I had observed last time. She had broad, soft facial features and a slightly wide figure, almost stocky but at the same time feminine, hinting at fecundity. Baz, as I still thought of him, smiled broadly as he gestured at me.

'Elizabeth, meet a man from my past. This is Monty – no, Bill Franklin. He used to be called Monty. We were at school together. No, not just at school; we were in School House together.'

'Good grief.' She smiled broadly at me as she held out her hand. 'I've never met anyone from Justin's boarding school days before. This is amazing. You look quite normal. I always understood from Justin that everyone was barking mad at that place.'

I grinned as I shook the hand. 'He's right. You have no idea.'

'I was beginning to think that the whole place was an invention of Justin's. Good for after-dinner stories without any factual basis. Is it true that some books in the library had slices of bread and butter compressed in them?'

'Absolutely. Roland Tertius's speciality. One called *Mountaineering in the Land of the Midnight Sun* contained a selection going over several years.'

'Heavens. And did you really throw them – the books – at each other?'

'On rainy days, often.'

'Hell!' She turned to him. 'I apologise.'

He made a mock bow. 'See what I told you was true. I am your husband. I do not lie to you.'

'Oh yeah?'

Just then, Marian came round the corner. There were introductions and exclamations. It turned out that the Harringtons lived in Muswell Hill, which was not far from us.

So Elizabeth invited us to dinner. Which is where it all began.

Chapter Fifteen

The offer from Tony Fitzsimmonds came with the morning post. It took the form of a letter of engagement with a confidentiality agreement attached. The letter was pretty straightforward. It offered me terms as a consultant to the proposed Art Investment Fund, with various clauses describing the duties required and offering a very acceptable retainer as well as hourly fees for attending meetings or special inspections. The confidentiality agreement was much more legal, required signing in three copies, and covered just about every piece of information that might be disclosed to me by Leggatt's. I'd seen many such documents in my previous business life and this one didn't frighten me. I signed it and wrote back a letter of acceptance, reciprocating Tony Fitzsimmonds' warm expressions of expectation of future mutual benefit and the joys of working together. Even if I had to suppress various suspicions that were surfacing, I felt like a man who has been welcomed back into a kind of fold.

That morning, a fold was what I needed. In a bad dream, Detective Sergeant Walters came to tell me that my alibi for the evening of Henry Roland's death was no good. Mrs Stanton denied being with me at the time I claimed. It brought me awake, shivering.

I sat at my breakfast table for a few moments of thought, going over my conversation yesterday with Ellen after she'd dropped her noisome little bombshell. I tried to keep things as light as possible. Of course, I told her, I had no intention of seducing the grieving widow. The idea was fantastic. Her marriage to Justin was a strange one in many ways but there are many forms of marriage and what different partners might accept from each other. My relationship with the Harringtons had been principally with Justin, not Elizabeth. The past was the past. I hadn't seen her for years. And having to do a little sleuthing to make sure the police didn't label me as principal suspect didn't include consoling the grieving widows of either Justin or Henry.

It was a tender spot, though, one I didn't want to touch.

'But did you hump her?' Ellen demanded.

'No,' I lied. 'You want a clear-cut answer? You've got one. No.'

'I think you're lying.'

'The past is the past,' I said, probably colouring at the intrusion, the seeming crudity of it, the reduction of something that was once so complex to such coarse simplicity. 'The past is the past. None of it matters now. Any more than yours with him belongs to me.'

'But I've been honest with you.' Now she was fulfilling Kingsley Amis's famous criticism of the character of women: the automatic assumption of the role of injured party in any argument. 'You're not being the same with me. I've been carrying my guilt about Justin and you've just sat, or rather lain, or even humped there without saying a bloody word about *her*.' She was playing that recognised feminine card as well, the one that spreads guilt all over the other party. 'I think I deserve more than that.'

'Ellen, what do you mean? He's only been dead a few days. I never once accused you of the possibility of going back to him while he was alive.'

'It was over. I told you it was over. I never hid it from you. I knew he was a fake very soon after it started and when I'd had enough I ended it. But she's free now and available. Oh, I bet she's available. And you have kept schtum all this time.'

'What makes you think that anything, if there ever was anything, with Elizabeth, is still continuing with me?'

'Because my gut feeling tells me you haven't levelled with me.'

'I've told you quite openly that I haven't been a saint since my marriage ended. I'm a normal man. But Elizabeth Harrington is not part of my plans, not in any way. Your intuition is wrong.'

'I think you're prevaricating. I have a sense of something impending, something you're holding back. Something you should but haven't told me, whatever it is.'

She rolled off the edge of the bed and went into the bathroom, trailing her wrapping sheet, and closed the door. I sat like a stone until she came out, dressed. There are things you can deal with and things you can't. I didn't understand the sequence of events.

'Well?' she demanded.

'Well what? I think this is very strange. Bizarre. I don't understand any of it.'

'It shouldn't take much understanding. You have to be as honest with me as I have been with you.'

'Why did you come here today? Why did you set this conflict going at the time you did? After the joy we'd just had?'

'Oh, I'm very sorry. Is my timing a problem?'

I thought of the purposeful way she'd set about me on arrival before replying. 'Yes, I'm afraid it is.'

She smiled ruefully and shook her head. 'You really are a cool customer, aren't you? Life in compartments, that's you. The big sex act mustn't be spoilt by a little bit of honesty afterwards, must it? Well, I'm very sorry if my timing was off, but maybe it suddenly occurred to me that yours has been just a bit too flawless. I came to this shop soon after I'd been made a widow and you got into the consolation stakes pretty damn quick. What is going to stop you from doing it again? With someone with whom I think you've got a back history? One which you've kept well under wraps.'

'Ellen, this is crazy. You and I – our relationship – is quite different.'

'Are we? Is it? Different from what?'

'Now you're trying to trap me. I haven't said that there is anything to justify, to explain away.'

'There is something though, isn't there?'

Yes, there was, but it was no good temporising. She wanted a conversation I wasn't prepared to have, not on the terms she was demanding. Ellen Stanton had abruptly become tough and territorial, it seemed to me. This sudden eruption froze my feelings into defence. She left, still obstinate, and I sat alone trying to unstitch my needled feelings. I thought she was unreasonable, a combination of the illogical and impulsive whilst pursuing an agenda. It was she who came to me after she was widowed, not vice versa. The sudden inquisition had caught me off balance though, it had to be said. Things I had put away for years, things not wanting to be faced, had started to surface. I wasn't ready to face them. Tangled webs are tangled webs; we flies take time to escape them.

Tony Fitzsimmonds' letter lightened a dank arising. After dealing with it, I went off to see Fat Arthur.

His workshops were in Ripley, on what was once the Portsmouth Road, but the village is now bypassed by the A3. Fat Arthur is not far from the Talbot Hotel, where Nelson probably stopped when posting down to join the *Victory* for the last time. The workshops occupy what was once a set of stables, useful for the enormous horse traffic of yesteryear but now converted for nefarious cabinetmaking and restoration purposes. Fat Arthur supplied the trade. Ask and it shall be forthcoming. You want a drum-top table? Here is a top and in the back room there is the base of an old breakfast table that will do fine. A marriage can be arranged. You want a walnut bureau? Fat Arthur used to take unsaleable old oak ones in bad condition, veneer them up in double thickness knife-cut walnut, bleach, wash, polish and sell as Queen Anne within the week.

To satisfy the demand for antique furniture with antique furniture would be beyond the bounds of possibility.

Want a Georgian wing armchair? A reproduction one with giveaway late cabrioles can easily be converted. Take a pair of straight old mahogany table legs from the pile outside; make the stretchers by knocking the fronts off Victorian tray drawers and plane them down. Cover all in black wax after you've button polished and buff to a deep shine, making sure not to overdo it where the piece wouldn't have got polished. Now you have a new structure under the old armchair but all made of good old mahogany in the mid-Georgian manner. Fat

Arthur and his men are nothing if not inventive. A dreadful little tambour-top Edwardian desk with tapering fluted legs? Veneer in satinwood to cover the flutes, do the rest necessary and off it goes as a Sheraton tambour satinwood *bonheur du jour* to a suitable auction.

A *bonheur du jour* like that is called, by those who know or get landed with it, as a *malheur du jour*.

I got there fairly smartly at eleven o'clock, still in a state about Ellen. Going to Fat Arthur's was a gamble; he was not particularly friendly due to my association, all those years ago, with Chess. I never used his services and so was of no financial benefit to him. But he usually managed to be curtly civil on the odd occasions I saw him. Our paths crossed at sales and sometimes in antiques shops where he might be delivering. I thought it worth a try to sound him out.

I arrived and began to pull myself together.

A dirty glue pot was bubbling on a gas ring, letting the distinctive sour aroma of hot cowhide glue mingle with those of shavings and sawdust. Benches were piled with pieces of wood and veneer. Broken chairs and pieces of furniture cluttered up spaces between boys and men in brown coats, white coats and no coats, all of them smudged. The man nearest me, in stained brown overalls, turned to look at me as I closed the glazed workshop door. A chair beside him, missing its front legs, had a back in one of the most popular Chippendale designs. The mortices in a pair of chamfered square section mahogany replacement legs were awaiting fitting to the tenons. Chairs were a speciality here.

'Well, well, Stan,' Fat Arthur said to him, coming out of a side office with a three-foot-long steel sash cramp in his hand, 'look what the wind's blown in.'

'Good morning, Arthur,' I said politely.

He was bigger and fatter than he had been in the Vallance Road days. Not much hair was left on his head but what was left was grey. There were big pouches under his eyes. Modern medical practice would classify him as a high risk for insurance purposes but what would they know? People like Fat Arthur ruin medical statistics.

'Haven't seen you for a long time,' he said.

'No, I suppose not.'

'You know Mr Bill Franklin, Stan?' He was still talking to the brown overalls. 'Lately turned antiques dealer after a life travelling in business?'

'No,' said Stan, 'I don't. Never heard of him.'

'Such is fame, eh?' Fat Arthur said, smiling nastily at me.

He wasn't going to shake hands; he just stood looking at me. Somewhere in the workshop someone put a plank through a band saw with a shriek of wood and saw blade. Craftsmen were looking at me curiously whilst pretending to get on with work.

'Is there somewhere we can talk?' I asked.

'Will it be worth my while?'

'I don't know until I talk to you.'

'I'm a bit busy, you see.' He gestured with the sash cramp. 'And I don't suppose you're bringing me any work, are you?'

'No. But information is always valuable.'

'What information?'

'Oh, things about Justin Harrington and Henry Roland, both deceased.'

'Bit late to come for info about them now they're brown bread, isn't it?'

'Not really. I was thinking more about outstanding monies and Chippendale furniture. And Ousedon Overwood Hall.'

His face twitched slightly, just once. 'No idea what you're talking about. I'm not owed any money. If you're owed money it's no good coming here. I haven't got any Chippendale furniture. And I've never heard of – what did you call it – Overwood Hall?'

His eyes, deep in tired sockets, stared at me in challenge. Suddenly I felt tired of being lied to. I decided to lie back.

'Oh well,' I said. 'In that case I'll keep going. To Basingstoke. To see if the police there looking into Henry's death will be interested in the concept of CKD furniture.'

'In what?'

'French furniture. Chairs in particular. Shipped across in component knocked-down form so that there's no Customs record of chair importation. Chippendale was doing it in the 1760s. Nothing new. Best way to create French chairs from nowhere. Leave no trail. Something you've been doing for a while. But this time I'm more interested – and so will they be – in the complete chairs, shipped over from Paris in their fully upholstered regalia – Gobelin tapestry covering and all – as the real thing.'

Suddenly he had paled. His grip tightened on the flat perforated metal bar of the cramp.

'I don't know what you're fucking talking about,' he snapped. 'I'm busy. Too busy to waste time with amateurs. Why don't you piss off and let workers get on with their work?'

'Don't worry. I'm leaving.'

I turned, opened the glazed workshop door and walked out to my car in the parking strip in front of the building. As I clicked the central locking keypad to release the doors, he came up after me, steel sash cramp still in hand.

'Piece of advice,' he snapped, coming up close so that his face was inches from mine and his big stomach almost touching my waist.

'Advice?'

'Yes, advice, *mate*. Don't get clever. Tell the police nothing. Fuck all, you hear me?'

'Really?'

'Yes *really*.' He jabbed a spare finger at me. 'You are out of your depth, you are. You go blabbering around and you'll find life very fucking difficult. In this trade we don't grass on each other, see? There are some very big forces at work these days and they don't like talkers. You go about saying things and suggesting ideas, you'll be very fucking sorry. Very, very sorry. Know what I mean?'

'Not really. Thanks for the advice all the same. I'm not going to Basingstoke, as it happens. But you've told me what I wanted to know.'

Suffused with rage, he brought the sash cramp round in a sweep to shoulder level, raising it with both arms for a blow. It left his face exposed.

Automatically, I did what Tomás Puig taught me to do, all those years ago, when I was thirteen: a straight left out from my shoulder, with the weight of a body swing behind it. I was rusty; I aimed at his nose but he was tilting his head back with his swing. I connected with the point of his fat jaw instead.

He went over backwards like a sack. The back of his head smacked the tarmac road surface and he let out a sound like a squeal as the breath went out of him. The sash cramp clattered to the ground. Prone on his back, he moaned, eyelids fluttering.

The workshop door flew open and the cabinetmaker called Stan in the stained brown overalls came out with another bigger fellow at his shoulder. As they quick-stepped towards me, elbows out, I picked up the sash cramp in both hands and held it high, like a broadsword, the screw handle at the working end pointed at them. They stopped dead in their tracks.

'He's not hurt. He'll come round in a minute,' I said. 'You need to put a damp cloth on the back of his neck.' I lowered the cramp. 'I'll keep this as evidence. You tell him that if he tries any funny tricks I'll have him charged with assault with an offensive weapon. For certain.'

I threw the cramp onto the back seat, got in the car, started the engine, and drove off. When I looked in the rear-view mirror they were still standing on the parking strip, staring after me. Fat Arthur was starting to sit upright.

I thought nothing changes over the years, nothing; Fat Arthur is just as greedy, nasty and frightened as ever.

Then my mobile phone rang.

Chapter Sixteen

They were waiting for me when I got back from Fat Arthur's. Three of them this time. They phoned me on my mobile to make sure I'd be available when they arrived. There was the same rather nondescript car, the same two men – Walters and Green – in token suits and another, taller man in a raincoat.

'This is DC Powell,' Sergeant Walters said, as I opened the shop door to let them in after I'd turned off the burglar alarm. 'He is from York.'

I smiled at him politely but he didn't smile back. He just nodded.

'DC Powell is coordinating our inquiries from the Yorkshire end,' Walters went on, 'in view of a possible connection between Roland and Harrington.'

A long way, I thought, to come on the off chance of seeing me. But then they probably had other fish to fry and had taken in Dorking already.

'So the connection is important?'

'We have yet to establish the exact nature of their

transactions,' Walters replied formally. 'But it is an area we are actively examining.'

'So Justin's death is suspicious?'

'At the moment we are considering the possibility.'

'Oh dear.'

He ignored my expression of dismay. 'You said that when Roland came to see you, just before he was murdered, he claimed that he was owed for a container-load of antiques shipped to America?'

'That's what he said.'

'You have no idea what was in the container?'

'No idea, no.'

'Any guess you can hazard?'

'Well, Henry was fixed on Georgian mahogany furniture. It was his life. He took the drop in trade hard. Henry had the turning circle of a supertanker. He wasn't flexible.'

'Odd, you see, Mr Franklin, because we can find no record of any transaction between Roland and Harrington for Georgian furniture. Nothing at all.'

'What about anything else?'

'Nothing so far. What sort of thing might we be looking for?'

The question wasn't put aggressively but the hint of suspicion hung over it. If I wasn't involved, which they evidently thought I might be, how could I refuse to assist?

'What about French furniture?'

'Why do you suggest that?'

'Because the day Henry was here it came up in conversation. We discussed the sale of the Fauville cabinet in New York last year – it made a million – and I recalled how Henry's father was sound on French stuff. He agreed but he seemed a bit strange about it.'

'Strange? In what way?'

'Oh, I don't know; a bit put out, somehow. He ended the conversation and left.'

'There's no record,' it was DC Green now, 'of any transaction between Roland and Harrington for Georgian or French furniture. Nothing.'

'Oh.'

'You don't sound surprised. Yet you say Roland claimed, when he was here, that Harrington owed him for a shipment.'

'Maybe they were both acting as third parties in a transaction between others.'

'Like commission agents, you mean?'

'Something like that, yes.'

'Maybe that transaction went through you.' Walters returned to the attack.

'I've told you it didn't. You can check my books.'

'We are doing that.'

'Without result, obviously.'

'We'll find out in due course.' Walters gestured at the York man, Powell. 'You've got a few questions, I think.'

'Just one or two.' Powell's Yorkshire accent was clear and pleasant. 'Have you any idea why Harrington was up in Yorkshire?'

'None. I hadn't seen him for a long time. We were not on good terms. Have you asked his TV company?'

'Oh yes, we have. And they say there was no reason of theirs why he should be there.'

'His wife?'

'She was away on the Continent. She knows of no reason, either.'

She's lying, I thought. But I didn't say anything.

'You say you were not on good terms?' Walters was back in interruption.

'Not really, no.'

'Why was that?'

'Mainly due to a disagreement over a book he commissioned from me. He reneged on the deal.'

'When was that?'

'About seven or eight years ago.'

'Oh?' Powell gave me a hard stare. 'That's odd. Because you see we have run through a great deal of footage the TV company provided and there's an unused record of you and Harrington at a café at an antiques fair about four years ago, or maybe even less. You seem to be getting on pretty well to me. Drinking coffee and chatting?'

Next to him, the other two stared at me, waiting. How do you explain that after years of association, conversations can be had which do not reopen old wounds or even friendships, nor regenerate the old warmth, that do not tread on swollen toes, but are still civilised?

'I didn't say we ever came to fisticuffs,' I said. 'And as it happened, that was quite a tense conversation. If I'd known we were being filmed for use in evidence four years later, I'd have shaken my fist at him.'

Powell suddenly smiled. 'I don't suppose the film is conclusive. But you do see that there are grounds for thinking your involvement with Harrington has been both long term and more recent, like that with Roland? And not necessarily hostile?'

'There must be many others of whom precisely the same can be said.'

'Indeed. Though not from the same school, the same boarding house.'

The three of them regarded me steadily once again. I had a vision, a memory photo-flash, of those ranked boys on the lawn by the big brick house, all unknowing, in that prelude, of what form the future might take.

I looked back at them. 'Tell me,' I demanded, 'how Justin was killed.'

'I'm afraid that the manner of his death is not for public dissemination. It contains evidence of a special nature.'

'But it wasn't a shot, like Henry Roland?'

'No. That's all I am prepared to say.'

'And you don't know why he was up in that neck of the woods? Apart from originally coming from Yorkshire?'

'He came from Leeds.' Powell spoke as though that were a foreign country. 'Not York or its environs.'

'You do know that he had a thing about Ousedon Overwood Hall? Was he researching that?'

'Ousedon Overwood,' Powell repeated slowly, as though savouring the name. 'The village not far from where he was found? What sort of thing?'

'He thought that the original hall contained furniture made by Chippendale. Hasn't anyone mentioned that?'

'No, they haven't.' Powell was suddenly more attentive. 'Ousedon Overwood hasn't had a hall for decades. I know it well. Why did he believe that?'

'He had sudden enthusiasms about things, particularly old things. But his interest in Ousedon Overwood went back a long way. He was convinced that Thomas Chippendale had supplied it with furniture. Or at least he wanted to be convinced. There was an oral tradition amongst one or two old villagers that the hall had once had some exceptional mahogany furniture.'

'Did he find any record of it?'

'Not that I know of. The house doesn't feature in Christopher Gilbert's work on Chippendale, so that makes it a very long shot.'

'Why would he visit the area?'

'To talk to someone, maybe. A local historian of some sort. Places like that generate local historians, some of them very good.'

'Interesting.' Powell made a note of some sort on a small pad.

'It may be a wild goose chase, of course,' Walters said, still looking at me.

'It probably is. But you asked me and I've told you. It's not a chase in which I participated, so I don't know how far he'd got.'

'But such furniture, if it existed, would be very valuable?'

'Very.'

'So that might be a reason for someone anxious to get their hands on it to keep him out of the way?'

'I suppose it's one possibility. But Justin had made enemies of all sorts in his time. He wasn't exactly popular with many people involved in antiques.'

'We're including that aspect in our line of inquiries.' Powell nodded once again. 'It would provide a more powerful motive if someone stood to gain financially by his demise, however.'

'I suppose so.'

'You don't know of anyone who obviously stood to gain, by any chance? Apart from his immediate family, of course?'

'I'm afraid not,' I said.

Chapter Seventeen

The offices of Harrington and Beckland were not far from Clapham High Street. The publishing company was on the first floor of a sub-classical block built in the 1930s, now divided into respectable premises in what was once a low-cost but not very fashionable area. Elsewhere in the building were various media enterprises, accountants and a firm of lawyers. The location, it seemed to me, was not very accessible and lacked both the ease of parking or, probably, the low rentals that had, years ago, made it attractive. It was almost a clandestine place, south of the river and wedged into congested obscurity, as though the address would discourage potential visitors. It smacked neither of inky scholarship nor trendy success. The entrance was clean and the feeling on entry anonymous. Inside, the place was tidy, without the atmosphere of frowst and stacked reams of dusty proofs I associated with publishing. To an outsider it might seem difficult, at first, to guess what went on here. Justin Harrington always met his authors in the West End, leaving most of the publishing mechanics to the staff in this place.

'I do keep an office in the building, though,' he once said to me. 'They call it the Erratum Room.'

It would have been useless to phone for an appointment. That way provides the easiest of those used to put visitors off. Taken aback by my unannounced arrival and cheerful request to see the head of the firm, the receptionist stared at me incredulously, as though I had made a preposterous suggestion. 'Celia Beckland? Have you got an appointment?'

'No. Just tell her Bill Franklin would like to see her.'

Her face tightened. 'She's in a meeting.'

To this girl my name evidently meant nothing even though, once, I had been one of the firm's authors.

'I'm sure she's in a meeting. I'd be disappointed if she weren't. That's what you all do, all of the time, isn't it? Just tell her or her secretary that I've come to see her about Justin Harrington.' I gave her a sunny smile as I did a repeat for her. 'That's Bill Franklin, about Justin. I can wait.'

The girl's mouth opened a little, as though this bandying about of the name of the firm's other principal was yet another disgraceful intrusion, but she picked up the phone.

A few minutes later a brisk middle-aged woman who said she was Celia Beckland's secretary showed me into a small, comfortable reception room furnished with a table and two chairs. I felt a return to my travelling days, like a print rep being set up to see the buyer.

'Would you like a coffee, Mr Franklin? Celia won't be long.'

'Thank you very much.'

She brought me a coffee and I scanned a bookshelf along one wall. It contained many of the firm's titles. Mine wasn't among them but there were plenty I recognised.

There was Dowdeswell on Regency furniture:

'I asked him if he'd ever been to the Brighton Pavilion. He said he had but I reckon his visit to Brighton was just a weekend with a tart on expenses. He probably never set foot in the place. One print of the library was all he had in the book. Mind you, Margaret Jourdain only has two glancing references to it in hers. Frances Collard was the one who covered most of it. Authors, Jesus, authors!'

There was poor old Harker, the architect, on rural timber-framed houses of East Anglia. That was a stressful one:

'At one point I asked him if he'd mind if we left out every other page. It would bring his rambling book to the right length and none of the meaning would be lost.'

Oh, and here was old Branksome on Gillows:

'The bugger wrote an entire book on Gillows without once mentioning their most celebrated contribution to the language of furniture: the Davenport. To Captain Davenport, a desk. I nearly threw his fucking proofs at him. Authors!'

Here was one that was a big success: an encyclopaedia of nineteenth-century furniture designs, collated by Justin and a girl researcher. It was expensive at the time but nearly every antiques dealer bought one. Justin did a lot of the bookshop selling himself, having to persuade many booksellers to take it. He found, on the next visit, that many of them had sold the one copy they had grudgingly taken but despite a quick sale of an expensive book, had not reordered. For them, the problem was over and they could carry on as before, flanked by their stock. It led to his bitter dictum about bookshops:

'A bookshop is a repository for books that do not sell.'

He liked to be a background man, though, in this publishing business. There was suddenly an accountant's caution about his role that was at odds with the later TV personality. There was a lot of hard grind, too, presumably leavened by Celia's attentions. The business had to grow, and to grow quickly.

'There's an optimum size to any business, and it's always bigger than you think it is.'

'Hello, Bill.'

Celia Beckland had come in quietly while I was scanning the shelves. I turned to face her. Slight shock: she had got older. So, I supposed, had I.

'Hi, Celia.'

She did not move to shake hands but gestured at one of the chairs and sat down on the other, allowing me to take in her appearance once again after a long break. Hair still fair; figure still slim; clothes quiet pastel colours but of twill texture; slender brown shoes; pale brown eyes; lips just faintly reddened; expression neutral but face now lined; overall image perhaps owing something to *Country Life* magazine but not wrong in town. It was an image hard to reconcile with muscular sexual grappling with Justin, salaciously describing her to me in bum-up position over the desk, but so often mistresses cultivate a respectable, even dull exterior.

'You're looking well,' she said.

I smiled ruefully. 'Thank you. So are you.'

'You've come about something to do with Justin.'

'Yes. I'm very sorry about the news.'

She nodded without speaking, her eyes looking at me unblinkingly in the interrogative. I decided I'd better press on without getting into lamentations.

'I'm sorry too about the sudden intrusion. I thought if I phoned you'd probably turn down my visit.'

She nodded.

'I would,' she said. Her eyes met mine directly, cool as can be. It reminded me that we were on different sides, different sides in a long history of complex relationships.

'In that case I'll be brief. I'm in a bit of a bind. The police tell me they are treating his death as suspicious.'

'Good. Because I'm sure that it is.'

'Sure?'

'Of course. Justin would never commit suicide.'

Well, I nearly said, I suppose you would know. Your reply is just like Ellen's. You and he were, to put it mildly, intimate for a long time. But I didn't; I temporised as usual and said:

'Neither do I. Think he'd commit suicide, I mean. The thing is, what with the murder of Henry Roland so soon afterwards, I'm put on the spot.'

She frowned. 'Henry Roland?'

'The dealer from Basingstoke. We were all in School House together.'

Her frown cleared. 'Ah. That school.'

'I spoke to Henry the day he died. He was worried about Justin's death because they had some sort of deal going on.'

'Did they?'

'You don't know anything about it?'

I got a very cool look as she replied. 'I haven't known anything about Justin's other business affairs for a very long time. He wasn't exactly involved here any more, either. Threw the odd book our way, of course. Came to the annual meeting last year but that was about it. Took a share of the profits. Have you asked Elizabeth about this deal with Henry Roland?'

'I haven't seen Elizabeth for a long time.' I ignored the implications of the question and persisted. 'Not very much involvement from a fifty per cent partner, then.' And, I thought, you went on seeing him privately, I'll bet on that. 'Although you published the book on Goderoy.'

Her face twitched just slightly. 'That was a one-off. I'm afraid I don't think I can help you much. I don't think you killed Justin but I have nothing concrete to say to the police.'

'I guess not, but thank you for the thought. You wouldn't be interested in a book on Georgian Revival furniture?'

'No. I wouldn't. And I think you know why he didn't publish that book of yours.'

'No, I don't.'

'It was rather obvious at the time.'

'Not to me, it wasn't. I thought the objection was yours.'

She shook her head. 'No. Justin suspected you and Elizabeth, so he spiked it.'

'I think Ellen might conceivably believe that, too.'

'Ellen?'

'Yes, Ellen Stanton. You do know her, don't you?'

Her face had set. There was a pause while she thought. Then: 'Yes, I know Ellen. She's it these days, isn't she? With you, I mean.'

So that's it, I thought, that's where it came from.

'Yes,' I said. 'She's it.'

'I thought so.'

'Look,' I said, 'it's been kind of you to see me. I much appreciate it. I'm sorry to have disturbed you when I'm sure you're very busy. I just had to see if anyone can shed light on what exactly he was up to when he died.'

'I think the TV people might help you better.' She stood up. 'Or Elizabeth, of course. Although he didn't confide in her too much, either.'

And what he did confide was selective or lies, I thought. But I said nothing and stood up. We moved to the door and I thought how well she'd controlled herself. But I was wrong. She couldn't help it, I suppose.

'Justin would be amused to find you picking through his leavings,' she said. 'Sexual and commercial, that is. Don't come back here though.'

That did it.

'I won't. After all, I expect you'll be even busier, now that you're sole proprietor,' I said.

She froze.

'I beg your pardon?'

'His share passes to you on his death, doesn't it?'

She glared at me now. I'd finally roused her. 'How do you know that?' she demanded.

'Justin told me,' I said.

Chapter Eighteen

'I hear you got so close to the pit that you fell in,' he said to me, on one of the last occasions I saw him in the flesh.

It must have been a short time after I'd gone into the antiques business. I was at a London fair, not exhibiting but looking round. I suddenly came across him, with an entourage including a TV camera, pontificating. At first I tried to avoid him, instinctively, as in that time at Vallance Road, like trying to avoid any bit of the past, but I was too slow. After guarded but civilised greetings, he insisted on a coffee break at a nearby table. A pretty girl got us two cappuccinos and he made a fuss about thanking her whilst making it clear that he was the boss and she was probably available.

'Something like that,' I agreed. It was always easier to agree with him.

He was wearing a beautifully hand-stitched middle-grey suit with waistcoat, which was just starting to fit a little too snugly. You have to be slender to wear a waistcoat, not barrel-chested like me, but he was tall, which helped. His shoes were hand-made, too, and his cream shirt looked silky, like his scarlet patterned tie.

By then he was with Connock and Lockie.

He took a sip through the powdered chocolate and froth, carefully, before looking at me with assessing brown eyes. It had been a long time, and emotions were complex, but the eyes were still deep set and his hair seemed to have got higher and thicker, with no trace of grey.

'The day job folded, then?' His voice was still slightly rough. It gave his speech a masculine, aggressive edge.

'No. I decided to pack it in. It was time to stop circling the globe.'

'No more gadding off to foreign parts on expense accounts?'

'Nope.'

'You'll miss it.'

'Nope.'

'You will. Oh, I know you always complained about the long lonely travels, with only the odd tart to fuck from time to time, but if there's one thing gets a man down, it's domesticity. Travel relieves the tedium. I always remember, when I started, my boss said to me that if you're a married man with three children, independent nights in a first-class hotel with a good restaurant are not to be sneezed at.'

'I remember. But I shan't miss it.'

'If you say so. Good payout? Lavish pension?'

'Have you read any newspapers lately?'

'And you've really gone into the trade?'

'I have.'

'How's Marian these days? Do you hear from her?'

'No. At least, hardly ever.'

'I'm not surprised. How's her married life now, do you know?'

He was on to marital differences like a fox to a rabbit. He got quite a few of his married women that way. But not Marian.

'She's bearing up rather well. She and her bloke have got a successful garden business on their hands.' I paused. 'How's Elizabeth?'

'She's bearing up. Not baring much else these days, though.' He squinted at me significantly as he made this coarsely humorous jest.

I absorbed it for just a moment.

'She's well, though?'

'Yes, Bill.' His voice was neutral. I let the subject subside. 'Celia?'

'Celia's well. Publishing suits her.'

'You used to say that next time you'll have a blonde.'

'I did. I will, too.'

'You're not bothering to wait much.'

He bared his teeth, even and white. 'You've been reading the gossip columns. Well, you know the old stockbroker's advice to his son: if it floats, flies or fucks, rent it. I haven't had to sign any permanent purchase contracts, or even pay rental, yet. Not in actual cash, anyway. Expensive restaurants and hotels and baubles, but not actual cash.'

'So I gather. But there's always a price to be paid.'

He ignored that and looked about us. Well-dressed people were sauntering round the stalls, looking at the polished furniture, the softly illuminated paintings, artefacts, textiles and all those ceramics. There was a hushed sort of reverence in the air, like there usually is when illusions are being indulged, when there is pandering to appetites.

He pulled a face. 'This business is buggered, you know that?' he asked. 'Utterly buggered.'

'You mean that once you see it on the telly, it's all over?'

He ignored the counterattack. 'Precisely, Bill. It's the old story. I try to avoid the obvious. When, on your New York visit, the hotel doorman and the taxi driver tell you to buy Microsoft shares because it's hot stock, you know it's time to sell Microsoft.'

'So what are you doing about it? Apart from rubbishing some of it?'

'I'm the doorman and the cabby. I'm telling the punters what to buy on telly. For as long as it lasts. It probably won't last long. I'll be moving on from antiques, Bill. Foot in several doors. I'm making hay while the sun shines.'

'Hay? Fat Arthur says you're making more than hay.'

By then Fat Arthur had his cabinetmaking business on the Portsmouth Road. Antique furniture restorations and rebuilds a speciality.

'Fat Arthur's a greedy bugger. Greedy buggers should keep their mouths shut if they want feeding.'

'All genuine restorations, of course. As in that book you published about the Fauville cabinet?'

'Of course. These days you have to sell the great *ébénistes* or the equivalent of Chippendale. Otherwise you're buggered. You find yourself grubbing along with bric-a-brac squitteries. Find anything good and you're elbowed out by Bond Street and ignorant showbiz millionaires.'

'Vile and Cobb might just do?'

He grinned. 'Or Ince and Mayhew. But Chippendale would be good enough.'

'When you say that the business is buggered, you mean it's all this information, on telly and in books, that's spoiling it?' I gave him a significant leer. 'All this openness? Everybody knows it all now? Like a mistress who's lost her mystery?'

'Exactly. Think of antiques dealers in the old days, Bill, when we started collecting. We missed the zenith of it. It was like the Stock Exchange. Or Lloyds. All insider knowledge. The real pros kept schtum and got rich. Wonderful. Like taking candy from a baby. It's all been shafted by publishers and the telly, casting bum know-how out to all and sundry like it's Maundy Thursday. Counterfeit pearls before genuine swine.'

I thought about Roland Senior, king of the Basingstoke ring in the days when no one knew anything and there was still mystery and scholarship in antiques, then I thought of Henry, pegging on in changed circumstances. I was silent for a moment before answering.

'The past was not always that great. Look what happened to Sam Wolsey over the Aga Khan's bed,' I said.

The celebrated story concerned the time when the property tycoon Maxwell Joseph died. His effects went to a famous firm of auctioneers for disposal. It was alleged that a carved Elizabethan oak four-poster bed the deceased had expensively acquired as genuine from Sam Wolsey, a superior oak dealer, was bought by the then Aga Khan at the auction sale. When it arrived in the South of France, the Aga Khan's expert gave it the thumbs down. The bed went smartly back to the auctioneers, who stepped sideways and passed the financial impact and the bed straight back to Wolsey. Big compensation was said to be involved.

He grinned. 'Poor old Sam. I thought of reprinting his book once.'

'Wolsey and Luff on early oak. I've got a copy somewhere.'

'Landing Maxwell Joseph with a duff four-poster and then having it hurled back at him years later. Painful. Before our time, but a salutary lesson. It might take a long time, but shit can catch up with you.' He looked thoughtfully towards an oak specialist's stand nearby. 'Mind you, most Elizabethan four-poster beds are dodgy. More of them have been sold than there were people to sleep in them.'

'Too true.'

He kept his gaze on the oak stand. 'Bad time to come into the trade, Bill. Leaving the pursuit of the present in favour of picking over the past. It's been a good run for many and it epitomises this country, but you've joined just as it's all over. The real stuff's too expensive and the real stuff's the only worthwhile game in town. A game that's pretty well tied up by the usual suspects.'

'It's always a bad time to go into any trade. The incumbents hate newcomers.'

'Needs a hell of a lot of capital. Lots of nerve.'

'Tell me about it.'

'A good hobby but a bad living. I remember Marian was always clear about that. She always used to say—'

'She's got what she wanted,' I snapped, stopping him. 'And surprise, surprise, she was wrong. But I agree with you. Once a business becomes part of the entertainment industry, it's buggered. There's nothing worse than showbiz. I'm avoiding that.'

'If you say so. Except that everything's showbiz now. The whole country is bloody showbiz. Politics. Private life. War. Women. Sex. Even the economy.' He suddenly drained his cup. 'I suppose you'll go in for Arts and Crafts furniture?'

'Amongst other things, yes.'

'It was a good book. Ahead of its time, though. Never be a pioneer.'

'Which argued for keeping it in print.'

He shook his head. 'It was just another book, Bill. Just another book. There are scads of them. Books are disposable; they get you nowhere.'

'So says every publisher, like farmers about sheep, with which they fill our fields. There weren't any others on the subject then. But it's no problem. I got over it long ago. And the Georgian Revival one you reneged on.'

He got up, ignoring my last sentence. 'I hate that Voyseyesque stuff. Boring oak sideboards and rigid chairs with rush seats. High-minded architects preaching precious interiors to the porcine masses. But I wish you well. Very brave. I must get on. Do my piece to camera.'

'Sowing further doubts? News of fresh disasters? Or just pushing something Fat Arthur's doing up for you?'

He smiled sardonically. 'No news is good news, Bill. The public love scandals and disasters.'

'You'll be into politics next, then? Or financial reporting. Or a new investigative programme? *Tonight With Justin Harrington*? Watch out, Baz. The telly always eats its own offspring. One slip and you're cooked, like Fanny Cradock.'

'I don't think so. I won't be doing cookery programmes, Bill.'

'It won't always be antiques, though, you said. I suppose you're right. You can't keep banging on about Chippenbum and Hepplecrap week in, week out, can you? Not even with Fat Arthur doing the necessary behind the scenes?'

'The roadshows have being going for twenty years.'

'You hate the twentieth century. Without twentieth-century stuff, the roadshows would have been gone long ago. What are you going to cover? Wire chairs by Race and sideboards by Robert Heritage? No, with you it was always Chippendale or nothing. In a way, you're just like the Rolands.'

His eyebrows shot up. For a moment, he hesitated. I saw a receptive, amused set to his face that was like the old days, when we were close friends. Before he agreed that I should write another book, one on Georgian Revival furniture of the late nineteenth century. I did a lot of research on it, late nights and early mornings; authorship had an allure. I thought he reneged because Celia Beckland wanted to do something else, on fashion. She thought they'd done enough furniture; furniture was boring. It was an issue with them in view of his interest in Chippendale and his time. I made myself believe that he gave in to her, presumably in return for some irresistible favours.

There wasn't a contract; I trusted him. I came to think that his mistress came first. Like David Lodge's novel about a fictional publisher, rogering his secretary on top of a pile of neglected titles, it put authorship into perspective. There were other issues between us, though; one in particular. The sensitive question he never asked about Elizabeth. Maybe my rationale was self-delusion; I hadn't faced up to that.

And I still had all that research, stuck in a big cardboard box waiting patiently for the right day to emerge. I'd probably never use it now; that riled me, really stuck in my throat.

Then again, I probably deserved it.

Surprisingly, he suddenly stuck his hand out, shook mine, smiled, said something like see you soon, and was gone. His crew trailed after him, two of them with cameras on their shoulders, working.

I didn't tell Ellen any of this. *En boca cerrada no entran moscas*. Literally, flies do not enter a closed mouth.

Chapter Nineteen

A casual, but maybe loaded, question: how long had I been in the antiques trade? How should I have answered that, to a policeman, in simple terms? Tell him I started in Bethnal Green or tell him I started a few years ago, here, on the road between Brasted and Westerham?

Why is nothing ever simple?

After Marian left me I went off the rails for a bit. Into recession, you might say if you were in business. All those years travelling, the well-paid time away chasing contracts for somebody else; I regretted every day lost. But life falls into patterns. It was obvious, afterwards, that the split was inevitable. Absence does not make the heart grow fonder. She met a gentle man at a local garden centre. He was a schoolmaster, divorced because his wife found the daily presence and predictability of life boring. He was mostly home.

That was what Marian wanted.

It was ironic. Ironic because although Marian loved antiques, she was frightened of them. Not the articles themselves, she loved most of those, but the trade in them. She thought that whole world was dodgy, best seen from the security of an outside, income-propped objectivity. Its practices might drag you down. There were criminal elements prowling on the fringes. She always clung to controlled solidity, a world with a monthly salary, a pension scheme, PAYE, products that were mundane, technical, not things for the satisfaction of illusions. She was risk averse, they'd say now. She couldn't shout 'stuff all that' and head for the open road. The fear was too great. The business excited her, always had, ever since we were first married and went to markets like the Portobello and Bethnal Green. On those Sundays, coming home was always so triumphant.

She always had a suspicion that what I would really like would be to buy in Bond Street, at Mallett's or Partridge's or Asprey's. It wasn't true, but the top end of the antiques business, about how wealth spent its money, fascinated me. When I was up in town, visiting the office, I often went to those famous shops, or to Sotheby's and Christie's to test my knowledge, match my wits against the specialists. I couldn't buy there but rich men's places were addictive. Whereas to her, street markets were the stuff of life. She loved markets, the people, the colour, even the shouting. To her, Bond Street shops were like mausoleums. Dark-suited lugubrious men looking down at you like looking at a poor corpse, knowing that you had no money. Grave dark furniture shining unemotionally in the gloom; she hated that. It wasn't decorative; it put her off antiques.

Chalk Farm Road was better. We had fun in the Chalk Farm Road. Good junk shops, antiques, all those areas up to Kentish Town where the wide streets of low, grey houses made you feel what it was like to have lived in Edwardian London or at least pre-war London, unchanged and scruffy and authentic. There were coal holes with cast-iron manhole covers like lids set into the pavement in front of each house, still being used for coal deliveries. All left as it was, unpainted, undeveloped; she loved it, the atmosphere, the feel of it, grey under a leaden sky. Just as London should be. She said she never thought a city could make you so happy. We were innocent then. Those were the days, my friend, those really were the days: buttonbacks at two quid and Victorian burr walnut oval loo tables for a fiver.

'Loo tables?' I can still hear Henry Roland snort. 'Loo tables? Victorian rubbish. In the Thirties my father's men used to split the tops in half to make walnut bedheads. They burnt the cabriole-legged, scrolled bases in the workshop stove. Kept the place warm. A fiver? You're wasting your money.'

After we got one home from Vallance Road, cleaned it and polished it, Marian and I would sell a loo table, on a weekday evening, for twelve pounds. Seven pounds clear profit, sold to a householder lured in by a card in a local tobacconist's window, saying we were leaving, going to South America, must sell a table or a buttonback chair or some other antique. And in the chill gloom of a London winter, late, it would sell, like Chester Goldman's bright shiny things in Cutler Street. We fell into it. It was a lark, a caper, not real life.

We never went to South America.

My travelling life had its own sense of adventure and excitement. There was a hunting feel to it, a chase, a sortie, a break from the daily round of domestic life, always an oyster to be opened. A South American posting fell through because the firm could no longer sell against the competition. The decline had started. It was inevitable that I would have to move job, to leave London for a suburb where antiques might still be a lucrative hobby but where no tobacconist's window was available to advertise trophies from Bethnal Green. Things change: Vallance Road was rebuilt and its trading disappeared. Brick Lane went ethnic. At the weekend Marian and I traded on the fringe between dealers until auctioneers took over as middlemen. Part-time was no longer possible. The structure was totally altered.

'Bismarck said,' I can hear Justin quoting, 'that a talent for languages is a useful attribute in a head waiter. But you'll be on an aeroplane for ever.'

'You've never read Bismarck. You got that from a Flashman novel by George Macdonald Fraser.'

Maybe he did, maybe he didn't. This was before we drifted apart, before Marian took, to use his own phraseology, the shits to him. Publishing caused all that. Publishing and Celia Beckland.

One dreadful day, I came home from a longer trip than usual. Marian was waiting in the front room, neatly dressed, almost demure, untouchable.

'We need to talk,' she said.

And so, with surprisingly few words, it was all over. It wasn't an unusual story. It happens all the time. She said I was away too much, that I had never settled down. Something in me was apart, didn't belong. Vallance Road and early community meant nothing; you live for now or never.

I went on working. I was well paid but it was risky. The technical business life can be just as illusory as that of antiques and paintings. Its decisions are just as emotional and its sands just as shifting. I made my base back in South America for a while, but not in Uruguay, which was in recessive turmoil, nor Argentina, which was on the slide. Brazil was the coming place. I came and went to São Paulo regularly, never severing my ties with England, keeping my eye on what was happening to antiques. I wrote my books on aeroplanes, in hotel rooms, at café tables. They kept me from going mad until the moment came that I realised the machinery game was over.

You never think it will happen to you, but it can. I came back from a trip to find upheaval at head office. The business had been taken over by foreigners, the pension scheme was going to be looted. I got out with the best deal I could, before they offered me one of their own. I knew it was time to stop; there's nothing sadder than an old salesman in a cheap hotel.

The odd thing was that once the plunge was taken, it went well. It was as though, having jumped off the diving board, I slid into the choppy water like a seal off an icy floe. I had an eye for things, which is more important than knowledge. You can always acquire knowledge; knowledge only needs memory. An eye is a gift. With what I'd salvaged and a big mortgage I bought premises on the old A25 between Westerham and Brasted. Both places had plenty of antiques shops already, even if some of them were struggling, and there's safety in numbers. There was passing trade. I lived behind and over the shop but that was no problem. There was a bit of a garden and two rough outbuildings for storage space. Despite my payout I was low on working capital, like all businesses are, but I was happy.

A couple of American dealers came to visit me and they bought – mainly Victoriana, but they were interested in Arts and Crafts and more recent things. They changed my eye from the eighteenth century I had been trained to revere. I had some contacts abroad from my travelling days, other Americans who liked Arts and Crafts, even though they had their own

– Stickley and those – to satisfy them. They remembered my book. I could live very frugally while I built up stock. I was full of purpose. Although I knew what I liked, I didn't stick totally to one period; I was in the interior décor business, using genuine things from different eras. I went to one or two fairs, taking a good stand but not too big. The shock of change gave way to a sense of future, of self-reliance. Everything seemed great. There was the occasional lady from time to time. Sweet were the uses of adversity.

I got to know the Stantons because Fred was a customer. Unusually for a retired man, he still collected all kinds of things, even furniture, right up to the time he died. And then, quite recently, Ellen Stanton came to the shop. Alone. That was another prelude.

People prefer simple answers to simple questions. I told DC Green: seven years. It was easier than telling him my life story. Or what I've left out so far.

Chapter Twenty

One of the tabloids wasn't satisfied with the police effort to date. *TV Presenter Justin's Death Baffler* it proclaimed, in a full headline outside a newsagent's shop in Oxted, where I'd stopped to get some provisions. I went in to buy a copy. No wonder Walters and Powell were a bit rattled.

Police looking into the mysterious death of controversial TV antiques presenter Justin Harrington, found dead near York ten days ago, seem to be baffled by the cause and circumstances of his death. Little progress has been reported. His BMW car, left parked near a local gravel pit, led to the discovery of his body. Police are not ruling out foul play but have not released any further details as to the cause of death. Informants in the area – the journalist would doubtless be relying on local pub gossip – have said that the car probably arrived after dark. Sounds of cars coming and going were heard by residents in a row of cottages not far from the gravel pit. Mr George Womersley, who has lived nearby for twenty years, said that it is very unusual to hear traffic late at night and that an old car was one of the vehicles he thought he heard on the night in question. The sound of an old engine with noisy gears was heard in addition to the more powerful tones of what may have been the BMW and another car during the hours of darkness.

Suggestions that there might be a connection with Harrington and the murder of upmarket antiques dealer Henry Roland near Basingstoke five days ago were not entirely discounted by the police even though some 200 miles separates the two events. 'We are keeping an open mind,' said Detective Sergeant Wagstaff in York. 'We appeal to the public to assist us in our inquiries with any possible relevant information.'

The article then went into some of Justin's back history and a bit about Henry Roland. I put the paper down on my car seat. A noisier engine or rather an engine with noisy gears? Not an old car with noisy gears, meaning transmission gears? It almost sounded as though they'd heard the camshaft drive gears on a pre-war Riley. I smiled at the thought and, thinking of Rileys, drove home wondering how I would tackle the thorny problem of Ellen.

My thinking was interrupted by the ringing of my mobile as I turned into my gate.

It wasn't Ellen.

'Mr Franklin?' the efficient secretarial voice queried. 'Could you make a meeting here? It's rather short notice, I'm afraid.'

'I'm glad you could make it right away,' Tony Fitzsimmonds said, green braces gleaming in the cold City light. 'We're anxious to proceed now, as quickly as possible.'

We were sitting in his office, next morning, with its panoramic view down one side and big brown horse painting on the other. On the same side of his desk as me, facing him, sat an alert Jim Macallister, one grey worsted knee cocked over the other. There was coffee on a side table and we had cups in front of us.

'I see,' I said.

I didn't, yet, but so what? I'd signed the confidentiality agreement so I presumed I was about to be let in on the family secrets.

'The fund has been set up. It will soon be advertised and announced. We've done our best to assuage the fears that investors have about previous art funds that resembled private equity closed-end funds. There've been some scams, a bit like those US real estate investment trusts which allowed small sums to be invested in large buildings about thirty years ago.'

'I remember those. Quite a scandal, one or two of them.'

'More.'

I tried to show I could keep up. 'But you're aiming for the market at present occupied by, say, the Fine Art Fund?'

Fitzsimmonds raised his eyebrows at his colleague.

Jim Macallister nodded on cue. 'In a way, yes. They have a galaxy of advisers and have attracted some forty million dollars of investment from about fifty, mostly European, investors. The fund is to be spread across old masters, Impressionists, modern and contemporary art.'

'Contemporary has become a scramble.'

'Tell me about it. They aim to achieve an annual return of between ten and fifteen per cent over ten or more years. They charge two per cent management fees and take twenty per cent of the profit over a six per cent hurdle rate. They also charge legal and other fees. One of the problems of art and antiques investment is the high transaction cost, as much as thirty per cent, which buggers up the nominal profits. So they try to buy and sell privately, cutting out the auctioneers.'

'Not always easy.'

'No. Not with art getting such publicity these days. The payment of death duties, divorces and debts provides the market with its major supplies. Those afflicted need not always go to auction, fortunately. But it would be illogical for us to try and emulate the Fine Art Fund as a kind of replica.'

I leant forward, showing I was keen. 'According to *Business Week*, there are plans to launch six new art investment funds this year. The four art categories you've named are presumably not the only ones they are aiming at. Nor you?'

'Indeed not. The number of categories defies description. From Chinese art and porcelain to American Indian head-dresses, motorbikes, Russian art, you name it. I think there are some seventy-odd categories in New York and London. The most important thing is the access to the top buyers and they are international. What they need is a blend of the reliable, the proven investments like the Impressionists or French furniture, together with a dash of riskier fliers, like Tabasco added to the stew.'

'By that definition all art, particularly contemporary art, is Tabasco.'

He waved a dismissive hand. 'We have yet to settle on the exact percentages of each category in which the Leggatt Art Fund will invest. If Justin were still with us it might have reflected the selections over the years he did with his TV programmes. He would have figured in the publicity, at which he was a professional. That would have provided a kind of figurehead character to the Fund, a sort of branding. But he's gone and we have to move on in terms of promotion. Like other investment funds we've got together a team of art and financial advisers who might be called the cream of those available. On furniture of the Georgian period we have retained Professor Patrick Gardene of the Park House Museum, Closterby.'

That made me sit back.

'Patrick Gardene!' I could hear Justin holler. 'The ancient obscene. That waspish old poof. Thinks he's an expert on Chippendale as well as Hepplewhite. Been waiting to fill Christopher Gilbert's shoes for twenty years.'

'You know Patrick Gardene?' queried Macallister.

'Indeed I do.'

'He sent me his book on appro. I sent it back. It was bloody terrible. Cranston's published it. I heard on the grapevine that they got him to contribute to the costs. Substantially.'

'I hope you approve.'

'He's well known. The Park House has both Hepplewhite and Sheraton furniture. He's written on Irish Chippendale, too.'

'Good. To back these experts up we have decided to engage a small, but very select, number of expert consultants who will act at a very practical level. Their job is essentially a form of insurance. This is where you come in.'

So, I thought, I am not an art or investment or furniture expert; I am your practical chap, a technician, boilersuited and spannered, gimlet at the ready for the bursting of bubbles. They've moved quickly to fill the Justin gap. He'd never have approved Gardene, who's Irish like Tony. Or me, come to that.

'The loss adjusters?' I queried.

'Not exactly. But let us say the unromantic pragmatists whose experience inclines them towards scepticism and challenge.'

'I'm not sure if I should be flattered or the opposite.'

'Take it as flattery, in view of Señor Carrasco.'

'Indeed.' Tony Fitzsimmonds was back into the conversation. 'How appropriate, in view of Justin's introduction of you to us in that case, that the first matter we would like you to investigate is one in which he wanted us to invest. It is intended as our first, and indeed a major, purchase of Georgian mahogany furniture. Chippendale furniture, to be precise.'

'Oh?'

'Indeed. He called it the Ooh Project. As in OOH.'

'Don't tell me: the initials stand for Ousedon Overwood Hall?'

'My goodness. You are indeed on the ball.'

'Justin was obsessed by Ousedon Overwood for years.'

'What are your views on it?'

'A long shot. Not impossible, in view of much unattributed Chippendale work, but definitely a long shot. No binding reference in any of the authenticated documents so far.'

'But a possibility?'

'New finds are made nearly every day.'

'I'm glad you're not entirely dismissive.' He pulled a file on his desk forward, in front of him. 'Justin put in an awful lot of work on this project. He traced descendants of the Thwaite family who confirmed that before its demise the Hall had a quantity of what was always regarded as genuine Chippendale furniture in it. Quite amazingly, he managed to obtain some photographs of the main interior rooms, taken some time around 1900. Here, what do you think of these?'

He opened the file and pushed some photographs in front of me. They were old and yellowing, even sepia, but they showed the sort of lush interiors you might see in back numbers of *Country Life*, or books on mansions published in the1930s. The first was of a large formal drawing room with a huge fireplace.

The room was elaborately overfurnished, with settees, chairs, tables, plants almost to the point of shrubbery, stands, screens, and paintings. I let out a steady low whistle.

'What's up?'

I put my finger close to the surface, pointing at a long ornate Chinese cabinet against a background wall. It had a pagoda-topped central section and wings leading to pagoda-topped end cabinets. It was all glass and scrolled glazing bars, ornate-ended support columns, finials, fretted brackets and fantasies. Inside, it appeared to be full of porcelain.

'That,' I said, keeping my finger rigid, 'is straight out of the 1754 first edition of Chippendale's *Director*.'

Tony Fitzsimmonds kept his face steady. 'You're sure?'

'Certain. It's called a "China Case". I've never seen one realised.'

'This could be unique?'

'It could be. Doesn't mean it's made by Chippendale, of course. Could be a copy.'

'What would authenticate it?'

'Original invoice. Contemporary estate records.'

'Maker's label?'

'That would help, but—'

'According to Justin, the documents pertaining to the furniture still have to be traced but the pieces are said to be labelled.'

'That's rare. Chippendale and Rannie, presumably.'

'Sorry?'

'The only Chippendale trade card I've ever seen is shown in Christopher Gilbert's book. Rannie was the finance man behind Chippendale when he started. But a trade card is not the same thing as a trade label on a piece of furniture, like those of Coxed & Woster earlier on. It would be a major find to discover a labelled piece of Chippendale furniture.'

'There are five items,' Macallister said. 'The china cabinet, a commode, a clothes press, a library bookcase and a set of chairs.'

'Wow. All labelled?'

'No. Not the chairs, the china cabinet or the clothes press. You say there's no Chippendale furniture with a label so far?'

'No. But authenticated furniture from his 1754 *Director* is very rare. The authenticated pieces are mostly from the later 1762 edition, in the Adam, or neo-classical style.'

Fitzsimmonds stroked his jaw. 'I'm not sure that the pieces are actually labelled. Justin talked of a trade card, not a label. Maybe the trade card was found in a drawer or something. Anyway, we have to decide whether to buy them or not.'

'Where are these marvels?'

'In a depository in Leeds.'

'Good God. Who owns them?'

'Ah. Apparently, title went to a creditor of the Thwaites when the estate was broken up in the Thirties. The creditor took possession of a range of furnishings and even a car or two in lieu of payment. The war broke out and they were preserved in Leeds, which being a producer of mainly off-the-peg suits, didn't cop much bombing. The creditor's widow was an eccentric old bird who refused to sell anything and kept the whole lot in storage, away from public scrutiny. It was a bit like the Tyntesfield situation; a sort of time warp. An interior preserved in aspic until Christie's were called in and then the National Trust – or was it English Heritage? – got its leg over.'

'Tyntesfield,' I interrupted, 'was a partial time warp, believe me. And this is beginning to sound like a similar case. So the widow owns the goods?'

'The widow died some time ago. Her executor sold the goods to a speculator-dealer for an unknown sum and they were moved to a new location. The speculator-dealer contacted Justin because he'd seen one of the TV programmes in which Justin mentioned Chippendale and Ousedon Overwood.'

'It's a small world.'

'Very.'

'There's Justin been looking all over for this stuff and the dealer contacts the one man who might be said to believe it existed. And no one else has been approached?'

'Your scepticism is understandable but TV is a great puller. The owner wants to sell. Justin said he is disillusioned with mahogany furniture in view of all the adverse publicity it's been getting.'

'So now would be a good time to buy?'

'That depends. What sort of figures might be asked for genuine Chippendale furniture these days?'

That was easy. 'The highest figures in recent years were things like a cabinet that went for four hundred thousand in 2006 and a library table that Sotheby's sold for nigh on a million in 2004. There was a secretaire display cabinet sold at Christie's for three hundred and forty one thousand pounds in 2003 and it had the cachet of the specialist dealers, Norman Adams, in its back history. A tea table went for two hundred and sixty five thousand. One of his hall lanterns went for a hundred and seventeen thousand or so. Had the Dumfries House sale taken place, there was a bookcase heading for more than two million. But Prince Charles saved the house for the nation and postponed the inevitable next record price. It's bound to come sooner or later. I've no doubt that the owner, like anyone else, can get all this info from the Internet. What matters is provenance; a Yorkshire country house provenance would up the stakes considerably.'

'Exactly. The owner's name is Kippax and he's expecting you to call him and arrange a viewing. He plays his cards close to his chest, Justin said, but he knows that if we buy he'll save the costs of auctioning. Like twenty to thirty per cent. So if you can get up there as soon as possible we can retain first option, which he promised Justin. If a whiff of the existence of this furniture gets out, there'll be a rush that'll make the California '49 look like a Sunday church promenade.'

'You want me to go pronto?'

He pushed the file towards me. 'Stand not upon the order of your going,' he said, 'but go at once.'

Which was a bit rich, I thought, seeing that he was quoting from the ghost scene in *Macbeth*. Without offering the banquet.

But I left. Without raising the subject of Henry Roland.

Chapter Twenty-One

'Cobbler's tingles,' Justin said triumphantly, producing a flat red Willem III cigar tin full of them, like something an angler might carry. Only this tin had tiny triangular spikes in it instead of a nest of writhing maggots.

We were in the spare room of his flat at the time, the one used for guests and as a workshop. In the centre of the floor was a walnut bureau lying on its side. An electric glue pot bubbled on a table. The piece, a victim of central heating, lay passively, like a sedated dog on a vet's operating table. Most of the veneer was off the exposed side, and the sheet which had been removed by steaming waited, dry, brittle, ragged and stained, to be put on again. He liked to devise solutions to problems like this by original but not necessarily sound methods. The idea was slap hot glue all over the exposed pine side, press the veneer back onto it, push down what could be pushed down with a veneer hammer, hoping that the glue would hold, then pin the recalcitrant, curling, bubbling rest of the surface down with the tingles, using only half their length.

Once the glue had set and the veneer was down, the tingles, like veneer pins, might leave tiny holes in the surface when pulled out, but these could be passed off as additional worm holes. There were plenty on the surface already, and galleries on the exposed pine side testified to the long presence of infestation.

Why he chose cobbler's tingles, which left tiny square holes, rather than veneer pins which, being round in section, left marks more like natural worm holes, I cannot remember. I think it was the consultant in him, always wanting to do something different from the established procedures of an industry, something that might go one better or, at least, cause a rethink of current logic. But not necessarily; he'd come across the tingles when he'd taken his shoes in for repair and couldn't resist them. They did have the merit, being wedge-shaped, of nailing the veneer to the surface rather more strongly than pins. On the other hand they were sharper and you tended to hammer your thumb and finger when tacking them into the sticky surface under repair. Frayed thumb and first finger ends were the usual result.

This was the zenith of our days restoring together. He would come home with a distressed trophy in the back of the car, such as a ragged Queen Anne walnut bureau, a longcase clock with cut-down base, a duff walnut kneehole desk that was clearly a Victorian repro, a mahogany wardrobe intended to be made into a glazed bookcase. Or a lowboy missing its cabriole legs – 'we'll get a good set of Hackney Road cabrioles made up by Mr Liebermann' – and a big oak-panelled mule chest to be made into a small two-drawer dresser. I remember another lowboy with its walnut-veneered, quartered and herringbone-banded top made up from two drawers taken from the undesirable bottom half of a chest on chest. It never stopped.

'How about,' I remember him saying, pointing at the bureau, lying on its side, 'inserting some pewter stringing lines? Then it could be a piece by Coxed and Woster.'

'It should be mulberry and burr elm for that.'

'It would be better, true, but mulberry is just dealer's fantasy. Coxed made ash and walnut furniture as well as the burr elm. What about an old label, clinging to the inside somewhere? John Coxed, at the Swan in St Paul's Church-Yard, London, all old and ragged, just clinging to the surface?'

'It hasn't got a label.'

'Labels,' his teeth flashed in a grin, 'like marriages, can be arranged.'

He loved it. He loved the whole of it, the artifice, the illusion, the cunning criminal skill of the faker, books like Cescinsky's *The Gentle Art of Faking Furniture* with its classic dedication to the memory of the late Adolph Shrager who 'acquired a second hand but first rate knowledge of both English Law and Antique Furniture by the simple process of paying for it in 1923'. As he gleefully rubbed his hands he would repeat the book's admonition 'Reader Do Thou Not Likewise.' Cescinsky was, initially, his bible. He wanted to know it all, everything, every trick of the trade, every sleight of hand. And, whilst acquiring this profound knowledge of the counterfeit, he hoped to uncover a masterpiece.

Deep down, initially, it was all to do with cocking a snook at society, with bamboozling the superior, Georgian Brown façade of the wealthy people he resented and from whom his father's Lille circumstances had alienated him. The excitement of conducting a successful fraud was like a drug. On one occasion he pointed at a panelled oak settle, purportedly monasterial but adorned with snake-like figures too bizarre to be genuine, and said:

'The start of my Royston Room, perhaps.'

This was an allusion to the late and unfortunate Adolph Shrager of Cescinsky repute, who paid richly for a complete oak-panelled and carved 'Royston Room' sold to him as having come from Royston Hall. There never was a Royston Hall and the room was made up of different panelled pieces but the defendant's experts in the court case described it as 'utterly genuine'. The fact that it came partly out of a local dairy and contained a high proportion of newly carved elements was the subject of court action, judgement, subsequent Divisional Court action and on to a Court of Appeal, which kept lawyers happy, but not the plaintiff. Shrager was also stitched up with a cream lacquer cabinet said to have been acquired in Barcelona but in fact modern, the stand of which Cescinsky claimed to have seen being made up in a kitchen, and a 'Tompion' clock with a forged dial. He obtained little support from the law on these either. More recent court cases against auctioneers have left plaintiffs baffled as to why wrong descriptions incur no redress.

Then, however, the excitement of learning through dirty hands and searching eye was intoxicating. I would come back from my travels and at some point over the weekend would go round to the Harringtons to see what Justin had most lately acquired. Marian and Elizabeth would brew up coffee whilst Justin and I pored and sawed over the current object. Marian and I still went out on sorties of our own, but they became more limited. Eventually we made our move to the suburbs. The Harringtons did likewise but to St George's Hill, the superior estate at Weybridge, evidence of the higher earning power of accountancy over engineering.

And then came publishing. It ruined everything.

'Books,' he said to me one day, sipping coffee over a mahogany pedestal partners' desk to which someone had added carved canted corners, 'leave one no option but to act. Current books are bloody useless.'

'Oh?'

'There's been nothing any good since the Thirties. Cescinsky and Jourdain and Rogers and all those were very good in their time. So were Avray Tipping and Macquoid; big thorough books about the top end. Country Life and Batsford: gentlemen publishing for gentlemen. Ralph Edwards is all very well but that's Country Life, too. RW Symonds was pretty good; I love that introduction by his friend, the collector Perceval Griffiths, that says he collected avidly for his first five years or so and put together the finest collection of lion mask furniture in existence. Then he found it had all been made for him.'

'At least he kept his sense of humour about it.'

'Indeed. Especially when he found his spurious pieces illustrated in art magazines and books as examples of masterpieces of eighteenth-century work. But for the next couple of decades antique collecting is going to be about populist things, nostalgia, collectibles on the one hand, and an upmarket sector needing the facts, not just a series of pictures of things in museums, on the other. There's a real gap.'

'Two gaps, by the sound of it.'

'Precisely, Bill! Two gaps. One must move with the times. I'm making my moves. Out of consultancy. One simply can not go on trailing from one desperately bad British company to another, like an army surgeon in a mobile wagon following defeat after bloody defeat in order to amputate gangrenous limbs.'

'How will you start?'

'With some money and Celia Beckland.'

'Who?'

'Celia at present works as an editor for a group of gentlemen publishers busily losing half a million a year. My current clients. They do not impress. They are very civilised men who believe that the way to run a company is to ignore the market but hope for a best-seller from time to time. It's no wonder that Jews and Scotsmen dominate publishing. Like the textile trade; they understand how to exploit outworkers in hovels, producing cheap popular output on cheap little machines.'

'Shocking. Is she efficient, this Celia?'

'Very. And,' he gave me a leer, 'she has other delightful attributes.'

'Oh no. You're not?'

'I am. She—'

There followed a lurid description of how Celia had obliged him bent over her desk, skirt pushed up her back, knickers stripped down, like something out of Simenon, after work in the evening, when the offices had emptied. He had a coarse streak when it came to women. He was tall, with deeply set eyes, dark, slightly saturnine and, then, vigorous. His humour was anarchic, mocking, quick to focus on weakness and muddle. I had no doubt that his comments on the gentlemanly publishing partners would have rendered Celia weak at the knees. He got a lot of his women that way.

In a sense, it was the end. Or, if you're in Churchillian mode, the beginning of the end.

Marian was affected first. Call it a married woman's outrage. Harrington and Beckland started in a small way, but the firm soon took up a lot of his time outside consultancy hours, while he still moonlighted. The need to be with Celia was added to the demands of the business. Elizabeth said nothing. Marian was at first suspicious, then angry. She had strong views on deception, on the effect things had on children, on honesty. I got back from trips abroad to find her fuming.

'It's obvious,' she raged. 'Absolutely obvious. He and that supposedly cool publishing piece are having it off like stoats. Elizabeth is turning a blind eye to it. He's disgusting. Preening himself about it. I can't stand that kind of slimy, self-satisfied adulterer. I thought he was flash to start with but now he's poisonous.'

Other women might have been amused, even excited by the scandal. Marian wasn't made that way. It caused a division. She didn't want to see Justin, not even to look at him. She was loyal to Elizabeth at first but when it became clear that Elizabeth wasn't going to do anything, felt that there was too much to lose, didn't make sexual fidelity an issue, she became estranged from Elizabeth too. It made life difficult: I had had no argument with Justin, enjoyed his anarchic company, loved the weekend analysis and practical work on pieces of furniture as contrast to business travel. But Marian resented my continuing relationship with him. It was implicit that he was a bad influence. Tell me who you are with and I'll tell you who you are; she didn't actually demand that I sever the friendship but somehow the time available became limited. It was embarrassing that she no longer wanted to visit the Harringtons. Inevitably, we drifted apart.

Some time passed. Occasionally I met Justin for lunch in an Italian restaurant in London. We visited auction rooms together and speculated on the authenticity of pieces. The restoration activities had to give way to other imperatives. One day he phoned me to make a lunch date out of the regular run of things.

'I'm leaving consultancy,' he announced over the antipasto. 'I'm finally making the break.'

'Celia will have your full attention from now on?'

He smiled. 'I shall become a publisher. Celia will be, as always, my business partner.'

'Does Elizabeth approve?'

'Elizabeth wants me to support her in the manner to which she has become accustomed. If Celia helps me to do that, she has no objection.'

'And Celia? Will she accept this arrangement?'

'Celia has made only one stipulation.' He poured us both another glass of Chianti classico. 'And this is between just you and me. In view of her efforts in getting the publishing going, my share of the company goes to her if I snuff it. It seems fair to me. I shall invest in a substantial pension to look after Elizabeth. That way the two of them are catered for.'

'Doesn't that rather leave Elizabeth at the mercy of Celia if anything happens to you in the meantime?'

'The publishing company won't be worth very much for some years yet. I've got life insurance for Elizabeth. And, in any case, once I tire of publishing I'll move on to other things.'

'You seem to have it all worked out.'

He nodded briskly. 'I'm doing my best. How's Marian?'

Some men acquire more women than they need. Some don't.

'We're getting divorced,' I answered.

Chapter Twenty-Two

In theory, the journey up to York should be simple. You leave at the crack of dawn so as to be on the M25 motorway in time to avoid the morning traffic build-up on the west side around Heathrow. You circle through to the north and turn off up the M1 motorway, jostling with heavy lorries. You listen to the radio and keep going until you reach a suitable service area, where you stop for ablutions, a big greasy breakfast and a quick read of the paper. By this time it is fully light and the world is buzzing about or towards its business. Full of calories and cholesterol, you stride confidently back to your car, throbbing with energy and high blood pressure, ready for the long stretch north.

At that moment, as you are about to slide behind the wheel, fortuitously, your mobile phone rings. Fortuitously, because you are not yet driving at high speed and liable to fines, imprisonment and obloquy if you respond.

With an inward curse, I answered the phone. Who would it be so early in the morning?

'Bill?' The voice was young, male and anxious. It was Steve Stanton.

'Steve? Hi, how are you? Everything all right?'

'I'm fine, but I've been talking to Mother. What's happened?'

'Happened?'

'Yes, happened. She sounds upset and won't discuss you at all. You've obviously had some sort of row?'

Pause, while the mind tries to decide what to say, how to smooth over something fundamental to a young man.

'Bill? Are you there? Where are you?'

'I'm on the motorway. At a service area, so I can talk.'

'Where are you going?'

'Leeds, as a matter of fact, Steve.'

'Leeds! Here? Why?'

'To look at some furniture.'

'Oh. I see. Can we meet?'

'Of course. It's a sudden visit, a moment's notice thing. I should be free by mid-afternoon. Look, don't worry about your mother and me. We had a disagreement but it'll sort itself out. I'll explain when we meet.'

'I would like to see you, Bill.' He still sounded anxious.

'Fine.'

We agreed on a rendezvous and I got behind the wheel. I put the key into the ignition and then stopped. It was time to think.

What in hell was I doing?

Chuck Vance was wary of Tony Fitzsimmonds and Leggatt's. Henry Roland, despite Tersh-Olly's denial, had been somehow involved with them. Justin Harrington was in deep with them. Henry and Justin were dead. My initial reaction had been to say no to them. But here I was, streaking up the M1, as deeply involved with Leggatt's as anyone. Why? Curiosity, boredom, a moth to a flame? Art, antiques and high finance had a relationship that always intrigued me. Was that it? Or was I playing the amateur detective to excess, behaving in a manner too clever by half? Just curious to know what happened to Justin and Henry?

No: I was in a police frame of some sort, that was clear. It was imperative to get out of it. Sergeant Walters had taken my books for examination. He wouldn't find anything there but he wasn't going to let go. Whatever Justin and Henry had been up to, I had to find out what it was. So far, there was nothing about the Leggatt involvement that put me in danger, from criminals or police. But it might throw some light on Justin's demise and, via Justin, Henry Roland.

On the other hand, this could develop into some sort of Harry Lime story with a dead third man but myself in the role of the hapless Holly Martins, the sidelined writer-narrator who becomes keen on Harry's girl but never gets her. Graham Greene deliberately made him a pathetic figure.

Disconcerting thought.

No, that wasn't a parallel; unlike Holly Martins, I'd had both of Justin's women.

Well, two of them, anyway. That made me think of Celia Beckland's sneer about pickings and my privileged knowledge.

I started the engine and drove off northwards.

The storage warehouse was nothing like I had imagined. I had thought of an old brick building in textile mill mode, with cobwebs and pillared gloom, shrouded in industrial antiquity. The warehouse estate, when I arrived on the fringes of Leeds, was modern, light, freshly minted and corrugated. Bright signs proclaimed new companies' names. Distribution was going on and vans were loading. In the car park outside the correct big warehouse, as I drove up, a suited, middle-aged man got out of a new saloon and greeted me briskly when I emerged from behind the wheel.

'Bill Franklin?'

'That's me.'

We shook hands. He was a fit-looking if heavy man in his fifties, with a short, greying beard. He wore a dark crumpled suit and had a strong Yorkshire accent.

'I'm James Kippax. You're dead on time. Reasonable drive up from London?'

'Not too bad.'

'Good. Could I see some ID, please? Sorry, I have to be careful.'

'Of course.' I got out my driving licence, one of the new ones with photograph, and showed it to him.

'Very good, thank you. You've taken over from Justin Harrington, I gather?'

'Yes, more or less.'

'Awful business. Very strange.'

'Tragic.'

'Did you know him?'

'We were old friends.'

He was looking at me intently. 'The police don't seem to know much, do they?'

I shook my head. 'They certainly give an odd impression. As though there's something strange about the way he died. Taking their time to explain.'

'I'm very sorry. He was lively company. I only saw him here, of course, so I didn't know him well. But I enjoyed his visits. It was extraordinary how he had been tracking the furniture down.'

'Oh?'

'It's a long story. Perhaps you'd better see it first, then I'll explain. Shall we go in?'

'That sounds sensible.' I gestured at the glass double doorway as we walked across from the cars. 'This all looks very modern. I was rather expecting a different sort of storage facility.'

He grinned. 'The furniture was kept in an old worsted mill building for ages. Decades, anyway. That was knocked down for redevelopment. Leeds is a modern city now, you know. I transferred the stuff three years ago, when I bought it along with a couple of vintage cars that went with it. I sold those and brought the furniture here. Fully protected and in a controlled atmosphere now.'

'I'm impressed. Lead on, James.'

The place had every modern security feature. He had to programme a number into a keypad at the main door. Once inside, in the empty corridors flanked by painted block walls, CCTV cameras eyed us bleakly. There was no one to be seen. He led the way down various lengths of empty passage and round corners until we came to a steel door set in the wall. He did more keypad programming and, using a large bunch of keys, unlocked a conventional lock.

'Here we are.' He swung the door open.

There was a moment of darkness while he found the lights, then the space became fully visible. It was a big square room, maybe thirty feet by thirty, with a tall ceiling height. The furniture was mostly against the walls, so we stood in a clear central area to look at it. I let out a low whistle.

Along one wall, occupying maybe twelve or even fifteen feet in length, was the long, high china cabinet I had seen in the photograph in Tony Fitzsimmonds' office, the photograph of the interior drawing room at Ousedon Overwood Hall. The cabinet was as fantastic, exuberant and Oriental as it had looked then, except that now it was empty of china. The central pagoda top almost touched the ceiling. Frets and brackets and scalloped roofs met the eye. Without any contents, the glazing bars looked even more like the tracery of wild but symmetrical invention.

'Ousedon Overwood Hall, Bill! Demolished in the nineteen forties to make way for council estate. Bastards! But the furniture was already long gone.'

'Quite an item, isn't it?' Kippax closed the corridor door and came back to stand beside me. 'Not my taste, but someone had their work cut out to make that.'

'They certainly did. It must have been hell to move.'

He chuckled. 'Not too easy, no. The wings and end cabinets come apart, of course. It's the amount of glass and fretwork that causes the worries.'

My eye moved round to take in the other pieces. Like the china cabinet, they were all mahogany. The clothes press was solid, like a wardrobe with a straight panelled upper section containing two rectangular doors below a dentellated top moulding. A bulbous-bellied lower section with deep drawers and canted corners had scrolled carving to the edges and serpentine bracket feet. The commode was a Chippendale *bombé* classic on curved cabriole legs, embellished with scroll and leaf carving. Against the opposite wall stood a huge breakfront bookcase, the upper doors glazed with astragal bars and the central section capped by a heavy broken pediment of classical design. Then there were ten chairs. They had a top rail which swept up to the inevitable pointed corners where it met the back uprights and a complex pierced central splat of Gothic design in one of Chippendale's most popular versions. The legs were square section with back bevel, not cabriole, which was the other Chippendale option.

'Wow,' I said.

James Kippax nodded approvingly. 'Impressive, eh?'

'The quality is incredible. And all from designs in the *Director*.'

'That's what Harrington said.'

'He was right.'

As I said that, suspicion was creeping over me. This was almost too good to be true. It was Chippendale furniture all right, but of what antiquity? Into my mind's eye came a photo in Christopher Gilbert's two-volume treatise on Thomas Chippendale, a photo of a china cabinet like this one, comparing its exactitude with an original design in the 1754 *Director* but the caption pointing out that it was made around 1900.

'All probably from the first edition of the *Director*. Ahead of anyone else in Yorkshire. Imagine that!'

As though reading my thoughts, Kippax spoke. 'The results of a dendrochronological test are on file. They took samples from one or two pieces. The mahogany is eighteenth century or earlier. There's no doubt of it. The paper for the trade card and label is two hundred and fifty years or so old, too.'

'Trade card? Label?'

He walked across to the *bombé* commode, opened a drawer and carefully took out a clear plastic punched pocket, A4 size, of the kind used to preserve documents in files or for presentations. In it was a piece of raddled white paper, thickish, about three inches by four. He handed it to me so that I could look carefully at the smudged black print.

The design and the lettering were very mixed. At the top was a drawing of a curvaceous armchair with upholstered back and seat, on cabriole legs. It was flanked by the name 'Chippendale' in copperplate to the left and '& Rannie' to the right. Underneath the chair legs in thick black Gothic type a German would have admired were two words: 'Cabinet Makers'. Below these the word 'and' came next in italic then below that in capitals of something like Times Roman but more spaced out: 'Upholsterers'. Back to copperplate under that for 'in St Martin's Lane, Charing Cross' the second 's' in Cross being a long one. Then, lastly, under that, 'London.' in the same sort of italic capitals as the 'and'.

'That's Chippendale's trade card of 1754 or thereabouts,' I said. 'I've seen it illustrated in Christopher Gilbert's book. There's one in the Westminster City Library.'

Kippax nodded. 'That's what Justin Harrington said.'

'You mentioned a label, too?'

'Labels, like marriages, can be arranged.'

He went across to the big pedimented bookcase and swung open one of the solid lower doors. Inside, clinging to the unpolished surface in peeling tatters, I saw the remains of a paper label printed with what looked like the duplicate of the chair drawing and lettering of the card.

'Voilà,' he said, with a grin. 'One label. Actually, the trade card was found in the clothes press, bottom drawer. I keep it in the top drawer of the commode just for convenience.'

I absorbed this staggering find for some long seconds without speaking. Most so-called Chippendale furniture found in neglected circumstances is Victorian or Twenties reproduction. Even though this was high-quality, apparently exact *Director* eighteenth-century furniture, it could easily be skilled Victorian work like Christopher Gilbert's astounding Chinese Chippendale china cabinet, very like the one on the wall behind me. Provenance and back history and documentation were the usual ways of establishing authenticity. I had recently seen an account of two Chippendale commodes sold in East Anglia whose provenance was said to start with a land agent of one of Chippendale's clients. The land agent was called Jones but no such Jones figured in Gilbert, nor any similar commodes. It was a minefield.

'What do you think?' asked Kippax. He was beginning to look a bit tense.

'I think this could be a very important collection,' I answered cautiously, keeping my voice steady. 'If provenance can be authenticated it is a very valuable find. You said that Justin had been tracking this down for a while? And you had it all the time?'

'Yes, he was amazing. He did a lot of research work in York and with local history societies. The interior photographs of Ousedon Overwood Hall were taken around 1910 for a county magazine that has long since gone to the wall. But they were great in that they showed this stuff in place.'

'Are back copies of the magazine in the York library?'

He hesitated just a fraction before shaking his head. 'Unfortunately not. The run that has been preserved is missing quite a few issues.'

'What was the magazine called?'

'Oh, something quite ordinary. I can't remember offhand. It went out of business in the Thirties. The photos were a brilliant find. A local antiquarian bookshop specialising in early photos – local views, that sort of thing – had some prints of them. The stock of the photographers was sold when they closed years ago and the bookshop snapped them up. Harrington went to browse there and found the Ousedon prints in a big random box file full of country landscape shots, snaps of local hunt meets and village fairs.'

'I can imagine Justin ferreting among that lot,' I said.

I could, too. A man who started by ferreting amongst the rubbish in Vallance Road on a Sunday morning, early, would get real pleasure from a treasure hunt amongst local photos in York.

'He was cock-a-hoop I can tell you. Bought them for whatever the bookshop asked and had copies made.'

'Pity he couldn't trace the magazine issue for which they were taken.'

'You can't have everything.'

'No. I gather from Tony Fitzsimmonds that you contacted Justin about this furniture you have here?'

'I certainly did.'

'Did you know he was tracking down the Ousedon Overwood Hall furniture?'

He shook his head vigorously. 'I'd no notion of that. I contacted him because he showed a page from Chippendale's *Director* on his TV programme and I thought: aye oop, that's like one of mine.'

'Amazing. What a small world TV makes it.'

'It does that.' He made a gesture of slight impatience. 'So what's your next move now, then, Bill?'

I didn't answer immediately. I walked carefully round the storage area, looking, assessing, wondering. Professor Patrick Gardene should take a look at this furniture. I had no doubt that Kippax had elevated views about its value – anyone with a computer can check on things like that – and would reject the first offer. It wasn't up to me to make the offer, though; Tony Fitzsimmonds would be doing that.

'Can I see whatever documentation you've got?' I asked.

'Certainly.' He turned towards the door. 'There's a copy of the dendrochronology report in my car. You take all the time you want here while I go and get it.'

'Thanks.'

He left me alone with the looming blocks of fanciful mahogany. I made a thorough tour of inspection and found nothing obviously wrong. Whoever made the pieces, if they were fakers, knew their stuff. There were no obvious things like dowelled joints – which mostly you can't detect without tearing the joint apart – wrong dovetails or drawer linings, wardrobe conversions, plinth-to-bracket foot jobs. These were all made from scratch, to eighteenth-century specifications. To Chippendale designs, straight from the first *Director*.

It had to be too good to be true.

And yet, and yet; a sense of awe was seeping through me. This was furniture of peak quality. Whoever made it, in eighteenth, nineteenth or twentieth century, were craftsmen of heroic ability. If you preferred it, you could go for the later, neo-classical inlaid stuff driven on by Adam – you could see that not so far away at Nostell Priory near Wakefield, where the most documented Chippendale collection, made for the Winn family, exists. You might prefer the ormolu-mounted extravaganzas of great French *ébénistes*, or you could extol painted Venetian fantasies, but you had to hand it to the men who made this stuff. Here, there was no margin for error, no hiding behind decoration. The use and blending of the mahogany had to be faultless, the carver's chisel could not slip. It may have followed the French lead, but it was a masterly continuation.

Kippax arrived with a file of papers. The dendrochronology reports were complex but, claiming the samples to be taken from unseen surfaces, said the wood was from the early eighteenth century. A paper expert had looked at the trade label and card. The paper was sufficiently old and the ink of an old type.

'OK,' I said, after reading the pages. 'I've seen enough.'

He was still tense. 'What now?'

'I'll report back. It will be up to Leggatt's to take it further.'

'But what will you say?'

'What I've seen. Can you send me some photocopies of the documents and the photographs, all of them? I know Tony Fitzsimmonds has got one or two but I'd like a copy of every one of them.'

He was looking disappointed. 'Do you think the furniture is genuine, though?'

'The evidence is strongly in favour. The furniture itself is massively convincing, too. But I'm sure you understand that I have to be cautious. This is such an unusually important find, especially with the trade card and the label.' I put some warmth into my voice. 'I find it very exciting. If Christie's or Sotheby's got wind of it there'd be headlines in all the trade journals.'

'I don't want that. I'm not letting any auctioneers take my money.'

'Very wise. I'll move quickly on this. Trust me. I'll be seeing Tony Fitzsimmonds again right away.'

He looked a bit mollified. 'Good. I've kept this under wraps and I promised Justin Harrington first option for Leggatt's, so I'll stick to my word. But I want an offer very soon. I've got pressures on me, you see.'

'I understand. All I can say is that this is exactly the sort of investment Leggatt's are looking for. It looks good. They will need further expert opinion, but that's up to them.'

'Huh! Bankers: they want their cake on a plate. Take no risks, but take all the money. I prefer antiques dealers in many ways.'

'Thanks. But not many antiques dealers could offer on this collection. And those that could would need big margins. Probably bigger than the auctioneers.'

'It's over to you and Fitzsimmonds then,' he said.

I pulled my small digital camera out of my pocket.

'Can I take some photos? We'll guarantee confidentiality, of course.'

He hesitated. An odd look came onto his face.

'We've already got the magazine ones of the pieces in the Hall,' I said smoothly. 'In situ, as it were. These of mine will just help to convince Leggatt's.'

He nodded, relaxing the look. 'Help yourself,' he said. 'But no one else sees them, eh?'

'Guaranteed,' I answered. 'Absolutely guaranteed. Leggatt's want this kept completely confidential.'

Chapter Twenty-Three

North-west of York on the B6265 road near Thorpe Underwood, I pulled my car in to a lay-by, switched off the engine, and phoned Tony Fitzsimmonds on my mobile.

The call was put straight through.

'Bill! Is it yourself? Good to hear from you.' He seemed to be in jocular mood. 'How have you got on?'

'Well.' I gave him a brief version of the events in Leeds. 'I'll give you a written report with illustrations very quickly. If everything is as it looks to be, it's an impressively important cache of Chippendale's work. Straight from the first edition of the *Director.*'

'Fantastic! But what's your view of it?'

'I've never been confronted with anything like it before so I'm keeping an open mind. Justin certainly put a load of work in on it. He must have been very excited. After all, he'd been searching for it for ages. I'll be very interested to hear Patrick Gardene's views. I certainly think there's enough evidence of authenticity for him to be brought in now.'

'Great! Well done, Bill. This is just the kind of investment we need to kick the Fund off with. Imagine the value to us once Patrick Gardene gives it the OK and we make a deal with Kippax. The acquisition could be memorable.'

'It certainly could.'

'You think Kippax will come to the party once Patrick says OK? He won't then try to conduct a Dutch auction?'

'I don't think so. There is always that possibility but from the way he talks he won't risk it at auction. On the day, the market may stall and he resents the margins. I think he'd rather get a cheque in hand from a firm buyer. There's always the risk that a dealer with a big-hitting client might step in, but Kippax would have to find a dealer like that for himself. There seems to be some kind of time pressure on him. He says he's giving us first option and I believe him. If Gardene gives the furniture his seal of approval and we make the right offer, it's ours.'

'Fantastic. I'll contact Patrick right away. Please do send your report in quickly so I can let him have a copy before he goes to look for himself.'

'I'll do that.'

Patrick, I thought, Patrick it is now? You know him that well already? And you just said 'once' Patrick OKs the furniture, not 'if'. Is that just wishful thinking?

Justin said, 'The thing to realise about the City is that no matter what they say, or whatever rules have been laid down, it's an insider business. Who you know, not what you know. If you're not in, you don't stand a chance.'

'Good man,' said Tony Fitzsimmonds. 'There's a great future in this, Bill, if we can play these opportunities right.'

'I'm sure there is.'

'I'll look forward to getting your report. And to seeing you soon.'

'Fine.'

'Well done.'

He rang off. I sat in the car for a quiet moment. Off to my right, well out of sight, the Yorkshire Ouse meandered. Upstream it went off towards the bypassed Great North Road at Boroughbridge, near where the river met the Ure, recently arrived past Newby Hall, and the Swale. Those two rivers create the Ouse. If Newby Hall could have Chippendale furniture – its owner, William Weddell, was a patron of Robert Adam and Newby has finely preserved Chippendale/Adam interiors – then why not Ousedon Overwood, this much nearer to York? Quite a few rich Yorkshire landowners, some using the York architect John Carr, decided they'd stretch to the successful, London-based, more expensive fellow-Yorkshireman Chippendale than, say Wright and Elwick of Wakefield, or Farrer, or Reynoldson, subscribers to the *Director*, but less costly than its author.

It was lush, rolling country, very English in the way that many areas from the Midlands upwards are, with thick hedges and trees concealing views over waving grass or green crops. Nutty dark brick houses dotted the sides of lanes or clustered in hamlets. Beningborough Hall was nearby, then those villages, or rather hamlets, that follow the meandering stream north-eastwards – Newton and Linton with its RAF base on the other side, going up to Aldwark and the golf course – flanked on this side by others placed a little back from the river. Ousedon Overwood was one of them. I was on a small country road with a straight run to Boroughbridge, but I turned off before Little Ouseburn to find the site of Justin's holy grail. And his last breath.

There was nothing much to see. I had imagined a vast estate of post-1945 council houses, stretching over rolling country. I was wrong. South was Green Hammerton and a stream that led via the Nidd back to the Ouse. Peaceful countryside slid past my car windows until I entered a straggling village. There was nothing to indicate that a great house had ever stood here until, as I drove carefully out of the end of a line of cottages, I came across a solitary pair of gateposts before reaching a small, typical post-1945 development. The redbrick council estate ran from the road southwards in the usual series of crescents and culs-de-sac, giving that rather maze-like impression that planners seemed to like fifty-odd years ago. The ways in and the ways out were limited, flanked by a bus stop on either side of the road. I sat wondering at the way isolated housing estates like this had been plonked down almost in the middle of nowhere, part of some long-lost master plan years ago.

'Art lost?' The deep voice, at my open window, made me jump. The speaker had come up from behind my parked car. He was old, in country clothing, his face weatherbeaten, but blue eyes keen. He leant on a rough walking stick. A short Jack Russell terrier, white body adorned with black spots but a brown face, peered independently into a clump of gorse nearby.

I grinned at him. This was evidently the local version of Neighbourhood Watch and I was prowling, a potential pervert after a schoolgirl. 'Yes,' I said. 'I am. I'm trying to work out where Ousedon Overwood Hall was located.'

'You're looking at it.' He gestured with the stick towards the nearest line of houses and the big stone gateposts. 'It stood here until after the war. Then they knocked it down. The drive met the road at the gateposts there. There was a gatekeeper's lodge but that's gone.'

'So there's nothing left?'

He shook his head. 'Not really. There's some old walls down towards the river. Nowt else left from those days.'

His eyes on mine were still keen, waiting for explanations.

'I'm in publishing,' I lied. 'Gardens. The Hall's were laid out by Nesfield and we're researching a book on him. Have to be sure what's still in existence. The landscape gardener, William Andrews Nesfield, that is.'

'I know. Not much by way of gardens left here,' he said, but his expression was relaxing. 'Not unless you're thinking of allotments.'

I grinned again, but I'd had an idea.

'There were some water features,' I said, 'according to the records. Maybe something nearer to the river?'

He shook his head. 'Nothing. I heard that the gardens were pretty grand, once, though. There's what look like big ponds but they're some old gravel diggings.'

'Oh? They couldn't have been formal ponds?'

'Not unless your Nesfield used bucket dredgers. There's an old one still rusting in the water near the river.'

'Looks like I'm out of luck, then.' I gestured at an eastward road flanking the estate 'Can I get through over the river to the Linton side this way?'

'No. You have to go towards Great Ouseburn and over the Aldwark toll bridge.'

'This just goes down to the river?'

'It does that. Down to where they found that TV fellow's car. Dead end, it is.'

'Oh? In more ways than one, then.'

'Aye. I thought you were maybe another reporter, looking for the site. Near the walls I told you about. They were the Hall boundaries once. Ruined now.'

'Oh. I might just take a look. My editor's keen for me to miss nothing.'

He chuckled. 'Now you sound like one of them reporters. All cordoned off, it was, down there. You can still find a couple of cones where they marked the car. Everything else has gone, though.'

'Funny place for him to be. What on earth was he doing there?'

'That's what everyone wants to know.'

'And there are no hedges, lines of trees, anything left of formal gardens at all?'

'Nay.' His eyes were getting shrewd again. 'You're best off with a helicopter looking for traces like that, aren't you?'

I pulled a face. 'You tell that to my editor. And ask him to pay for a helicopter. We're not the BBC, awash with money.'

'They always use a helicopter for those lost garden programmes. The wife's dead keen on them. Like she was on Harrington.'

'Thanks all the same. Harrington and helicopters are not my editor's thing.'

He nodded, suddenly abrupt at this mention of wives and editors. 'Mine neither. I must get on. Good luck to you, anyway.'

'Thanks. And good luck to you too.'

He gave a short, low whistle and the Jack Russell came out of the gorse bush. The two of them moved off, the old man poling along on his stick. I drove carefully down the eastward road past the estate, slowing as the way narrowed through hedges towards the river. The single-track lane was metalled but the verges looked dodgy except for passing places at field gates or brief widenings of the road. Houses were sparse, fronted by pretty gardens but isolated. Eventually, with a couple of stretches of tumbled wall coming up, I came to an open grassy patch at the side of the road, wide enough and long enough to park more than one car. A pair of cones leant against the hedge, spaced about fifteen feet apart. I stopped and pulled on to the grassy patch, switching off the engine. I was there; I was sitting there, where Justin had last sat, breathing his last breaths.

My mobile phone rang.

I almost switched it off in irritation, but the repeated imperative of the tone was too much to resist. With a silent curse, I answered with my usual hello.

The responding voice was brisk, strong, American.

'Hi, Bill! It's me. Chuck Vance. How are ya?'

'Chuck! I'm fine. Where are you?'

'New York, where else? Where are you?'

'I'm in Yorkshire. I'm sitting in my car, on the very spot where Justin Harrington snuffed it.'

'What? You *ghoul*. Are you crazy? What are you doing? The cops'll fry you alive. They think murderers always revisit the scene of the crime.'

'I'm investigating.'

'A *sleuth*, are you? You're plumb crazy. Listen, shipmate, belay that detective nonsense and get back to your shop, pronto. I bring good news. I've sold both your Arts and Crafts pieces.'

'What?'

'You going deaf? You got shit in your ears or what? I'll repeat what I just said. I sold both your Arts and Crafts pieces. The Ashbee and the Blomfield. For the price.'

'Christ! You unbelievable, inspired, wonderful maniac! Who to?'

'A big-time client in hedge funds. Setting up a special collection. Don't worry: I'll pay you against shipping documents. Banker's draft. OK?'

'Of course! Wow! Christ!'

'Thought you might like to know. I expect the best lunch in Surrey when I next see you. But there's a hitch.'

My excitement drained. 'Hitch? What kind of hitch?'

He chuckled. 'You have to find more. This is only the beginning. The guy wants the best of American and British Arts and Crafts. I'll find the Americans. I need you to find the Brits. OK?'

'OK. It won't be easy but OK. I'm obliged to you, Chuck. That's fantastic, utterly fantastic.'

'Good. And I have news about the other thing.'

'Other thing?'

'The Fauville cabinet. It was purchased at auction by an investment outfit called Stargaze. Rumour has it that they are going into French furniture in a big way. Stargaze Investments is the creation of a guy called O'Hanlon. Rory O'Hanlon. They recently took a shipment of French chairs. Eighteenth century.'

'Don't tell me: they came from Henry Roland.'

'I don't know who they came from. I don't know if Harrington was involved either. These people play with their cards close to their chests.'

'Do they have any connection with Leggatt's?'

'I checked. The answer is no. There is no financial connection. But strangely enough O'Hanlon and Fitzsimmonds both own stock in a Kentucky stud farm. And some horse outfit in Ireland.'

'How strange.'

THE CHIPPENDALE FACTOR 201

'Yeah, ain't it?'

'One does French furniture, the other does English. And maybe both will do Irish.'

'Could be. But what in hell are you really doing, up there in Yorkshire?'

'I've been looking at a hitherto undiscovered collection of Chippendale furniture found by Justin Harrington.'

'Horse shit. Undiscovered Chippendale furniture? Does the ownership of Brooklyn Bridge come with it? Undiscovered Chippendale furniture is on a par with undiscovered gold bars and an old map of Treasure Island from the trunk in my attic.'

'You're a sceptical man, Chuck.'

'Go home. Go home and pack those cabinets. Then go find some more. Please. I beg you. Please go home.'

'I'm on my way.'

'Promise?'

'Promise.'

'See ya, Bill. Take care.'

'See you too, Chuck.'

He rang off. I sat grinning like a lunatic, alone in my car, thinking of those cabinets and money, and Chuck. Fantastic! Amazing. I wanted to shout out loud, punch the air in triumph. Around me was the calm countryside only broken by the ruined bits of wall, and the narrow road heading towards its end at the river, where the diggings made ponds. Excitement thrilled through my veins, buzzing the blood, stirring my loins. Men excited by success, by a win, by anything, get worked up that way. I started to think about Ellen. I could have done with her, there and then, in the car, any old way, skirt hitched up, breath panting, celebrating, the two of us humping like a pair of mad stoats. The cabinets are sold! Get your knickers off, girl, quick!

I stared out of the window at the remaining boundary walls of the demesne of Ousedon Overwood Hall and the isolated country this side of the river as realisation dawned.

Of course! That was it; that was why he was here. That was what Justin Harrington – Baz Stevens was doing here.

He had a woman down here, humping for his life. He was celebrating.

He had a woman here.

Chapter Twenty-Four

'The thing is,' Steve Stanton said, over his cup of tea, which he was using as a sort of facial shield from time to time, 'I had this idea about setting up a vintage car business when I leave college.'

'Very good. But you weren't going to confine yourself to Rileys, were you?'

He blinked. 'Actually, yes I was. Which is why I thought you would be an ideal co-director in it. Without interfering with your antiques business, of course.'

It was incongruous, really. We were sitting in a café near his college, one we had agreed to meet at, and having the sort of tea and cake that a visiting dad might buy a son at boarding school. He was horribly embarrassed but determined, in the way that youth can be determined, to go through with what he wanted to go through with.

I smiled at him. 'It's a great idea. And I'm flattered. But you see, I think you'd have to do more than think of just Rileys. By all means be a specialist in them because you love them, but do one or two other marques as well. The thing is, you see—'

'*There's an optimum size to any business, and it's always much bigger than you think it is.*'

'– there's an optimum size to any business and it's always much bigger than you think it is.'

He nodded vigorously. 'That's what one of my lecturers keeps saying.'

'I'm glad he agrees. What you should consider, as well, is storage.'

'Storage?'

'Yes. There are several specialists who have set up in converted farm buildings, or custom-made buildings, to store vintage cars in the right environment. Near Goodwood or Silverstone or other circuits. Or some central, convenient location. They look after rich collectors' collections, service them, repair them, provide all the facilities necessary. It solves the collector-investor's problems, especially if he or she lives in London or a big city. People who own several cars, and you'd be surprised how many there are, can't garage them easily in towns. But they can drive out to a storage unit, take out the current favourite car, do a rally or a race meeting or an outing to impress their friends and mistresses, and pop it back in when finished. It's kept dry, exercised when necessary – cars are a bit like horses that way – and groomed ready for use. You charge an ongoing monthly fee plus whatever work is required. The cash flow is much improved. An operation like that is far better than getting all oily in a backstreet workshop, waiting for old Rileys in need of repair to roll up.'

'You've got it.' He put his cup down in excitement. 'I knew you'd have it. That's why I thought of you from the beginning. And with you and mother—' He broke off and picked up the cup once again. 'At least, I thought, with you and mother – but now – I mean, is it all over?'

I smiled at him again. 'No, Steve, it's not all over. It's just a temporary hiatus. These things happen. I'm sure you know that.'

He stared ferociously out of the café window. 'There's somebody else though, isn't there?'

'No, Steve, there's nobody else.'

'You mean you haven't—'

'No, Steve, I haven't. Look at me. I haven't.'

He looked, but still flinched before he spoke. 'Mother mentioned Elizabeth Harrington.'

'It's a long time, a very long time, since I saw Elizabeth Harrington.'

He was brightly flushed. 'I hated him. *Hated* him. On top of what he was doing, he tried to cheat Father over investments. That skunk: I loathed him. It's good riddance. I'm glad he's dead. I hated him.'

I had a thought, of rattling gears down a lane near the Ouse, in the dark. Why would an old car be down that lane at night? Was that when Steve had the Kestrel Nine up at college?

Ellen had been up here then, too.

He was silent, flushed, waiting. There was no time to speculate.

'Well, that's all over, Steve. We all have to move on. And I'm delighted with your idea. I'd be honoured to be part of your vintage car venture. And I'd put some money into it. I'm sure you'll make a success of it.'

His face cleared. 'You do? You will?'

'I will.'

'That's great!'

I held my hand out across the table. 'We'll shake on it?'

We shook.

I sat back, thinking.

'What?' he asked.

'Could you do something for me? A bit of research over in York? I might be a bit conspicuous but a student wouldn't. I'll pay you a fee for your time.'

He leant forward, excited. 'What research?'

I explained to him all about Ousedon Overwood Hall and the Chippendale furniture, and the photographs from the missing magazines. Then the back history I needed and where to start looking.

'Fantastic,' he said. 'I'm glad I brought the Riley back up again. I'll do it in no time.'

'Go carefully. Be as discreet as you can.'

'You can rely on me. Wow! I wonder if it really is genuine. What a great project to work on.'

'And don't fret about me and your mother and the Harrington thing. It will sort itself out. The main thing right now is to track down what Justin was up to.'

He looked at me curiously. 'You really were a friend of his once, weren't you?'

'Yes,' I said. 'I was a friend of his once.'

Chapter Twenty-Five

The day after Justin's memorial service, I went upstairs and reopened my old school trunk. The service was somewhat impromptu. The police had held up a proper funeral for as long as whatever post-mortems were necessary could be completed. So someone, being in showbiz, organised a memorial service in the meantime. It was in London, at one of those fashionable churches in which they hold such services. It seemed irregular, even hasty, but they'd done it. I got a call from Bert Higgins, who I knew from attendance at fairs.

I'd sent my report off to Fitzsimmonds. I'd tried to phone Ellen. There was only an answerphone recording at the other end. I drove to the house but she wasn't there. It was going to take time. I went to the memorial service in sombre mood.

As I looked into the trunk my mind flicked back, just for a moment, to the ceremony. Not as many of the School House lot as I'd expected, really. From my rearward pew I'd watched them come and go. Foster, larger than ever, his dark clothes straining at the seams. Baker, no longer possessed of a sober suit that fitted, in a navy blue blazer and charcoal trousers.

Rampson, sepulchral in a long black overcoat. Draycott, saturnine and gap-tooth-grinning from his lined lean face, fleeting at the end of the ceremony. Podge Chinley, still pasty, fatter than ever, features almost subsumed into his pudding of a head. But of Carroll, Harris, O'Hara, Tertius, there was no sign. Some weren't from the same intake. Some despised the deceased. Some had long fled the country. Some were dead. Brigham was the first to go, by heart attack in a hotel. Pernambuco, of all places. Geisler of the thick horn-rims was said to have met a sated end in louche circumstances in Egypt. I had my doubts about that. The yearly magazine glossed over the past and I wasn't in the old boys' club. I didn't go up to the annual dinners in town. But I was surprised that the funeral hadn't produced a bigger gathering of people I knew. The last one was for Tubby Edwards, conked out on his tractor in the middle of a ploughed field. The turnout was better for him.

Henry Roland went to that one.

Not that the service lacked a crowd. I saw Tony Fitzsimmonds and Jim Macallister, suitably in subfusc clothing, and got an approving nod from both. Their relationship with Justin must have developed more than I realised. Celia Beckland, cool as a cucumber and dressed in smart grey, went gliding down towards the front, presumably present as a business partner rather than her more personal status. There were many others from the later periods of Baz Stevens' life, some of them well known to the media. They were the prominent majority, flash-snapped by a group of photographers along with some Mayfair dealers led by a glum-faced Bert Higgins, who was probably a creditor. The media didn't know the deceased as Baz Stevens, of course. He was Justin Harrington to them, a face and a name from TV appearances that were part of a knowing, celebrity culture.

Editors had to make sure they'd clocked the event, especially the presence of a couple of well-known beauties whose names gossip had linked to the deceased at one time or another.

'The TV antiques crowd,' I could hear him snarl. 'French-polished parasites with satinwood smiles on their dentil-moulded mouths. Look at 'em, leering at their painted doxies.'

'You're misquoting someone,' I'd say. 'Or paraphrasing him.'

'So what? I am right. I've had my cock in most of those cleavages. Crap. All of it is crap. Celebrity or bust.'

'Then why did you pursue it?'

He'd never answer that. The celebrity and the doxies were like drugs to him. Tactless of the two at the funeral to come. But typical of anything connected to Stevens-Harrington. Even his *pompes funèbres* had to be *pompes célèbres*. His widow was different. Flanked by her two children, now adults heading for their forties, she kept a cool dignity in the face of the photographers. She passed close to the pew I occupied and I saw her very clearly, closer than for many years. She looked much the same as I remembered her but older, thicker in the way that we all get thicker whilst fighting off getting fat. But still attractive.

She didn't seem to see me.

I had to pause for a moment to think about the sight and memory of her. Elizabeth: my mind went away for a suspended moment, immeasurable, and when I wrenched my eyes back to the trunk, I had no idea how long a moment had elapsed or why I was bothering to look.

My focus had gone. More effort was needed.

I put the first School House photograph to one side and carefully went to the fourth one, the one before my last house photograph, thank God, the one where I now sat on a chair at one end of the power row, arms folded, staring aggressively at the camera. Was that really me? Thinner, leaner, more cynical, addicted to the writing of Somerset Maugham? What had I been made into? Where was Baz Stevens? I scanned the faces along the seated line, then again along the standing rows.

He wasn't there.

Henry Roland had been right. Baz Stevens wasn't there. I had long known it but some shutter of the mind had dropped, refusing to accept the pictorial gap. His absence had been blotted from my recollection. Strange how the memory plays tricks over time, taking out some years and etching others onto the brain. The last time I had taken out these photographs, I only looked at the first one, where my unformed face – pudgy, Marian called it – stared out at me.

Harris wasn't there either. Henry Roland said he had been given the chop, too. What for? I had forgotten all about Harris but slowly, dimly at first, an idea about what Harris used to do was coming back to me.

Printing.

Under the school photographs the jumbled packs of images still recorded moments and people, sunlit days and cloudy events innocently unaware of future scrutiny like mine. The schoolboys in front of Montevideo's British School, like those on the lawn at School House, stared blandly at the camera, not at the narrowing eyes of later knowledge. Some time, some time soon, an order should be imposed to make sense of these disparate occasions, significant perhaps for what was not there, for occasions never recorded.

History books are arranged so as to do that.

Arranging a life story from these random flashes of illumination might be more difficult, though.

I shut the trunk and went back, down the stairs to today.

Chapter Twenty-Six

They told me, long afterwards, that Fat Arthur was in a very bad mood that day. He had always been nervous and irritable, not like a normal craftsman, for as long as anyone remembered, but of late he'd got worse.

Anyway, he was always the last to shut up shop, so everyone had pretty well gone when he came out of the front door jangling his big bunch of keys. His man Stan was already in his car just about to start up and leave when Fat Arthur came out, still in his stained long brown coat. He was a grubby dresser, wore dirty old trainers, a pair of grey worsted trousers spattered with God knows what, a blue shirt with fat on the frontage.

There was a short length of service road alongside the workshops, separating them from the main road, and Arthur normally parked there. So did Stan, but a bit further back. He said he could see that Fat Arthur was still in a bate because he was muttering to himself as he walked the few steps from the door across to his car.

He was standing by the driver's door, fiddling with his keys, when the motorbike came off the main road and slowed up as it rolled down the short service strip. It was green, powerful, and there were two people on it. Both wore dark leathers and both had those all-embracing crash helmets on, the ones that conceal the head entirely. Arthur looked up from his bunch of keys, a bit surprised, as the motorbike throbbed up, and half-turned towards it. The pillion rider put his arm out and there was a sharp noise, Stan said like a dull crack, and Fat Arthur's head jerked sharply. He dropped his keys and his legs gave way so that he fell sliding down the door of his car.

The motorbike still kept rolling down the service strip until it reached the feed-in back to the main road. It seemed quite unhurried until then but once the wheels were on the main drag it accelerated away steadily, no roaring noises, just a motorbike heading off towards Send or Burnt Common or maybe Guildford.

Stan the man got out of his car and went to look at Fat Arthur, lying in a pile in the road, with a bullet in his head, stone dead.

Or brown bread, as he would have put it.

The doorbell rang without glad anticipation as the two policemen came in. The sergeant, Walters, looked tense; the constable, Green, was his normal rather impassive self.

'Good morning,' I said. I was waiting for my packers and removal men to come for the Ashbee and Blomfield cabinets. There's nothing like making a hole in your stock to cheer you up. Empty spaces stimulate activity, providing they step up the cash flow too. But Ellen Stanton was casting a shadow on my joy. At least, her absence was doing the casting.

'Good morning, Mr Franklin.' DS Walters did at least return the civility before opening fire. 'Where were you yesterday, late afternoon, around five thirty to six p.m.?'

I looked him straight in the eye. 'Yesterday, I went to the memorial service for Justin Harrington up in London. It started at two p.m. or thereabouts and lasted an hour. I came home after it, so I guess by five-thirty I was back here.'

I didn't tell him that I'd phoned Ellen Stanton and left a message for her, for the third time, without result. She seemed to be away.

'Can anyone confirm that you were here then?'

'No one called, no.'

'When did you last see Arthur Brigley?'

'Fat Arthur? Four days ago, in Ripley. He was sitting in the road when I last saw him.'

'You hit him, didn't you? In fact you knocked him down.'

'I certainly did. In self-defence. He was attacking me with a three-foot sash cramp. It's on the back seat of my car.'

'I shall need to have that as evidence.'

'You're welcome. What's happened?'

His face darkened. 'Arthur Brigley was killed yesterday, outside his workshops, by an unknown assailant.'

'Don't tell me: he was shot, like Henry Roland?'

'He was. How do you know?'

I ignored that. 'I do wonder why it is that every time someone gets shot, you come here. I haven't got a gun. Nor a green motorbike.'

'How do you know the assailant was on a green motorbike?'

'Because Henry's was. You didn't tell me that either; I'm guessing because I think it came to look me over, too.'

'You don't seem to be very upset by this news.'

I was; I was shocked; but I wasn't going to show it to this accusatory policeman.

'Fat Arthur was a nasty piece of work who produced more fake furniture than anyone I know. His methods were dreadful. Men like Fat Arthur ruin the trade. He was rude, aggressive and frightened. Some disgruntled customer was bound to catch up with him sooner or later. And he knew it.'

'Like you, you mean, bashing him in the street? That sort of disgruntled customer?'

'I've never been a customer of Fat Arthur's. I went to ask him, with great courtesy, about Henry Roland and Justin Harrington and maybe some French chairs. He turned nasty and attacked me. A steel sash cramp is a grisly weapon. To me his behaviour confirmed his guilt.'

'I don't think you quite understand how serious your position is. There is now one thread of close connection between the deaths of Justin Harrington, Henry Roland and Arthur Brigley: you. What is more, you've been prowling around in Yorkshire at the scene of Harrington's death. With some cock and bull story about garden books.'

'Oho. The old guy with the Jack Russell dog rang in my licence number, obviously. I wondered if he might.'

'There is enough material to justify my running you in to the station for questioning under caution.'

'Then do so or stop blustering. You'd be much better off asking me for help. Especially about a French consignment of chairs. Tell me: did Justin Harrington die of a heart attack?'

'His death is not now being treated as suspicious. The cause is still not for publication.'

'I think a woman got to him before the mob. Was there evidence of a woman in his car?'

Walters gave me a curious stare. 'Actually, no. Forensic didn't come up with anything like that. Apart from his wife, that is.'

'But he died unexpectedly, so that means something he ingested. Perhaps an overdose of a stimulant like, say, Viagra or another aphrodisiac?'

DC Green made a curious spluttering noise, then, catching his sergeant's eye, straightened his face.

'Why do you think that?'

'Just conjecture.'

'If there is one thing I can't stand it's suspects who play at being amateur sleuths. I think you should come to the police station.'

'If you want to waste your time as well as mine, fine. But as an antique furniture dealer rather than an amateur sleuth – or a suspect – I suggest you follow another line of inquiry involving French chairs. I think that Justin Harrington and Henry Roland set up a deal to sell some French eighteenth-century chairs to an investment outfit in America. A long set, possibly a whole container-load. They got them from a French dealer in Saint-Germaine-en-Laye called Dubois. The chairs were shipped here first for Fat Arthur to do some dodgy provenance work on them – what work I can't say but maybe the idea was to give them an English country house provenance, Chippendale supply, something like that.'

'Chippendale didn't make French furniture.'

'If there's one thing I can't stand it's amateur furniture experts. Chippendale imported lots of French chairs – and mirrors – and supplied them to his clients. Mostly he bought them as frames ready for upholstering, which he did in London, in his premises in St Martin's Lane, with imported French tapestry. In New York they love French furniture. A set of French chairs with additional Chippendale involvement would be big money. The Chippendale factor ramps things up.'

'But these would be dodgy?' DC Green sounded really interested.

'Almost certainly. And when the New York end found out, they made sure the people concerned would never do it again.'

'What New York end?' Walters sounded testy.

'You could try an investment company called Stargaze Investments. They may not have been the importer; a subsidiary company would do that. But Henry Roland was a key figure in the supply despite your drawing a blank. Maybe a business name of Fat Arthur's was used. I'm sure you've got his books.'

'We'll get them.' Walters was still abrupt but I could tell he was rethinking, hard.

'I wouldn't waste any time if I were you.'

'This all sounds like a strong, muscular red herring to me.'

'You're mixing your metaphors. Hares are muscular; red herrings aren't. And actually, I'm trying to help you. You know for certain I didn't kill Henry or Fat Arthur and I have no idea how to commission hit men on motorbikes. What would I gain by these deaths?'

'They would conceal forgery, for a start. They would also leave you as sole beneficiary of these frauds.'

'Well, I'm not. But I am interested in one thing, and that is who blew the gaffe?'

'What?'

'The purchasers of those chairs got to know that they were fakes *before* they paid up. Someone told them the whole story. When Henry Roland came to see me he said his payment was still due – from Harrington. So Harrington set the whole thing up and was handling payment. He was dead when Henry called to see me and Henry was shot that same evening. It looks as though it took a few days to track back to Fat Arthur's role in the scam. Now Dubois must be in danger.'

Walters was listening at last. 'It seems pretty drastic to bump them all off over a set of chairs. The purchaser could simply have withheld payment and made them take them back.'

'There are people who take that sort of thing personally. Particularly people who have dodgy money. And right now they have both the chairs and their money.'

'Not much good if the chairs are dud though, is it?'

'Who can say the chairs are dud? Once everyone involved in their production is dead?'

'Dubois?' he snapped. 'Saint-Germaine-en-Laye?'

'You've got it.'

He turned on his heel and Green shot through the door after him. I heard their car start up and shouted, but it was too late. They left so quickly that they forgot to take Fat Arthur's sash cramp with them.

Chapter Twenty-Seven

Steve Stanton's voice, on the telephone, was a mixture of apprehension and excitement. He'd turned York Public Library upside down.

'Seventeen ten,' he said. 'The original house at Ousedon Overwood was built in 1710. By a man called Francis Smithers. A wool merchant.'

'What else?'

'Quite a modest place. A gentleman's residence. Queen Anne style, of course. He died in 1743 and was followed by William Smithers. Who died in 1781 and in turn was followed by Benjamin Smithers, born 1737 died 1801.'

'Did he or his dad buy any Chippendale furniture?'

'No mention of it that I could find at that period but the house was said to be well appointed. He had no sons and his only daughter Dorothy married a guy called James Allgood. They had a daughter Mary Allgood in 1791. She too was an only child and in 1811 she married Thomas Thwaite.'

'Aha! At last. *Aquí vienen los* Thwaite.'

'What?'

'Nothing. I wondered when the Thwaites would turn up.'

'Well, that couple don't seem to have lasted long because in 1824 the property belonged to a George Thwaite. He did well somehow in the coal trade.'

'Wool and coal. Like the Winn family at Nostell Priory. An encouraging combination for Chippendale.'

'Is it? Well, he prospered Yorkshire-fashion and in 1840 he financed a rebuild on grander lines. Decimus Burton was the architect and William Andrews Nesfield landscaped the grounds.'

'Ha ha.'

'What?'

'That's a joke. Nesfield invented the ha-ha. I wonder if there was one at Ousedon Overwood.'

'I've no idea. There is a print of the house and grounds done by some local artist in the 1850s. Quite impressive in a thick-set, squarish style. Sort of sub-classical in that early Victorian way Burton did for the house, with a porticoed front door, and formal landscaping with shrubs and rose beds and rectangular ornamental ponds. No interiors.'

'Pity.'

'The Thwaites prospered in wool, coal and shipping, rather than land, but they don't seem to have left much social record. Anyway, George both earned and spent heavily. He died in 1875 and Albert took over.' He paused. 'Albert was artistic and did not marry.'

'Oh dear.'

'You guessed: Albert embellished the place until his death in 1906. Lavishly. Things were getting mortgaged. Income had fallen. By 1914 the exchequer was looking bad and his nephew Edward was struggling.'

'Don't tell me, I know. Lloyd George's death duties put the boot in after 1918.'

'Exactly. Edward's son was killed in the trenches in 1916. The old Thwaites struggled on until 1932 when the house was sold to a property man called Brotherton. His idea was to develop a country house hotel and golf course.'

'There's a golf course at Aldwark.'

'I don't know the date of that. Maybe it came first. Anyway, nothing came of it and the place just languished. During the war the house was an overspill RAF and Canadian officers' mess for Linton, then it had some Free French and Polish troops billeted in it.'

'I bet that finished it off.'

'It did. They did a lot of damage. After the war the buildings were torn down and the council estate built. It was intended to build a bigger estate, which seems ridiculous, but the plans were shelved. End of Ousedon Overwood Hall.'

'Sad. Very like Kenneth Clark's family house at Sudbourne. It doesn't sound as though the eighteenth-century Smithers were grand enough to buy top-rate Chippendale furniture, but they might have gone for the plain mahogany. What did the article in the local magazine say about how long the furniture in the photographs of the interiors had been there?'

'Ah. There's a bit of a problem about that. The librarian remembered the old magazines – the *Swale and Ouse Illustrated Recorder* – a monthly job which went out of business in the Thirties. She got them out for a visitor some four or five weeks ago. She took me to their storage shelves for 1910, which was the year of the article, but she couldn't remember which month. We got out the stock for that year and two issues – June and July – are missing.'

'What?'

'Yep. And they have the article about Ousedon Overwood in them. It was in two parts. The house and gardens were in the first and the interiors in the second part. We checked all the other issues that year and there's nothing about Ousedon Overwood Hall in them. It has to be those two. They've gone.'

'Shit.'

'She says that the visitor must have taken them. She was really upset – their security is supposed to stop that kind of theft but hardly anyone ever looked at the magazines and they had no security strip or anything to them. She remembered him, though. He was a tall dark man, late middle age, well dressed, with a high forehead.'

'Justin Harrington.'

'You bet. I asked her if she watched him on telly but she didn't. But if I take her a photo, I bet she'll identify him.'

'The bastard. He snitched the magazines. That could only be because the articles said something he wanted to hide.'

'Correct. There must be something dodgy about that furniture.'

'Shit. Bugger. Damn. Blast.'

'Succinctly put, Bill.'

I had a recall of James Kippax's hesitation before he responded to my question about copies of magazines in the library. How did he know that the key ones were missing? Justin must have told him. But why?

'Are there no other records in that library?' I asked Steve. 'About Ousedon Overwood Hall, I mean.'

'I checked with the librarian and we went through her computer records. Zilch, except for some post-1945 planning committee records.'

'I'll phone the British Library magazine section at Colindale and see if they have any runs of the *Swale and Ouse Illustrated Recorder* in their archives but it's a long shot.'

'I thought about that. You'd be more likely to find copies here in Yorkshire, in private collections. We could advertise.'

'I agree. Let's try it. Put something in whatever local papers and magazines you think are read by Yorkshire magazine collectors. I'll pay for the ads. Try local history societies, too. Concentrate on York.'

'I will. I'll try the Internet, too. This is exciting. You can get a taste for this sort of thing.'

'Don't neglect your studies, for God's sake, Steve.'

'I won't. But about that other business we discussed?'

'What?'

He hesitated. 'There's a Riley Gamecock coming up for sale at a local car auction in Leeds. It's in poor nick but a Gamecock is always a good seller. This is a 1932 model. I thought it might make a good start to the venture.'

'It might indeed. Do your research. Make a quick estimate of the cost of doing it up. You know what a good example will sell for. Go to the auction and bid for it, leaving plenty of margin. I'll finance it if you get it.'

'Great. It would be a terrific start. Although now I'm nervous.'

'You can do it, Steve. Just don't get carried away at the auction. Set an upper limit and stick to it. I'm sure you know all this but you have to start somewhere. But for Heaven's sake don't neglect college. Your mother will kill me if your work is affected.'

There was an interrogative silence.

'I've tried to contact her,' I said, 'but she seems to be away.'

'She was here.' His voice started to go hoarse. 'I told her what's going on. And I told her what you said.'

'What did she say?'

'She didn't say anything. She changed the subject.'

'Has she gone home?'

'No. She's gone to stay with my aunt in Manchester. I don't know when she'll be home.'

'Don't worry about it, Steve. Just carry on as we've discussed. I must ring off now.' I hesitated, thinking. 'I'll follow up another line of inquiry about those magazines.'

I didn't tell him where.

Chapter Twenty-Eight

St George's Hill still had that calm, tailored look that comes from placing houses carefully in spaced, park-like settings. The sense of privacy inspired by making traffic pass through gates, even open gates, felt well conceived. After all, they could be closed to fulfil legal privacy requirements but they are just there, reminding those entering that they do so by permission of some kind. Inside the stockade, lumps of rhododendrons add thick masses of dark green screening to the clipped hedging and mown grass fronting. This is still an estate of executive achievement, I thought, the object of commercial and social ambitions, the epitome of plot acquired by plotting.

I slowed the car down as I approached the house, feeling a certain degree of nervous tension creep over the calm outward appearance I had planned. It had been a long time; there was a huge gulf; you never know how a woman might react.

Bracing myself, I parked in the drive, got out briskly, went to the front door and rang the bell. There was an agonising wait whilst nothing happened, then there was a surprise: it was opened by Elizabeth herself. She looked tired but good, casually but expensively dressed.

'Christ,' she said, staring at me. 'I don't believe this.'

I resisted a flippant response. 'Hello, Elizabeth.'

'You've got a nerve.'

'I'm nervous, certainly.'

'You must be bloody desperate.'

'A little edgy, let us say.'

Her face creased into a slight smile. 'You were always lucky. The kids left half an hour ago. Otherwise they'd have answered the door for me and chucked you out. It's the maid's day off, too.'

'A bit like old times,' I said. 'But not quite.'

Her smile vanished. 'Certainly not quite.' Then she frowned slightly. 'I thought I saw you at the memorial service.'

'I was there.'

'Ah. I knew it.'

'You did a good job of not seeing me.'

'What did you expect?'

'Nothing. I thought you were the most dignified part of it.'

'And now?'

'Nothing. Except maybe some help.'

'So you just turned up?'

'The phone is a barrier.'

'True. You want to come in?'

'Yes, please.'

She stood back and opened the door a little wider. 'You'd better come in, then.'

I passed through into the flowered hall and she led the way into a small sitting room. There was a bookcase and desk and two chintz armchairs. Light came in through paned Georgian-style windows with chintz curtains. She motioned to one of the armchairs and sat in the other, facing me. Just like it was with Celia Beckland.

'You look well,' she said. 'If stressed.'

I smiled ruefully. 'Thanks. You look as good as ever. Maybe a bit tired. How are things going?'

She made a gesture that waved the question aside. 'I'm managing. What I can't believe is that you are here. But then you often did that. Turn up out of the blue, I mean.' A slightly mocking look came to her face. 'I'm told it's Ellen these days.'

Just like it was with Celia Beckland.

'Yes,' I said. 'It's Ellen these days. I suppose Celia told you?'

'Yes. She did.'

There was a short silence full of suspense. Strange connections, implied actions, wonderings of how often who saw who, how they arranged their meetings, and what they said to each other passed through my mind. This was a woman with whom I had done everything, who had called out in passion as she clutched beneath me, yet here we were, talking like stiff repertory actors in a hack matinée scene.

'I'm in a bind,' I said. 'The police and others think I was involved in some scam of Henry Roland and Justin's. And now someone has shot Fat Arthur.'

'How's Marian?' she asked. 'Do you ever hear from her?'

'Yes, I do. She's fine. The life suits her. They got a silver gilt at Chelsea. And now I've got Tony Fitzsimmonds to deal with.'

'She's good at gardening.'

'*Gardening is what people do when the sex is over. If they aren't waspish designer queers. Which a lot of them are.*'

'Yes,' I said. 'She's a good gardener.'

'You never took it up.'

'No. Never.'

'*A gardener is a man or woman who digs a hole, sticks some shit and a plant in it, waters it and thinks it's a miracle when the bloody thing grows. As though they'd just invented the system themselves.*'

'Not quite the Latin image, gardening?'

'I didn't think I had that. More of an Englishman abroad, perhaps.'

'Or the half Uruguayan at home.'

I shrugged. 'Whichever you prefer.'

She didn't answer. The half Uruguayan, I thought, was what caused the clutching and the calling out. But silence is golden.

'Why do you think I can help you? After all this time?'

'It's to do with Justin, up in Yorkshire.'

Her face went guarded. 'What about him?'

'Did you know what he was doing?'

'I wasn't there. As I've told the police at length. I assume he was still pursuing the Chippendale chimera.'

'Did he bring any magazines home in the weeks before he went? I'm looking for two copies of an old journal called the *Swale and Ouse Illustrated Recorder*. June and July 1910.'

'The *what*?'

'The *Swale and Ouse Illustrated Recorder*. He pinched two copies from the York Public Library.'

'He did *what*?'

'He stole them. They had evidence in them. Something he didn't want made public. You know the whole story about Leggatt's and the furniture?'

'No.'

I gave her a brief resumé of the Ousedon Overwood furniture story to date. As I told it, she began to relax. By the time I finished, the half-smile was back on her face.

'What a hoot,' she said.

I nearly answered I'm glad you think so, with two men shot dead and your late husband's demise still unexplained. But I didn't. *En boca cerrada no entran moscas.* I reflected how she had always been the opposite from Marian, who loved antiques and took them seriously, like her plants. Elizabeth loved them but saw them all as an opportunist's game. Justin had trained her well.

'Illusions,' he said. 'We are in the business of illusions. Like Ferrari salesmen. The greater the con, the more effective the illusion.'

'Not true. We are talking of beautifully made things.'

'The magazines,' I persisted. 'You never saw them?'

'Of course not. If what you say is true, he would never have shown them to me. I explained all about that to you years ago. Have you forgotten?'

'Of course I've not forgotten.'

Years ago, at the height of our affair, between snatches of frantic coupling, Elizabeth had explained the territorial nature of her life with Justin. How he kept to his territory and she to hers. The nature of the bargain that kept her in luxury while he was free to roam. The bargain she broke when, one day I was back from a trip to São Paulo and, at a loose end, went to an antiques fair in London. Harrington and Beckland had a stand there to promote their books. Celia and Justin were staffing it but I avoided them. The coolness caused by Marian's reaction to their relationship had affected the way I thought about them. Joking with Justin over lunch was one thing; dealing with them together a very different matter. Celia was never pleased to have me around, knowing all I knew.

On the other side of the exhibition hall I came across Elizabeth having a coffee and looking pensive. Down in the mouth. She seemed glad to see me and we talked over coffee of the old days in Vallance Road.

'Things were great then,' she said, brightening. 'Do you remember...'

We talked until it was lunchtime and on through lunch. And that was how it started. It went from there. Brief hours snatched in my flat, or in hotels, or in the back of the car. It could have been squalid but it wasn't. Oh, I know, everyone says that. We are all unique in our deceits. But I was at a loose end and she was thrilling and full of mischief.

Did Justin know? I think he guessed. Did he care? Of course; what he did was to take wives, not have his taken. He never said anything directly to me, but there were shadows between us, not just those induced by Marian, before the Georgian Revival book got binned.

It was fabulous.

What ended it? Children, what else? Hers were growing up, becoming curious. They started to bring boyfriends and girlfriends home. They had an image of her, in opposition to their father's, that it was important to preserve. They nearly caught us out a couple of times. Elizabeth became afraid, tense. Respectability had become very important. I was too proud to wait in the wings for the rare beckoning gesture. I was in love and it hurt, even though I knew the whole thing was impossible. It's an old story. Their marriage would never break up.

End of affair.

'I'd offer you some tea,' she said now, her manner warmer, 'because it's one of Justin's more hilarious escapades and I'd not have heard it if you hadn't come here. But the kids will be back soon. And I don't think – the widow being consoled is not—'

'No,' I said. 'I suppose not. You can't help with the magazines at all?'

'I'm sorry, Bill. I can't help you.'

Her voice had a kind but obvious finality to it that said don't ask any more and don't try asking again.

'I understand,' I said. 'One last thing: had he seen Harris – that's Bob Harris, from School House – at all lately?'

She frowned. 'God, that school. I don't think – although yes, there was a call I took from someone I think was called Harris quite a long while ago. Why?'

'Thanks.' I stood up. 'It's probably nothing. Just a thought I had about printing. Harris used to make up false postmarks for a hobby. At school, that is. He could produce ones that looked really old.'

I didn't say that's why they both got chucked out. It didn't seem the right moment.

She got up too, then hesitated. 'About Ellen. Is it—'

'Yes it is. Serious, that is.'

She looked troubled for a moment, then nodded. 'You better go,' she said. 'This is no place for you.'

It emphasised the finality of my departure.

But she did say 'Good luck, Bill,' as I left.

I took my leave decorously and drove away quickly so that my car wouldn't embarrass anyone. I was thinking hard. She knew all about Ellen. So it was odds-on that Ellen knew all about her. I had to deal with that.

But, more important, I had to deal with the thought that one of them might have been the woman with Justin when he parked his car on the grass near the ruined walls at Ousedon. Despite what Sergeant Walters said, a woman was there, had to be, I knew it.

Celia, or Elizabeth, or Ellen? Or someone else?

Chapter Twenty-Nine

After I had opened the shop next morning the phone went and the secretarial voice said she had Mr Tony Fitzsimmonds for me.

'Bill? How are you?'

'Fine, Tony. You?'

'I'm fine. Great news: Patrick Gardene has OK'd the furniture as utterly Chippendale. With enthusiasm.'

'He has? Without reservation?'

'Absolutely. He is really very excited about it. Wants to publish a learned article on it. I've told him fine, just as soon as we've tied Kippax up and the pieces are the Fund's property. It will be good PR of course.'

'You've spoken to Kippax?'

'I've made him an offer. A million. He says will we confirm in writing and he'll take it seriously. He'll try for a bit more, I'm sure.'

'I bet he will. Amazing. So Patrick Gardene is all fired up about it?'

'He certainly is. He says the commode, the chairs, the clothes press and the china cabinet are astonishing. The big bookcase is a bit more straightforward – not exactly run-of-the-mill, it's high quality – but you know, one of those big, sober Georgian pieces. Not up to the others. Worth money all the same.'

My thoughts were racing but I kept up the platitudes to conceal them. 'Well, this is a turn-up for the book.'

'Fantastic. A major find.'

'The sort of thing Gardene's been looking for for ages.' I couldn't resist that.

'Has he now?'

'He certainly has. It's a great breakthrough for him.'

'Do you think he's overreacting?'

'Oh no.' I hastened to make amends. 'I'm sure he must have been very thorough. I expect he'll write up chapter and verse to prove his point.'

'I'm sure he will. Do you not think he's the leading authority these days?'

'I'm sure he must be in the top echelon. You might argue that there are other curators – at Harewood House, Newby, Nostell, Temple Newsam, the V&A no less – as well as a few well-known top dealers, who might rival him. But from the point of view of your investors you've got one of the top dogs.'

'I'm glad you say that.' His voice had gone very soft. 'On the basis of Patrick Gardene's seal of approval I've committed us now. It's virtually a done deal. I wouldn't like to find any subsequent skeletons in the woodwork.'

'I'm sure you wouldn't.'

'Let us not look for any, then.' It was a flat statement; an instruction, no less.

'Best not, of course, Tony.'

'Good. I'll be in touch again soon, Bill. Let me have an invoice for your fees, won't you?'

'I'll do that, Tony.'

'We'll meet up soon, Bill.'

'Fine.'

He rang off. I sat staring at the instrument on my desk. *Let us not look for any, then.* The soft voice had not concealed the threat about skeletons in the woodwork.

What was my role, then? Why hire me?

Something to do with Justin Harrington, of course.

For some reason I started thinking about Cescinsky and his story about the Royston Room. Then Perceval Griffiths and his lion mask furniture. Once it appears in books as examples of the real thing it becomes the real thing. Just like *The Man Who Shot Liberty Vallance.* He didn't, but forget the truth and tell the legend. Patrick Gardene's imprimatur was similar; it was as though it had been arranged, trade card, label, expert opinion and all.

I'd been warned off. What would he do if I found a skeleton? Thoughts of Henry Roland and Fat Arthur were not very far away, along with green motorbikes. I'd started Steve looking; he was probably safe right now, but it might be best to stand him down. He'd be disappointed but at least he wouldn't be in danger.

In any case, what did I stand to gain? It would be my word against Professor Patrick Gardene's. I had Arts and Crafts to look for.

I decided to call the whole thing off.

Then the shop doorbell rang.

'They do say,' Spikey Yelland squinted at me over his mug of coffee, 'that just before he got shot you duffed Fat Arthur up good and proper. Right there, in the street. Clobbered him to the ground smack on the very spot where he was croaked.'

'You have introduced a slight foreshortening of the time scale. Some three days between the events have suddenly disappeared. And who are "they"? The Dorking crowd again? Or his man Stan?'

'Oh, you know,' he gestured vaguely. 'The trade generally.'

'All of it?'

'Local, sort of.'

'What's the betting? Odds on for me in leg irons by the weekend? Eugene Aram move over, my gyves are bigger than yours?'

'Well, you know how the fuzz work, Bill. Interconnections and all that malarkey. With three in a row you must be in the frame.'

'How heartening of you to simplify the situation so graphically. The police have already been here, yesterday morning while you were presumably scoffing sausage rolls at Stanley's, and left to pursue more likely lines of inquiry.'

'Really?' He looked quite disappointed. 'What lines would those be?'

'You'll have to ask them.'

His face fell. Spikey was hoping for insider knowledge but I wasn't forthcoming. My information to Walters was speculative; there was no point in spreading gossip that might turn out to be wrong.

'How about this then?' he asked.

Out of his pocket he produced a solid silver vase about six inches high, slightly trumpet-shaped, with a flat base, the body decorated with raised whiplash foliage.

'Liberty's,' I said. 'Designed by Alexander Knox. Arts and Crafts bordering on Art Nouveau.' I handled it round a bit, looking at its stamped marks. 'Nice. What's the date?'

'Nineteen hundred and six,' he responded promptly.

'Very good. How much?'

'Ah,' a sly look came into his face, 'I'm not much up on this Arts and Crafts stuff. What do you reckon?'

I frowned at him. He knew he was breaking protocol. He looked back innocently.

'I am in your hands,' he said.

'An auctioneer like Woolley & Wallis would estimate it at six to nine hundred,' I said.

A look of pleasure came into his face. 'I reckoned around that,' he said. 'How much will you give me?'

'Six hundred.'

'That's a bit on the low side.'

'Seven, then. I'd rather have one of his clocks, but I'll give you seven.'

He smiled. 'Done, Bill. Done. You are a scholar and a gentleman.' He let the smile stay in place and stood up. 'Now let me get something a bit special for you.'

He went outside to his shabby van and came back holding a big flat brown-paper parcel. With an air of triumph he planked it down on the table in front of me and opened the wrapping. I stared in disbelief at the leather-bound quarto-size book that came to light.

'Your part of the world, that, isn't it?' he asked.

I was looking at a fine copy of Ackermann's book of colour aquatints of the Argentine and Uruguay by Emeric Essex Vidal of 1820. Unique. Amazing. The only notable colour-plate book of its kind in English dealing with Argentina and Uruguay. Right in front of me.

The only other time I'd seen one was in New York, years ago, in Kraus's rare bookshop on East 46th Street.

'*Picturesque Illustrations of Buenos Ayres and Montevideo,*' I said out loud. 'L Harrison for R Ackermann. London, 1820. Christ. Where in hell did you get this?'

'Old lady customer of mine. Widow. Husband collected prints. Bit short of cash.'

'Originally issued serially but this is a complete edition.' I racked my memory. The Kraus lady assistant had let me look wonderingly through theirs. It was a kind act, for in no way could I afford six thousand eight hundred dollars whilst travelling on business. The red morocco volume had had the bookplate of a Yorkshire family called Todd in it. My part of the world, Spikey said: there was a view of Monte Video, as it was called then, the gentle *Cerro* hill that gave the place its name, along with Buenos Aires – its 'market place' – ostriches, gauchos, Pampas Indians and other plates.

I thought of Del Castillo, Obis Otero, Irureta Goyena and the sardonic Tomás Puig smiling in the photograph in the trunk. The Ombú tree, if it existed then, must have been in the middle of fields when this was published. Pocitos was still rough coastline. I couldn't believe it. This was unbelievably rare. Vidal was a navy purser who published drawings of St Helena as well as these unique illustrations.

With a cautious hand I opened the book. There was an armorial bookplate stuck inside the front cover, with a light pencil inscription.

Thwaite – the writing was faint but clear. *Ousedon Overwood, Yorkshire.*

This, it meant, was the armorial bookplate of the Thwaites of Ousedon Overwood. I sat almost paralysed. Which one? George most likely, the one who did well in the coal trade. He owned the Hall in 1824 and was a tradesman seeking gentility, building up a library. The date would fit.

'Are you all right?' Spikey sounded quite concerned. 'You've gone pale.'

'Where did you say you got this?'

He bridled slightly and his smile vanished. 'It's dead kosher, you know. I wouldn't bring you anything hot. My widow's a genuine client. Her old man collected some nice things. I sold a lot of hunting prints before we got to the topographicals and travel.'

'What did the Dorking print boys think?'

There was a silence.

'Come on, Spikey, you're bound to have shown this to them.'

He coughed. 'Out of their league. One offered me five. Didn't seem much to me. Then I remembered you saying you'd had family in that part of the world, once. And –' he gestured at the *Patoruzú* cartoon figures on the kitchen wall – 'I remembered them. I know you don't do prints but I just thought, it's worth a try.'

I was still feeling numb.

'This would be for me, not for trade,' I said.

'That's nice. I could tell the old lady it's found a good home.'

I paged through the beautiful, old, formal sheets. Watermarks were right: '1818 J Whatman Turkey Mills' for the plates, twenty-four of them, all in place. No one had pillaged this book. I thought carefully. Six thousand eight hundred dollars, that's about three thousand six hundred pounds, top retail whack in New York. Halve it at auction. Take off thirty per cent auction margin. That leaves twelve hundred. Only fifty quid a print; too low.

But Thwaite? Ousedon Overwood?

'How much?' Spikey couldn't keep quiet any longer.

'Fifteen hundred.'

'Fifteen hundred?'

'Fifteen hundred. A hundred and fifty for you, cash, and a cheque for one thousand three hundred and fifty for the old lady. Top whack, final offer.'

He smiled again. 'I said you're a scholar and a gentleman. You are. You really are. That's a done deal, Bill. Bloody hell: I shall have to look after you, not be your *Fúlmine*.' The smile faded slightly. 'Otherwise, if the police don't get you, the motorbike will.'

Spikey had changed everything.

I phoned the British Library magazine section at Colindale and they said no, they didn't have any copies of the *Swale and Ouse Illustrated Recorder*. They were helpful and took me quite seriously, much more seriously than an old mate in the book and magazine trade I phoned who said no, he didn't have any of those. He also said that strangely enough he was a bit short of pre-1914 stock on the *Chipping Sodbury Gazette* and the *Little Pocklington Courier* too, being a funny swine.

My best hopes lay with Steve and the Internet.

I went into my living room, where I had put the Ackermann book carefully on the table, and paged through it again carefully before looking at the armorial bookplate and the pencilled inscription. *Thwaite. Ousedon Overwood.* Those country house libraries all got broken up when the families fell on hard times and the properties were sold. But what synchronicity was this? What serendipity?

Not look further? When Uruguay and Ousedon were linked in some sort of message to me? No way, Tony Fitzsimmonds, no way!

Then my telephone rang again.

'Mr Franklin?' The voice on the phone was tight, clipped.

'Yes, Detective Sergeant Walters?'

'We've just had confirmation from our opposite numbers in Paris. A dealer from Saint-Germaine-en-Laye called Thierry Dubois was found dead in his car yesterday. He'd been shot. Once, in the head.'

'Oh dear.'

'You are a bit of a cold fish, Mr Franklin. It's not just oh dear. It's oh bloody murder.'

'I didn't know Thierry Dubois.'

'How did you know about him? About his dealings with Henry Roland? Remind me, please.'

'Tersh told me.'

'Who the hell is Tersh?'

'Henry's younger brother. Tertius. The third in Latin. His proper Christian name is Olly for Oliver. Oliver Roland.'

'Is he in the business?'

'No. He is visually impaired. Tell me: did you have any joy with Fat Arthur's books and records?'

A brief silence. Then: 'A chunk of Arthur Brigley's paperwork seems to be missing. Someone rifled his office.'

'Oh dear. The same someone is doing everything they can to eliminate records and people who know all about the origins of that French furniture shipment.'

'Who else might they go for? Who else might be able to make the connection?'

'Well, Tersh could connect Henry Roland and Fat Arthur with Dubois, I suppose. And he now has all the Roland accounts left to him.'

'And where is this Tersh or rather Oliver Roland of that ilk?'

'At his mushroom farm near Frimley.'

'Give me the details. We'll pay him a visit.'

I gave him the details but I was already getting out my car keys. Tersh would be in the earthy-smelling sheds, oblivious to calls. They were nearer but on current form I'd probably be there well before Walters and Green.

There were still no sheep in the straggly fields of tufted, lumpy grass. The same bits of spiky machinery rotted quietly to themselves in a field corner. The old blue Mercedes estate car was parked outside the mobile office cabin but there was no white van this time. It must have been out on delivery.

As I drove into the yard the forklift driven by the mad lad came bellowing out of the far shed, buffeting the plastic doors open wide and swerving sharply as it did an arc to enter the middle shed. As it banged those middle plastic doors inwards, with me stopped to watch it, a brown-coated figure came out of the side door of the middle shed, talking into a mobile held to its ear.

I could have called him after all, I thought, as I watched him gesture angrily at the passing forklift with the big pallet-tray of compost on its mid-placed forks, if only I'd noted his mobile number. I'm too old-fashioned about phones and visits.

It definitely was old Tersh, peering quizzically in my direction, head back, with his fuzzy vision, frowning as a deeper engine note throbbed above that of my car. He took the mobile away from his ear and peered away to the side of my vehicle. That was when I looked into my rear-view mirror and saw the big green motorbike cruising in behind me.

There were two men on it, wearing those spherical helmets like space helmets with tinted visors that completely conceal the head of the person inside.

I gave a great shout of warning which was useless inside closed car windows and, too late, tried to swerve across the motorbike's path as it passed by me. The driver turned his handlebars briskly in avoidance and I missed the back of the bike by about six inches. It motored smoothly across the yard in front of a mystified Tertius and did a tight circle to come round towards him to get closer as the pillion passenger raised his right arm.

I jumped out of the car, shouting, seeing at the same time that the bike was turned to pass close by Tersh and that it was lining up straight towards me once it had dealt with him.

The middle shed doors banged open and the forklift came bellowing out, another heavy pallet-tray set lower on its forks. The bike was poised right in its path. There was no time for the mad lad, peering through the uprights at this unimaginable presence, to stop. Even though he jammed on his brakes, the pallet-tray and forks caught the bike and passengers square at about seat level. The bike went over and the forklift reared up to mount it, the pallet-tray falling off forwards and the terrible vehicle weight crushing, mangling, stalling and settling on the machinery, limbs and bodies beneath it.

I started to run across the yard. Even though they had helmets on, you could hear the screaming. From inside the helmets came screaming and screaming and screaming as the panicking mad lad reversed to try and back off. It was a terrible mistake. Things were too entangled for the forklift to come away cleanly, let alone the big flat box full of compost.

The screaming didn't die down much as the nondescript car containing DS Walters and DC Green drove slowly into the yard.

Chapter Thirty

There comes a point, in the investigation and progression of murderous criminal activity, when events dictate that a sergeant is not senior enough. It seems that we had reached that point.

A detective inspector arrived to take over.

It took an enormous amount of time to sort out. An ambulance came first, but the ten minutes it took seemed quite dilatory after a group of us had got the two mangled men in leathers out from under the wreckage. Any movement provoked cries of agony and rage. With their helmets off they looked ordinary, slightly grizzled bikers in their thirties, like skilled tradesmen you'd see anywhere except that now they were broken craftsmen, legs twisted inside shapeless leathers, faces contorted as they lay on the gravel.

Tertius was in a state of shock and so was the mad lad. They went inside the office cabin to be given tea. DS Walters grimly picked up the automatic pistol he found lying near the broken motorbike and put it in a plastic bag he got from his car. Police vehicles and forensic vans, far too many of them it seemed to me, kept coming in and filling the yard. A great deal of time went by after the ambulance departed, closely followed by a striped police car.

Then there were statements to be taken. The detective inspector was called Baxter and was larger in size than Walters or Green who, as a mere constable, was required to fade into the background. DI Baxter had a cropped bulbous skull with a high forehead creased into what looked like a permanent frown.

'Why did you go to Frimley?' he demanded irritably, across a police interview room table at his local headquarters. Walters sat beside him.

'What kept you?' My words were aimed at Walters. 'You only had a quick trip down the M3 to get there. It was much further for me.'

'Answer the question.'

'I wanted to warn Tersh that he might be in danger.'

Baxter leant forward. 'Either you are an interfering amateur or you set up his intended murder and rushed to see it done.'

'Oh dear. I was the next victim, but you lot simply will not accept any help, will you? Do you think it likely that a professional would give you the details I provided and then suddenly arrange to be on site for this debacle?'

'No, I don't, as a matter of fact. Which puts you in as an interfering amateur.'

'Have no fear. I shall interfere no more. From now on you are clear to solve this whole thing by yourselves.'

'I must warn you that it is an offence to withhold vital or even remotely relevant information from a police inquiry.'

'Oh, have it both ways. Damned if I do and damned if I don't.'

This irritable interchange ceased as a uniformed constable came to beckon Baxter away to some other debate. Walters looked at me gloomily.

'I don't suppose either of those two will tell us anything,' he said. 'They'll say they met a man in a pub somewhere and he paid them. That sort are too frightened to talk. They'll be in hospital for weeks.'

'At least you can check if the same gun killed Henry and Fat Arthur. And maybe Thierry Dubois.'

'Of course forensics will do that. But even if it is and we charge them, the trail probably ends with them.'

I shook my head. 'You're undermining my faith in the force. Surely you can get further back up the chain? There must be pressures you can exert on them?'

He pulled a face and got up. 'We'll see. Wait here until your statement is typed out.'

'Just a minute: we've had four similar motorbike attacks but you still haven't said how Justin Harrington died.'

'I know.'

'I think there was a woman with him at the time.'

'Why do you think that?'

'From my knowledge of him.'

Walters sighed. 'It certainly seems that his heart stopped due to ingestion of an overdose of a stimulant drug. On top of a hot curry.'

'A sexually stimulating drug?'

'Yes.'

'Where did he eat the curry?'

Walters shrugged. 'In York, I suppose. What does it matter? If he ate it with some bird, he had her somewhere other than in his car. The York boys aren't pursuing it because there's no reason to.'

'My God, you're reluctant, nowadays. You were all over me until recently.'

'In deference to the feelings of his family this information has been strictly embargoed. We can be tactful, you know.'

'Foul play is no longer suspected?'

'No. The York boys are on to other things and we're not exactly underemployed.'

'What are you – or they – going to tell the media?'

'That he died of a heart attack.'

'What does his doctor say?'

'He had a heart condition. He should not have taken the stimulant but there is no evidence that he was forced. The curry didn't help.'

I thought for a moment. 'The woman must have had her own car. Otherwise she'd have had to walk a long way to the nearest transport. He was found alone in his own vehicle.'

'Cars were heard in the lane that night.'

Including one like an old Riley, I thought. But said nothing.

'Now that I've let you in on this knowledge, is there anything else you want to tell us?' Walters asked.

'If his death is not being treated as suspicious, it doesn't matter who benefits from his death?'

He gave me a curious look. 'No, it doesn't. Anything else?'

'I don't think so. Has your man in York followed up what I told him?'

'Our inquiries in Yorkshire are proceeding,' replied Walters formally as Baxter came back in to the room. 'If we need you any further, Mr Franklin, we'll let you know.'

The shop had a gap in it where the Ashbee cabinet had gone. So did my sitting room where the Eastlake-Blomfield chiffonier had stood. I was cash rich just for the moment but I felt a bit stripped, deprived.

Ellen didn't answer her phone.

I took a slow look round the place, assessing. There were still some good-quality things in it but nothing important any more. The two pieces bought by Chuck Vance would be difficult to replace. It was time to get out and about again, back on the trail. There were auctions coming up. I had money, I had a new buyer for the best in Arts and Crafts. The police didn't want me interfering in what was clearly some kind of vengeance vendetta over bogus French furniture sent to New York. I should get my own business going again.

Somehow, I didn't feel like it. My taste for trade had gone flat. Like Larkin's rapist, with the sale of my two best pieces I had stumbled up the breathless stair into fulfilment's desolate attic. In the back of my mind, all the time, were distracting thoughts about Justin, and Ellen, and Elizabeth, and Celia. And the fantastic coincidence of the Vidal book printed by Ackermann: picturesque views of Montevideo and Buenos Aires with the Thwaite bookplate from the library at Ousedon Overwood in it? What message was this?

The telephone rang.

'Bill?' Steve Stanton's voice was excited, enthusiastic. Youth was coming to my rescue.

'What, Steve?'

'I didn't get the Gamecock. It went for too much. But I got a much better bargain.'

'Good! What?'

'A Lynx. A really nice one.'

'Good boy! What kind of Lynx? A 12/4 Sprite?'

'No such luck. This is an earlier Nine. 1933. But it's a really pretty car and it doesn't need much doing to it.'

'Excellent. Bravo. Well done. When can I see it?'

'Up here any time.' His voice went cautious. 'Can we go halves on it?'

'Of course. I said I'd help with finance.'

'There's something else. About Ousedon Overwood.'

'What?'

'I've found a guy. On the Internet, but he's in Harrogate. He says he's got a run of the *Swale and Ouse Illustrated Recorder*, pre-1914.'

'Fantastic! How much does he want for them?'

'There's no sale, Bill. He just responded to my Web posting.'

'What does he want?'

'I phoned him. He's an absolute anorak, a real magpie, but he says I can look through them if I want. He won't release them. They're in a pile in his storeroom. He says I can go over there tomorrow and see if the June and July 1910 issues are among them. He isn't sure if it's a complete long run and he won't get them out unless I go there. I'll go if you think it's worth it.'

I thought quickly.

'I'll get an early train. Meet me in Leeds at the main station tomorrow,' I said. 'I'm coming with you.'

Chapter Thirty-One

The great thing about going to Leeds by train was that I could read the newspaper at leisure. I took my time, leafing through the parish-pump trivia and Middle Eastern horrors before absorbing the editorial comment and opinionated articles.

It was a horse that stopped me.

I had almost reached the end, slightly lulled by the fast rhythm of the train, when the sports pages yielded a picture of a horse and, inset beside it, another of Tony Fitzsimmonds in one of those trilby hats that seem to be compulsory at race meetings. The headline arrested my attention.

Row Still Festers Over Fauville Goderoy

Fauville Goderoy? It took a second or two to realise that this was the name of the horse.

The dispute between the New York financier Rory O'Hanlon and London's Tony Fitzsimmonds reached a new pitch yesterday when solicitors acting on behalf of O'Hanlon served an injunction on Fauville Goderoy's Wicklow stables preventing any use of the horse at stud. O'Hanlon and Fitzsimmonds have been in dispute over the syndicate-owned

*stallion, in which they both have major stakes, since rumoured
financial conflicts in alternative investment markets triggered
a spat between the two powerful owners. A spokesman for
O'Hanlon yesterday said that until full details of various
rights were clarified, an embargo has been placed on the horse,
currently located in County Wicklow. Tony Fitzsimmonds was
not available for comment yesterday but on previous form he
will contest the injunction vigorously. Fauville Goderoy is a
recent acquisition by the two men, who have joint equestrian
interests in Kentucky and Ireland...*

I put the paper down. Suddenly I felt like a minor cog in
a very big wheel. Or, more likely, a small disposable pawn
in a big, dirty chess game in which minor pieces were being
knocked off the board. Just as Henry Roland and Thierry
Dubois and Fat Arthur were disposable. And Justin Harrington,
maybe, in his way too, had been disposable. Something had
clearly enraged O'Hanlon, who seemed to be eliminating
Fitzsimmonds' pieces from the game...*rumoured financial
conflicts in alternative investment markets*? I had had nothing
to do with the Fauville cabinet, nor the mystery shipment of
French chairs, but if the acquisition of the Chippendale pieces
got enmeshed in this turf war, I was as vulnerable as Spikey
Yelland had jokingly stated.

My mind began to work overtime. Was O'Hanlon caught
up in Leggatt's furniture investment in some way? Why had
Fitzsimmonds involved me at all? He had Professor Patrick
Gardene up his sleeve all along. Justin had done the research
and set up the deal. Between the two the Fund was primed
for action. Justin's death must be the answer: his death upset
the smooth passage of the scam. After it, Fitzsimmonds needed
someone who knew Justin, knew furniture and was sceptical,

to test the soundness of the proposition. And I had fallen neatly into place. I had recorded no obvious flaws, made no call to dispute the whole thing, finally yielded meek agreement not to look in cupboards for skeletons. If I could be persuaded, and with Gardene's imprimatur, the investment fund was primed to go Chippendale with full fanfare. Only Justin knew about those magazine articles. And maybe Kippax.

Almost certainly Kippax. But with a million at stake, he could be relied upon to keep his mouth shut.

I had almost forgotten what it was like to ride in an old Riley. The smell of leather and hot oil – only a tobacco aroma was missing – the feel of the chassis flexing as Steve whirled round the corners, the rattle, bump and thud, the separate headlights up front, my legs channelled into the space alongside the warm transmission, the whining change of the preselector. He drove it well, mostly at a steady forty-five but with faster bursts, providing plenty of sensation of speed and noise. He was full of enthusiasm about the Lynx he'd bought and described it avidly, saying we'd go to see it once we'd been to Harrogate.

Not long after we'd left Leeds on the A61, Harewood came up and I thought of that splendid later Chippendale furniture in Harewood House, the inlaid commode with Diana and Minerva, the patronage of Lascelles, the pages and pages of detailed accounts in Christopher Gilbert's book. No worries about provenance there. What was I doing? What was I hoping to achieve? Simple truth and self-flattering knowledge, what? Had Justin transferred his obsession to me? Maybe he had.

We reached the outskirts of Harrogate, not its elegant centre. An unassuming road of neat bungalows and chalet-bungalows came up in front of the Kestrel's gleaming bonnet. Steve slowed down, peered steadily for house numbers, pulled into the pavement.

'Here we are. His name is Shipley, by the way. Ralph Shipley.'

The chalet-bungalow was unremarkable and the front garden had been halved by asphalt, on which a saloon car was parked. A thin old guy in a snuff-coloured woollen cardigan and brown corduroys opened the front door. He peered at us over half-moon reading glasses.

'Mr Shipley?' Steve was brisk. 'I'm Steve Stanton. We spoke on the phone. About the Swale and Ouse magazines?'

'Oh, yes.' There was a smile, but he peered at me in query.

'My uncle,' said Steve firmly. 'Bill Franklin. He's keen on local history, too.'

The smile stayed in place. 'You'd better come in,' he said.

The entrance passage opened into a small hall lined with shelves full of books. I caught a glimpse, through an open doorway, of a room stacked with teetering piles of magazines. A staircase led upwards, presumably to his bedroom. There was a smell of toast.

'Come through the kitchen,' he said. 'It'll save going back outside.'

We went through a neat kitchen with linoleum flooring, an elderly gas stove and dated cabinets. A back door opened outside into a small yard. Across the yard was a wide wooden building with an entrance veranda like a cricket pavilion but the pitched roof stretched back into the garden like a long chicken shed. I gaped a bit and the old guy smiled again.

'My hobby room,' he said, as he unlocked its door. 'I'm afraid it's getting a bit full.'

This was an understatement. Inside, the length of the space was choked with piles of paper. Most of the piles were magazines. I caught sight of *The Graphic* heaped beside copies of *The Studio*. They were all old.

'My interests,' he said modestly, 'include the arts as well as local history.'

'Very good. Mostly Yorkshire?'

'Mostly. Despite the way it looks, I have a system of storage that enables me to know where most things are located. My computer indoors has a record I try to keep near enough updated but not for everything. Ah, your *Swale and Ouse Illustrated Recorder*s should be here.'

We were well down the long shed and he switched on a light. There was room in the central passage for a man to walk the length of the building without hindrance and racks allowed access to the sides here and there. It smelt damp and there was a lot of dust. The air seemed muffled by paper.

'A remarkable collection,' I said, putting as much admiration into my voice as possible.

'Quite unique,' he agreed. 'But although I have offered it to various libraries and bodies in this country, they don't seem to be very enthusiastic. It is likely that when I pass on, it will all go to America.'

'What a shame,' I said politely. 'Surely there's a library or museum here that would value this collection?'

'Lack of space and lack of funds. I do not want the collection to be broken up. I want no money for it, but it needs proper cataloguing, and that takes time.' He gestured at a set of collapsing shelves loaded with magazines, which went up as high as the cross beams of the roof's A frame. 'These have not been disturbed since I acquired them. You are welcome to look through them. All I ask is that you replace them much in the way that you found them.'

'We certainly will.'

He nodded in a strange bobbing way and then said, 'If you find the details you seek, I have a photocopier indoors which can be used to copy what you need. I'll leave you to get on but do give me a shout if you need any help.'

'That's very kind.'

'My pleasure. These magazines are very rare, by the way. To my knowledge only the York Library has any similar run of them.'

He trundled off back through the door as though leaving us there with his treasures was the most natural thing in the world. Steve gave me a wink.

'The Americans will really snap this lot up,' he whispered. 'I don't think.'

'You'd be amazed. They just might. Here, you take the left-hand stack and I'll take the right. June and July 1910, eh? Let's go.'

The amazing thing is that it took us only fifteen minutes. The magazines were an odd old size, yellowing, with advertisements on the front. Pictures of local worthies dotted fine print articles along with views of bits of river. There were articles on monuments, buildings and houses. Pictures of men at cricket grounds added to the summer months' activities. The copies were stacked more or less by year and Steve found those for 1910 in his pile. With excitement he took the dozen copies for that year and put them on top of a smaller pile so as to extract the June and July issues with ease.

'Here we go in June: *Ousedon Overwood Hall* by local historian Giles Oust. Look, there's a photo of the outside of the hall and pictures of the gardens. Impressive. A lot of guff about Burton and Nesfield. History of the Thwaites.'

I wrenched my eyes off pictures of the bulky porticoed hall and hedged gardens.

'The interiors must be in the next issue, July.'

He put down June and picked up another copy, thumbing through it quickly. I stopped him as the picture of the room with the full china cabinet I'd seen in Fitzsimmonds' office appeared.

'There it is! The same one!'

'Got it, eh, Bill?'

He opened the pages to show three more interiors. In them, the pieces Kippax had shown me appeared in their domestic settings. Commode, chairs, clothes press, china cabinet were all accounted for. Then, over the page, was a picture of the big bookcase with its broken pediment. With disbelief I read the caption beneath it:

The Original 18th Century 'Chipindale' Bookcase which served as inspiration to Mr Albert Thwaite.

'Bill?' Steve's voice was wondering. 'Are you reading what I'm reading?'

'The text, Steve! We need to read the text.'

In 1898 Mr Albert Thwaite, in addition to his other schemes of interior décor, commissioned four pieces of furniture from the highly praised Larwood and Brown of Curtain Road, London. These were exactly to designs illustrated in Chippendale's 1754 Director *and of more elaborate conception than the great bookcase bought from "Mr Chipindale" in 1757 by Mr Thwaite's ancestor, William Smithers. Mr Albert Thwaite, the present owner's uncle, was noted for his excellent taste and many decorative schemes of interior and exterior improvement.*

He felt that the great bookcase, one of the few pieces remaining from the original eighteenth-century hall after its rebuilding by Burton in 1840, should be joined by mahogany furniture in the best Chippendale style. The designs for the chairs, commode, clothes press for Mr Albert's bedroom and the elaborate china cabinet may all be found in the first edition of the Director. *Other interior improvements included the splendid brocade curtains established in the…*

We stood in the extraordinary shed for a few breathless seconds more before I broke out into laughter. Professor Patrick Gardene had it exactly the wrong way round. The big bookcase was kosher, the other pieces were repros. Fine repros, but repros.

So much for Gardene and his learned article.

'Bill? Are you OK? Why are you laughing?'

I explained to him and he grinned.

'I knew that bastard was up to no good that night. Knew it. No wonder he stole the mags from York Library. But surely the firm of Larwood and Brown can be checked?'

I shook my head. 'Curtain Road still has veneer suppliers but the district got plastered in the war. Lots of it was razed to the ground. All that area has changed. Larwood and Brown will be long gone. Many Shoreditch furniture firms have simply disappeared. Justin will have checked on that.'

'Surely he didn't think he could get away with it though? Look how we've managed to find out.'

'You heard Shipley say that these magazines are rare. Legend has it that Ousedon Overwood had Chippendale furniture in it. It did. A bookcase. Only obsessive anoraks do the kind of research into obscure little magazines of the kind that we're doing. The Fund investors have a learned professor to reassure them. He could dispute the local amateur, Mr Giles, Oust's history. That trade label on the bookcase might just be original. The Kedleston bookcase by the Linnells went for a million and a half at Christie's last summer. The Ousedon one isn't as fine but it's original. Who wants to rock the boat?'

'You?'

I smiled. 'Not just yet. I bet Kippax thinks the whole collection is repro, though. Justin won't have told him about the bookcase. Kippax'll be delighted to accept Fitzsimmonds' offer.'

'Do you think Fitzsimmonds knows?'

'That's a good question. It may explain my presence in a way I haven't understood up to now. If Fitzsimmonds had suspicions about Justin, death intervened before he could voice them.'

'Good riddance.'

I frowned at him. 'I didn't hear that. Come on. Let's get this photocopied and get on our way.'

Maybe it was the rattle of the Riley's timing gears as we burbled along the main road. Maybe it was the tumult in my brain. Maybe it was the Harewood House sign we passed on the way back to Leeds. Maybe it was my worry about Ellen.

'Pull over,' I ordered Steve abruptly.

'What?'

'Pull over. There's a lay-by coming up. That'll do. I need to talk to you.'

He pulled over obediently and we stopped. He switched off. 'What's up?'

I sat back in my bucket seat, then looked at his competent hands on the steering wheel, with its advance and retard lever and hooter button. Behind the rim was the gear selector lever in its quadrant. In front the wooden dashboard and instruments. Outside there were green fields and trees.

'You were there, weren't you? When Harrington died? This was one of the cars the locals heard.'

He started in his seat. 'What? No, I – that is—'

'You said back there in that paper igloo that you knew he was up to no good *that night*. That night? Could only be one night, couldn't it? You were there in Ousedon, weren't you? Following him?'

His hands gripped the wheel tightly. 'Bill, I don't know what you—'

'Come on, Steve, we're friends. I don't know why you haven't told me before but now is the time to cough it up. Now. You can trust me.'

His hands relaxed. I was dreading what he might be going to say but I waited.

'Wetherby,' he said at last. 'It was in Wetherby. Off the Great North Road. The A1.'

'Wait a minute. Was your mother there?'

'Good God, no. I dropped her off at Leeds station that afternoon. She went back to London, then home. We were still arguing over my career.'

Relief flooded through me. 'So what took you to Wetherby?'

'A bunch of the lads from college. They set up a rock group in a pub there. I went to join them. I was on orange juice because I was driving but none of them wanted a lift from me. I had enough of the rock – it was terrible – and I was going back to where I'd left the car when I saw this couple come out of an Indian restaurant. I knew it was Justin Harrington as soon as I saw him. He was laughing and strutting, taking the woman's arm and pulling her to him. They went to the car park ahead of me.'

'Did you recognise the woman?'

'No, I didn't. But then I never knew his wife or any of his other girlfriends, except those tarts in the newspapers.'

There was a moment's silence. I quickly filled it.

'Fairish hair?'

'Yes.'

'Clothes? Skirt or trousers?'

'Skirt.'

'Pastel shades?'

'What – oh, I see, her clothes, yes, more or less.'

Celia Beckland, I thought. 'Where did they go?'

'That was the funny thing. They were getting steamy but got into separate cars. His was a BMW, she had a Mazda sporty thing, red.'

'You followed them? In the Riley? Why?'

'I don't know why. Some kind of anger. When they set off it wasn't even my direction: up north. Some sort of curiosity, perhaps. I hated that bugger but I wanted to see what he was at. I suppose it was obvious really, but I had some sort of impulse to catch him out.'

'Bit difficult, wasn't it?'

'Hell of a job. He went lickety-split up the A1 with her trailing. I nearly gave up after five miles. But then they turned off right at the A59 and slowed to go cross country. Off to the left.'

'To Ousedon Overwood.'

'Yes. Down some bloody narrow lanes. They seemed to go on for ever. I thought this is it, they'll see me, time to pack it in. Let him shag her wherever they stop, I'm no peeping Tom. The impulse, whatever it was, had gone. I pulled up on a rise by a farm gate entrance to turn round. That's when I saw the lights of their cars about five hundred yards away, down gently sloping country below me. They'd pulled into the side, like me. The lights went off. That's it I thought, they'll be at it on his back seat in just a tick. I left only the side lights on to turn round and while I was turning, I saw a set of headlights come on again, with a car turning tight in the road. That's odd, I thought, that didn't take long. I was close in to the hedge at the farm gate. If I drove back up the lane anyone coming back would come up right behind me. I switched everything off and tucked myself down behind the wheel. The Mazda came back past the entrance going fast, too fast for the lane, really, back the way we'd come. I sat and waited. Maybe she changed her mind, I thought, he missed his nookie after all. I eased out of the car to look but the BMW's lights never came back on way below me. I got a creepy feeling, like there's something wrong but I don't want to know what it is. They hadn't had time to – you know – not nearly time enough.'

'So you left?'

'I left. Then I read about him, dead in there, a day or two later. No one has said of what.'

'You've kept this well under your hat. Or have you told Ellen?'

'Not likely! I deal with Mother on a need-to-know basis.'

'I can tell you how he died. He took a sexual stimulant and it gave him a heart attack.'

'Christ. He didn't look as though he needed one in Wetherby. All over her, he was.'

'He was excited. He thought he'd set up a wonderful deal. He wanted to celebrate there and then, in the place it all started. The nearest he could get to the site of Ousedon Overwood Hall. He ingested a stimulant. It killed him.'

'God. Do you think she slipped it to him?'

'I don't know. He knew he had a heart condition. But knowing how he liked to live on the edge, he might have taken the risk.'

'Have the police interviewed her?'

'The police are not treating his death as suspicious. There was no forensic evidence of a woman's presence in the car.'

'I'm not surprised. No time. But she was there.' He thought for a moment. 'Am I a witness?'

'Only marginally. What did you see? Nothing criminal.'

'He tried to ruin my father. He was a bastard. I don't want to grass on her.'

'I'm not sure there's anything to grass.'

He looked across at me curiously. 'You know her, don't you?'

'Yes. But don't get the wrong idea. She dislikes me intensely. In her eyes I have always belonged to the opposition.'

'That's a relief. What do we do now?'

'We keep schtum. In the meantime, we go and look at that Lynx of yours.'

'Oh great.' He started up the engine. 'I forgot to tell you, by the way. Mother said to let you know she's back home again.'

Chapter Thirty-Two

When she opened the door, she stared at me with mouth slightly open, as though my appearance was a surprise but not quite such a surprise as, say, Elizabeth had found it at her front door in St George's Hill. Or Celia, enclosed in her Clapham office.

But then, it hadn't been as long as it had with Elizabeth. And it wasn't a surprise. I just couldn't help the brief comparison, apart from the slightly open mouth, which told of something other than surprise.

She was wearing a rather full cream blouse tucked loosely into a pleated cotton skirt. A pair of light canvas shoes. Couldn't have been better.

'We need to have a serious discussion,' she said.

I stepped through the door and closed it firmly. Then I put my arm round her waist.

'Hey! Just because you've spent some time buttering up Steve, you needn't think you can—'

I brought my left hand under her knees, lifted her off her feet and half carried her, half struggling, through the door on the right, one that led into a small sitting room with a TV set and a large sofa in it.

'Stop it! Bill? Put me down! I'll scream!'

I stopped her mouth with mine, holding her firmly with my right arm as I put her feet back on the floor. With my left I pulled the blouse clean out of the skirt at the front. As I hoped, she was wearing no bra under it. She jerked her head back from the kiss.

'What the *hell* are you doing? I'll scream, I mean it!'

I dropped her onto the settee and ignored the resulting shout of protest. The blouse rode up high under her armpits. The volume of the pleated skirt allowed plenty of scope for revelation and access. There followed a token struggle during which modesty conflicted with desire until a disbelieving voice said, as they passed her knees, that I was tearing the last token shreds of respectability off her. Then resistance ceased.

Some time later as we still lay clumsily engaged, as Lawrence Durrell once put it, like the victims of a terrible accident, I said:

'She told you, didn't she?'

Ellen looked up through lowered eyelids and smiled a languorous smile.

'Yes, she did.'

I waited for her to say which one of them it was that told her, since I had said it to both. But she didn't elaborate. She just said, 'You're getting a little heavy, Bill.'

That was easy to deal with. I put my mouth close to her ear and suggested one or two solutions.

'That is *coarse*,' she said. 'Really coarse.'

But she soon obliged.

And, while sounds and events proceeded along their gratifying, passionate and varied path, I couldn't help wondering, between bouts that dizzied rational thought, whether it was Elizabeth or Celia who had told her that I said that she was it, really it.

Or both of them.

Afterwards, long afterwards it seemed, sated, showered, spruced and polished, sitting on the Yorkshire Windsors at the kitchen table, coffee in front of us, it was confession time. I went through it all, the history and the recent visit to Elizabeth.

'She told you,' I said.

'Yes. She told me.'

'Elizabeth?'

'Yes.'

'Did you go to Weybridge or was it just a call?'

'We met. Fortnum's.'

'How traditional. Tea and cakes and intimate girl talk. And Celia?'

'She came too.'

'Extraordinary. What did she say about the Ousedon business?'

'Nothing. I didn't ask her. Celia and I are not that close. It's just a selected information thing.'

'Elizabeth must have told her about Justin's heart condition. He wouldn't have told her himself; he didn't admit to weaknesses.'

'That's true.'

'I think she may have slipped him an extra dose while they were eating at the restaurant in Wetherby.'

'You don't know that.'

'She's a cool customer. She must have been prepared to get into the back of his car and perform until he dropped. But she was lucky; he snuffed it still sitting at the wheel. So she never got in his car. She probably opened his door, saw him, and scarpered. My God, what animosity he generated.'

'Steve's never said a word to me. My own son.'

'He's too emotional about it just now. Give him time. But he mustn't know what we know.'

'You say Celia gets the publishing company?'

'Yes. All of it.'

'My God, she's earned it.'

I chuckled. 'In her own way, yes. She lied to me about Justin's distance from the publishing business, though. He must have been much more involved than she said.'

'He was. And he was demanding. In every way. Interfered in everything, she says. She wanted it all to end, both commercially and personally, but he wouldn't.'

'So she had both motive and means.'

'Now you sound like a policeman.'

'Not me. My lips are sealed. So are Steve's. Actually, if she or his desire pills hadn't got him first, the motorbike certainly would have. So Celia, who just happened to be one step ahead, would have got her wish anyway.'

'What about the furniture? And all these murders?'

'That, or rather those, are a different matter altogether.'

Chapter Thirty-Three

The sports page the next day had a small headline: *Agreement Reached in Fauville Goderoy Dispute*. I sat having coffee with Spikey Yelland in my kitchen and read the article while he got two small silver pincushions out of his pocket and set them up for me to admire.

'Members of the Fauville Goderoy syndicate in Ireland have brought the two major disputees together to come to an agreement. Yesterday Tony Fitzsimmonds and Rory O'Hanlon from New York appear to have put aside their disagreements and provided the syndicate with the go-ahead to put the stallion out to stud. All appears now to be sweetness and light. They left together for London, where they are to explore joint investment projects. Tony Fitzsimmonds' Leggatt's Finance is rumoured to be forming an art investment fund in which O'Hanlon, who has similar interests in the USA, may participate. At Dublin Airport, Fitzsimmonds said...'

I put the paper down and looked at the clock. Ten-fifteen. I picked up my mobile and dialled Leggatt's to get the cool secretary.

'I'm afraid Mr Fitzsimmonds is in a meeting right now, Mr Franklin. He's not available.'

'Jim Macallister, then. This is urgent.'

'Mr Macallister is also in the—'

'When I say urgent, I mean like disaster urgent. Mahogany hall stomping is off. The furniture ain't Chippendale.'

Macallister came on about three minutes later.

'Look here, Franklin, this is most—'

'No, you look here, Macallister. Has a cheque gone to Kippax yet?'

'That's confidential.'

'Has it gone? Because I have incontrovertible evidence that four fifths of that stuff is dud.'

'But Patrick Gardene—'

'Patrick Gardene is either ga-ga, professionally mendacious or bribed. Has the cheque gone? Because if it has, you've just lost about half a million.'

His voice dropped. 'Kippax negotiated to the end but we reached agreement yesterday. It's been drawn up for signature. There is to be an announcement to the press this afternoon.'

'Hold the presses. I'm coming up to your office. Now. It'll take me just over an hour. Tell Tony and O'Hanlon to be there, no messing.'

'What? You here? Impossible. Look here, O'Hanlon is an important—'

'Tell them to be there! If O'Hanlon buys into that furniture you're both dead. So think: I'll save you a fortune and bullets from motorbikes. In your heads.'

'But—'

'Tell them! You make that press announcement and you'll

be sprayed with shit so thick you'll need a chisel to get it off. Before O'Hanlon gets a chain saw to you.'

'What on earth—'

'I'm on my way.'

I put the mobile down. Spikey was staring at me across the table, mouth open. I got up and looked at him, assessing. He was wearing quite a respectable lightweight jacket, good trousers, striped blue shirt, Italian shoes. His hair was short and neat. He was shaved and clean.

He shifted uncomfortably. 'What are you looking at?'

'Are you going somewhere? You're dressed up like a hambone.'

He bridled. 'I like good clothes. Nothing wrong, is there?'

'Indeed not. Spikey – no, tell me: do you have a real name?'

'Funny you should ask that. I have been going to ask you to drop the Spikey bit now. Time to move on.'

'In favour of what?'

He looked a bit sheepish. 'Lionel.'

'*Lionel?* Your Christian name is Lionel?'

'What's wrong with that?'

I grinned. 'Nothing, actually. Lionel Yelland: not a bad name for a silver dealer. It'll take a bit of getting used to, but I'm game. So come on, Lionel. You're coming to the City with me.'

'Eh? The City? What for?'

'I'll explain on the way. Don't worry; I'll see you right.'

'Now?'

'Now.'

'Why me?'

'Because if it hadn't been for you, and your book of Ackermann's Uruguay, I wouldn't be going.'

Chapter Thirty-Four

'Who the hell,' Jim Macallister demanded, at the entrance to Fitzsimmonds' office, 'is this?'

Inside, Fitzsimmonds was sitting at his desk. Near him, facing the same way, was a small neat man in a Boston three-piece suit, nice smooth buttoned waistcoat, floral green tie, cutaway shirt collar. Not like I imagined O'Hanlon at all. More like a neat, quiet businessman than a lethal presence. He looked at us, saying nothing.

'This,' I said, 'is my colleague, Lionel Yelland.'

Spikey smiled cheerfully and held out a hand. Macallister ignored it.

'Colleague? What kind of colleague?'

'He is my security consultant.'

Macallister blinked. Then he said, 'He can't join this meeting. He hasn't signed our confidentiality agreement.'

'Lionel is my *confidential* security consultant. Under agreement to me. He is fully up to speed with your documentation and will observe what is required.'

'Natch,' said Spikey, still smiling and showing small gaps

in his front teeth, like a crocodile yawning. He looked round, taking in the view, the horse painting on the wall, Fitzsimmonds' green braces, O'Hanlon's three-piece, and kept smiling.

'That still doesn't mean he can attend this meeting. There has been no clearance time allowed.'

'Jim,' O'Hanlon's voice was quiet, not very American but still American, 'why don't you just quit the grey suit routine shit and let these gentlemen in? We want to hear what they have to say. We're kind of on a schedule here.'

Grudgingly, Macallister drew up another chair and we sat facing the three of them.

'Well?' Tony Fitzsimmonds didn't sound pleased and doubtless wasn't. 'What is this new *incontrovertible* evidence?'

'I'll come to that in a minute.' I kept my eyes on O'Hanlon. 'I have two stories to tell you. They won't take long. The first concerns a set of French chairs, which Justin Harrington arranged for Henry Roland to sell to a subsidiary of Stargaze Investments. The chairs actually came from a dealer in Saint-Germaine-en-Laye called Dubois, who made them.'

Fitzsimmonds frowned. 'This has nothing to do with the Chippendale furniture from Ousedon Overwood that we are about to buy.'

'No, not yet. But it shows what can happen to you if you get it wrong. The chairs were shipped to Arthur Brigley. He not only aged them suitably but got, from a friend of Justin Harrington's called Harris, a set of forged documents verifying their supply by Chippendale in the eighteenth century to some English country house, possibly even Ousedon Overwood, since it would be almost impossible to check if such chairs ever existed there. The chairs went to America but an unknown person blew the gaffe. He or she phoned the purchaser and told them the whole story. The purchaser was already pissed off about owning a rather overpriced cabinet made by Goderoy – the Fauville – which was expensive to buy but soon exposed as nothing like the quality it had been cracked up to be in a book published by Harrington.'

I kept my eyes on O'Hanlon but he showed no emotion. Fitzsimmonds was staring at me intently.

'Harrington then died of a self-induced heart attack in his car at Ousedon.'

'Self induced?' Fitzsimmonds leant forward.

'He took a sexual stimulant which killed him. He was, in a way, lucky. Because the pissed-off purchaser of the chairs hired a pair of hit men to bump off those concerned. Harrington would have been the first to go. As it was, Roland, Brigley and Dubois all got murdered. Then the purchaser tried to include anyone who might know or be able to prove that the chairs were bogus, like Olly Roland. I was on the list, too. This was like King Canute ordering the sea to withdraw. The purchaser hasn't paid for the chairs so no money has been lost. The killings are for pride. I know, and so does Lionel here, and so do men in Dubois and Brigley's workshops that the chairs are duff. So does Harris, wherever he is, and the informant, and Tersh – Olly Roland. You can't kill us all. The best thing you can do is to flog the chairs in some low-profile auction.'

'I can not think,' O'Hanlon's voice was still quiet, 'why you are directing this crap story at me.'

'Because you are both the pissed-off purchaser of the goods and commissioner of the retribution I have described.'

He stood up. 'That's slander. Actionable' He nodded at Fitzsimmonds' desk and its equipment. 'Got that, witnessed and recorded?'

'Spikey,' I said. 'Now.'

Spikey got up, leant over the desk, flipped a lid open on a box on it, pulled out a small tape and, as Macallister jumped at him, fended him off with one hand while he stripped the tape out of its housing.

'Hey!' shouted Macallister.

Spikey put his face in Macallister's, his nose about three inches from the other's. 'I've destroyed more fucking pirate tapes at concerts than you've had hot dinners. And their fucking owners with them. So sit down.'

Macallister turned furiously to me. 'I'm calling the police!'

'Do that. They'll be very interested in my story. And the next one. My advice is to hear it before you call them, and don't try unauthorised recordings on us again. Lionel really hates them.'

Macallister paused for a moment, got a nod from Fitzsimmonds, and sat down. So did O'Hanlon, slowly. Spikey put the tape in his pocket and sat down, too.

'Let's let that pass,' I said. Now I turned to Fitzsimmonds. 'This is the other story: Justin Harrington had, all his life, two great ambitions. One, to find the Chippendale furniture he believed had existed at Ousedon Overwood. The other was to pull off some huge, Cescinsky-style antique furniture fakery, one of his cobblers' tingles jobs but better. When Kippax contacted him, he must have gone nearly crazy. Here was the chance to fulfil both. His research in the York Library told him the real story: the bookcase is genuine, the rest are late nineteenth-century reproductions. Brilliantly done, copied straight from the first edition of the *Director*, but copies. He did a deal with Kippax to diddle you. He couldn't help gilding the lily, though: he got Harris to make a label and a trade card. Kippax knew the whole story; if the later pieces could be verified as Chippendale, the value would be multiplied by five. The trade label would add even more. Justin fixed it and he stole the truthful story from the library. He had you set up and doubtless did a deal with Kippax. He went out to celebrate, a bit prematurely. Then he died.'

'This is pure speculation. Where is the evidence?'

'You hired me to check, didn't you? Something about Justin made you suspicious. You knew I'd known him for a long time. You asked that when you first rang. Well, I checked.' I turned to Spikey. 'Show them the magazine extract.'

We'd made three photocopies and he handed them over. There was a silence while they read them.

'Patrick Gardene would dispute this,' Fitzsimmonds said.

'Patrick Gardene has been waiting for something like the Ousedon furniture all his life. Either that blinded him or you've paid him to authenticate the stuff regardless.'

'That's a slander, too!'

'Is it? I hired a research student to check on this and it took him just three days to find another set of magazines with the truth in them. Three days, for no expert on Chippendale. Of course, Justin was banking on plenty of time elapsing before anyone got really curious, especially with Gardene's rubber stamp on the furniture. The investment fund is supposed to be long term, anyway. Poor old Sam Wolsey's four-poster bed took a long time to come back but, sooner or later, this lot would have come back to torpedo you, too. Remember that. And that not only do we two here today know but the researcher and my solicitor know.' I was looking at O'Hanlon again. 'I've deposited the whole story in case anything should happen. Like motorbikes coming out of the woodwork. To get me or Kippax or Harris. By the way, I have no idea where Harris is; the school old boys' association doesn't keep addresses of those who were expelled.'

O'Hanlon looked up from his copy sheet. 'You were at school with these crooks?'

'I was.'

'Some school.' He looked at Fitzsimmonds. 'You nearly sold me a real bummer. What do we do now?'

'You could buy the furniture,' I said. 'If you don't, I will.'

'What? You? For how much?'

'With this authenticity, the big bookcase must be a good buy at three hundred thousand. There's a market for the copies at about ten grand each, minimum.'

Macallister spoke for the first time since we'd sat down. 'That's not what the Fund is about.'

'If nothing under a million interests you, my advice is to stay away from English furniture. The number of Kedleston bookcases or Badminton cabinets or Chandos chairs available is pretty limited. Which is why,' I looked at O'Hanlon again, 'French is a more fertile field.'

Fitzsimmonds looked up from his page of the *Swale and Ouse Illustrated Recorder*. His face was congested.

'Scrub the cheque,' he snapped at Macallister. 'Phone Kippax. Tell him we'll give him quarter of a million for the lot. Take it or leave it, the bastard.' Then he looked at me and Spikey. But I was already standing up.

'I don't expect you'll be inviting us to lunch,' I said. 'In any case, we must be going. We'll let ourselves out.'

And we moved to the door. Surprisingly, Fitzsimmonds got up and came with us, waving Macallister back. We walked past his secretary and across a hall to the lift. He thumbed the button to call it.

'It's not over yet,' he said. His voice was low. 'That was a good job you did. I'll be in touch with you later.'

We went down in the lift and out into the fresh air without saying a word. At the kerb a dark green Bentley Mulsanne with a uniformed chauffeur stood waiting. Spikey turned to me on the pavement.

'That Bentley his? Fitzsimmonds'?'

'Yes.'

'Shit.'

'Think of it as a trade vehicle.'

'Like my van, you mean?'

'Exactly. Thanks, Lionel,' I said. 'You were great.'

'Jesus, Bill. Was all that true?'

'All of it.'

'What did he mean, it's not all over yet?'

'I really don't like to think. We mere pawns can only keep a low profile and our powder dry. Now, I have to make a telephone call.'

He stood close to me while I walked to the next corner and dialled, glancing this way and that into the City traffic, as though a motorbike might career up to us.

I got straight through.

'Sergeant Walters? Bill Franklin. Any luck with the motor-bike men yet?'

'No.' Walters was abrupt. I guessed Baxter was listening. 'They say they can't identify their client and they've got a London brief giving us trouble over questioning in view of their injuries.'

'You need to find a man called Harris. Bob Harris. Specialises in printing old documents. He was in contact with Justin Harrington some weeks ago, must recently have been close to Fat Arthur Brigley, certainly Henry Roland. Tersh – that's Olly Roland – should be able to dig his address out for you from Buckton House. Find him and you'll find who took the container of French chairs. That's where the contract killings come from.'

'Why haven't you told us this before?'

'Think,' I said, 'what I've told you before. This is a fluid situation.'

I switched off and put the phone back in my pocket.

'Bloody hell,' said Spikey. 'What happens next?'

'We grab a taxi and go to the West End.'

'What for?'

'For a really good lunch. On me.'

Chapter Thirty-Five

Across the yard from the kitchen the big doors of the coach house were open. In one bay the chrome radiator nose of the Kestrel gleamed in the sun. Next to it the slightly more upright lines of the Lynx tourer, with its hood and tonneau cover removed, stood by sedately in companionable approval. Steve had got a friend of his with a big trailer to bring it down from Leeds. It was white, with black mudguards and running boards.

It looked pretty good to me.

'Wish it was an MPH or an Imp,' said Steve, looking at it wistfully.

In 1934 Riley cars came outright second, third, fifth, sixth, twelfth and thirteenth at Le Mans, only yielding first place to a bigger, supercharged 2.3 litre Alfa Romeo driven by Chinetti and Étancelin, the sole survivor of three Alfas entering the race. The Riley MPHs won the 1500cc class and the Imps the 1100cc class both outright and Dorothy Champney won the Ladies' Prize in an Imp before marrying Victor Riley. They thrashed Aston Martin, MG, Lagonda and Singer as well as the foreign competition except for the surviving Alfa.

'Give it time,' I said. 'And a lot more money.'

'There's quite a lot to do to the Lynx bodywork. I think it might be better with some replacement valves in the engine, too.'

'In machinery the better is always the enemy of the good. Or, to use an old American expression, if it ain't broke, don't fix it.'

He grinned. 'I'll remember that. I want to get on, though. You should go and have your coffee or there'll be trouble. I'll be in for mine in just a minute.'

I went obediently into the kitchen and sat at the big fruitwood farm table with his mother. Cups and plates, cutlery, letters and papers littered its morning surface.

'He's changed completely,' she said. 'He's even working at his college work.'

'It's called motivation. With motivation you can do anything.'

'Is it a good buy? That car, I mean.'

'Yes. It's fine.'

Her face cleared. 'You're not just saying that? To reassure me?'

'No. As someone who owns half of that car, I'm relieved to tell you that we won't lose money on it. He'll learn from it, that's the main thing. He'll learn that his labour time won't earn what a professional mechanic would charge but that's fine, too. Next time the costing will be more accurate.'

'Thank heaven.' She put a mug of coffee in front of me. 'He's really grateful to you. You really are a smooth, sly, underhand, conniving rapist.'

'I didn't rape you. You collaborated enthusiastically.'

'You as good as. And I wasn't, well, sure. I never thought you'd go for me like that. Like a storm.'

'Watch this space.'

'I liked the calm after it.' Her eyes were on mine. 'I'm glad we cleared all that up.'

'Me too. But talking of conniving, what about you ladies? Especially Celia Beckland.'

'I've told you I'm not close to Celia.'

'Quite apart from Justin, she has three deaths and an attempted murder down to her.'

'What? How's that?'

'She must have been the tip-off to Stargaze that those French chairs were dodgy. Justin must have been boasting on their pillow. Quite apart from his deal with Kippax. It's ironic, really.'

'Ironic? Why?'

'It obviously didn't occur to her, when she blew the gaffe, that O'Hanlon would react with savage gangster methods. He really was smarting over the Fauville cabinet. Coming on top of that, the news that he was being suckered over the French chairs sent him into orbit. What Celia didn't know when she went north was that O'Hanlon was going to kill Justin anyway. She didn't need to give him a heart attack down a Yorkshire lane after a hot promising supper. O'Hanlon's motorbike men would have done the job for her.'

'You don't know that she did it.'

'It's a pretty good guess. I think she fed him an extra pill or two. I bet if I showed Steve her photo he'd confirm that she was the woman in Wetherby.'

'Oh God, please don't involve Steve any more than he already is.'

'Don't worry, I won't. He must get on with his final college exams.'

'While you look after his mother?'

'While I see to his mother.'

'Don't be coarse.' She frowned in mock disapproval before going on. 'I'm worried about those bankers, though, Bill. I don't understand what they mean by saying it's not finished yet. But by the way, the police seem to be satisfied about Justin, so that's all over.'

She gestured at her copy of the *Telegraph*, which lay open on the table. A small inside article she'd kept in view said *TV Presenter Died From Natural Causes*. Under it there was a slightly dated photo of Justin and Elizabeth at some function or another, arm in arm. The article was brief; without murder, Justin was no longer news.

'I haven't seen that in my paper. DS Walters said as much when I last saw him, though.'

'So there's no point in going on about it any longer.' Her eyes looked straight into mine.

'No, of course not. I'm not going to.'

Steve came in, wiping his hands on a rag, and looked over his mother's shoulder at the photograph of Justin and Elizabeth. His face lit up.

'That's her. That's the one. In Wetherby.'

It took a few seconds to take in what he'd said.

'What!' I heard the shock in my voice. 'It can't be. You've made a mistake. That's Elizabeth Harrington.'

He pointed at the photo. 'That's absolutely her. Is that Elizabeth Harrington? I've never seen her before. It was her all right.'

'But – it couldn't have been her! She was on the Continent.'

Ellen was still looking at me. 'She was on the Continent when they found the body. Travelling. It was a day or two later, remember? She would have had time to drive down to the Channel and cross.'

'A red Mazda? Does she have a red Mazda?'

'She has some sort of red sports car. Celia has a grey Mercedes.'

I sat numb for a time that seemed infinite, feeling as though I had been kicked in the solar plexus, whilst staring at the photograph. Its image, man and wife staring back, mocked me.

After a while I heard Steve say, 'Are you all right, Bill? You've gone as white as a sheet.'

'No, I'm not all right. She sat there and pretended she knew nothing about Ousedon Overwood or anything. All the time I was telling her. All the time. The story amused her in a detached sort of fashion. And yet she – and she tipped off –' I heard my voice turn desperate. 'She can't have! It couldn't be her. Steve, you described the woman's clothes. Pastel shades. They shout Celia. She could have hired the car.'

'I've often thought,' Ellen said, 'how Celia and Elizabeth dressed in the same tones. Something to do with Justin, I expect.'

She was pale-faced, too.

'So she – she—'

'What passes between husband and wife has to be a mystery to outsiders.' Her tone was low.

'Well, it isn't. It can't be. There are three murders and—'

My mobile phone rang. I sat looking at Ellen and Steve, ignoring it as my mind went round and round until I felt dizzy.

It rang again. With a curse, I pulled it out of my pocket.

'Mr Franklin?' DS Walters was abrupt once again.

'Yes, Sergeant?'

'We've found Harris. At his house near Reading. In Winnersh, actually; a bungalow on the A329 into the city.'

'What does he say?'

'He hasn't been able to say anything for about two weeks. His body has considerably deteriorated. But it is him. Or he, if you're pedantic. My inspector – Detective Inspector Baxter – says he'd appreciate a bit of assistance at the site. As soon as possible.'

'My assistance? What with?'

'Documentary matters.'

'You need an accountant, surely?'

'These are antique documents.'

Ellen was staring at me, still pale, with all the anxious lines in her face well marked. I hadn't touched my coffee yet.

'Give me the address,' I said. 'I'll come over right away.'

Chapter Thirty-Six

The bungalow was even less remarkable than the one in Harrogate. It was in a line of bungalows on the main road, each set back slightly behind a small front garden which, in many cases, had been adapted for extra parking.

There were two police cars outside, scene of crime exclusive tapes, a white van and two officious cops in uniform to get past.

'The remains have been removed,' Walters said to me as I stood outside.

'That's a relief.'

'They were just inside the front door. Very unpleasant. Didn't half pen and ink, Trevor.'

'How did he die?'

'Shot in the head.'

'Nobody local noticed?'

'He kept himself to himself. Went away from time to time. Loner.'

'No paper? No milk?'

Walters gave me a leery look. 'Constables are looking into these matters. Bit short-handed. You want to join them?'

'Sorry.'

'Come through round the side. He worked in a big shed in the back garden.'

'Like much of Blair's Britain.'

The shed at the back wasn't as big as the one at Harrogate but it had a similar feel to it. I was kept outside but allowed to peer in through a pair of open doors. There was a smaller amount of paper about but there was the same musty smell as there had been in Harrogate. I took in the ancient printing equipment, the many letterpress racks, all of it old, the flat tanks where paper must have been treated. Chemicals in bottles ranked along shelves or stood on tables. There were little stacks of paper of different sizes all over the place. DI Baxter stood in the middle of it all, talking to a man in white overalls. He was in overalls himself but broke off and came to the door, nodding to Walters.

'Technically a crime scene,' he said. His big bulbous head shone. 'Inside the bungalow's where it all happened but we have to treat this as one too. Can't let you in. Much appreciate your coming, though. Now: what is the connection to this guy?'

'We were all at school together. Harris and Harrington – he was Stevens then – were contemporaries. Henry Roland was older. Tersh – Oliver Roland – and I are younger. Henry said there was a scandal of some sort over stamps. Postmarks, that is. Harris was said to have faked them. For Harrington.'

Baxter grunted. 'Some people never change. This place is almost a model forger's workshop. What should we be looking for?'

'Old fake invoices for French furniture. But they'd be written in ink using copperplate script.'

'Not printed?'

'No.'

'Letterheads above the writing?'

'Maybe.'

'Hm. There's some old written documents – wills and things – in a chest. We'll check those. What about printed stuff?'

'A trade card from Chippendale and Rannie. Size about three inches by four. Or a similar label on paper. Several fonts and a sketch of a chair at the top. They may have photocopied an example from a book by Christopher Gilbert on Chippendale.'

'Where would we get an example?'

I thought of Kippax. 'Has your Yorkshireman Powell followed up the Ousedon lead?'

'Yes. No progress. Harrington died of a heart attack.'

'Kippax has two examples he can show you. The label in his bookcase may be genuine but the trade card could be dodgy.'

'I'll get Powell to check. What else?'

'Anything relating to a cabinetmaker called Goderoy and the Fauville cabinet. Old French documents, invoices, that sort of thing.'

I thought: Bert Higgins will love me for this. But they probably took him in brilliantly while he was writing his book.

'Right. Make a note of that, Sergeant. What else?'

Cobbler's tingles, Bill.

'Try a label for John Coxed or Coxed and Woster. Got a swan on it.'

'Oh, I've seen that. On a desk. Wait here.'

Cobbler's tingles; he came back with an old tattered piece of paper carefully laid on his palm. It was printed with a sketchy pillared arch with a swan in it. Under that *John Coxed, at the Swan in St Paul's Church-Yard, London, makes and sells Cabinets, Book Cases, Chests of Drawers, Scrutores, and Looking-Glasses of all sorts...*

'That's it.'

'That's what?'

'A fake trade label ready to be pasted on a piece of furniture of about 1715, or purporting to be, made preferably in burr maple or yew, with inlaid pewter stringing lines.'

'Eh? Where do I find this piece of furniture?'

'Fat Arthur probably made it. Harris just provided the label. I imagine it's somewhere in America by now. That will just be a proof label, for practice. You'll need to check Arthur Brigley's books.'

Baxter suddenly looked tired. 'I can see this is going to be a long job. Thanks; we'll call you when we need you.'

'My pleasure.'

Walters walked me back through the uniformed sentinels to my car. On the way, I said, 'Mrs Harrington was on the Continent when Justin was found, wasn't she?'

'That's what the York boys say, yes. Somewhere in Brittany. Or Normandy. I forget which. I'm not on the York bit.'

I started unlocking the car. He stared at me curiously.

'Why do you ask?'

'No reason,' I said.

I drove home rather slowly. I didn't call Ellen and I left my mobile off.

I didn't feel well.

Agonising about what Elizabeth had done, and how she had misled me and concealed it, wasn't just a matter of hurt pride. I felt physically ill. After a while I pulled into a lay-by and sat there, wondering whether to get out and risk vomiting onto the grass verge.

Not a good day: delayed reaction setting in.

I had been in love with Elizabeth once. I thought that had been something special. Oh, it was a long while ago, but it was special. Even with Justin bursting about, and searing feelings of guilt, it had been unique for me. But not for her, obviously. She'd sat there and listened after she'd reminded me, in that confidential way that made you feel like someone close, that she'd told me years ago that Justin kept his secrets. That he would never have told her about stealing those two magazines.

What a hoot, she'd said.

She'd probably got them hidden somewhere.

A hoot: there were four men dead now, and one they'd tried to kill. And Justin himself, gone to glory in the seat of his car with Elizabeth, not Celia, looking on, expected in for excitement.

She's not baring much else these days, he'd said, over coffee at the fair.

But she'd gone north with him, or been called to go, once he'd set up his deal with Kippax and was nearly frantic with excitement about the big bookcase being genuine, the climax of so much research.

He sent for her, not Celia.

The image came to me of Elizabeth pushing the pram down Vallance Road in the early morning light all those years ago, the brisk excited stamp of her feet, the hunt sending the electric shivers of anticipation through her. Do people change? The cool matron of St George's Hill hadn't. All it took was the thrilling call, *come and see what I've got*, and she was off. He must have intended to take her to Leeds the following day to see Kippax's haul. But first the celebration nearby. Then the consummation on the spot.

But *she's not baring much else these days*? Was the Ousedon tryst to be the reaffirmation of his possession, the means of re-entry to his conjugal delights after all those other dalliances? And had she intended to cooperate with that?

When did she decide her chance had come? When she got the call and he asked her to join him? Or on the journey up north, cool reflection taking over?

I've brought your pills?

Or was it during that curry dinner in Wetherby, he flushed and in full spate, she laughing and keeping him going, thinking, all the time, I'm not living with this any more, I haven't been given the chance until now and it may be a long time before there's another one? Waiting for the moment he'd gone to the loo to slip an extra dose into his lager?

She would have had her passport with her in pre-meditation? Or gone back to Weybridge in the night, collected it and headed for Dover? Her crossing time could easily be checked. But the police weren't suspicious. Why should they be? They'd had to locate her in Normandy or Brittany, being tactful about the cause of death.

You can make a booking for a ferry crossing early, miss that sailing, and go on a later one. There'd have to be a detailed investigation to check on all that sort of thing. Given Justin's reputation it was no wonder the police were letting tact overcome suspicion. The DPS would laugh at the idea of preparing a case on my wild speculations.

Not surprising that there was no forensic evidence of Celia in the car. There wasn't enough evidence to bring a prosecution against anyone. Only Steve knew where they'd eaten their curry – the police would naturally think of York first – and the Indian restaurant staff in Wetherby hadn't come forward. They probably didn't know who their guests were anyway. How many Indian waiters watched *How Old Is It*? Or wanted to draw the police into their premises?

The look on Ellen's face told me of her shock, too. That was another blow, something hard to be absorbed, a tea at Fortnum's full of deception. Clichés about tangled webs to be avoided; sophisticated attitudes to adulteries could not paper over the shock of death.

I must get to Ellen soon.

After a while I found that the roadside with its bedraggled green grass and scraps of plastic had come back into focus. My vision cleared. Cars and lorries were speeding past, buffeting the air. I eased out into the road and drove carefully home.

In the car parking space outside the shop, the dark green Bentley Mulsanne was waiting, chauffeur at the wheel, banker in the back.

Chapter Thirty-Seven

'I couldn't raise you on your mobile,' Tony Fitzsimmonds was looking round my kitchen as he spoke, taking in the print of the brainless moorhen by Detmold, the figures of Bólido and Fúlmine from *Patoruzú*, a bit of Leeds pottery, odd glasses and other bric-a-brac, 'but I thought I'd drop by in hopes you'd turn up.'

'Lucky, then,' I said.

The chauffeur was outside, in the car. There was no sign of Macallister.

'I somehow knew that if I waited, you'd turn up. I don't know why. And you did.'

'Irish intuition.'

He smiled thinly and didn't respond. I handed him a glass with a big shot of Bushmills whiskey in it, having offered him Irish then remembered that this was a Northern Ireland distillery, and thought what the hell, I need it more than he does. He put a small dose of mineral water in his, held up his glass and said, 'Absent friends.'

'Absent friends,' I echoed, and downed mine neat.

He raised his eyebrows. 'Bad day?'

'Very bad. I've been to Wokingham, at police behest, to look at the place where a man called Harris, paper forger, was shot dead two weeks ago. Not nice. He was good at eighteenth-century cabinetmakers' trade labels, amongst other things like false copperplate invoices. For French furniture, like the chairs your friend O'Hanlon took such objection to. He was another school friend of Justin Harrington's, too.'

I poured myself another shot of Bushmills and waved the bottle at him interrogatively. He shook his head.

'I came to tell you,' he said, speaking rather deliberately, 'that Rory O'Hanlon was arrested on his arrival back in New York yesterday. The FBI were waiting for him at the airport.'

'What? What for?'

'Financial irregularities of a major order, I understand.'

'Not murder?'

Fitzsimmonds shook his head. 'No. The charges are financial. Nonetheless, they carry severe prison sentences if he is found guilty. Long sentences. It seems there are grave criminal offences involved. The Yanks go for white-collar crime prosecutions in a big way.'

'Good heavens. I still think he was behind all these deaths except Justin's.'

'The investigations will take a long time and other revelations may come to light. They will, of course, take precedence over anything our police want to arrest him for.'

'Why have you come to tell me this?'

'Can we sit down?'

'Of course. Forgive me: bring your drink into the sitting room.'

We left the kitchen and went into the sitting room. There was still an obvious gap where the Eastlake-Blomfield cabinet had stood but he didn't comment and I wasn't going to explain. We sat down.

'You're familiar with the case of the Enron or NatWest Three?' he asked.

'Bermingham, Mulgrew and Darby? It's in all the papers, yes.'

'The Yanks are misusing that treaty to extradite anyone remotely involved in fraud. Without reciprocity. If my company had investment funds from O'Hanlon I'd be fending off the FBI myself, too, right now. Even though I'm Irish, Leggatt's is subject to UK law and I'm its CEO. But our police have no priority in the US courts, even if the charge is more serious.'

'I understand.'

'O'Hanlon was going to invest Stargaze funds heavily in our art fund. Prior to other investments. Jim Macallister was keen on the idea, too. Thanks to your intervention the other day, O'Hanlon cried off pretty sharply. He was very abusive. Jim was very miffed with you over that meeting, I can tell you. He took deep exception to your man Yelland.'

'Spikey – Lionel – meant well.'

'Doubtless. The manner of it was unfortunate, though.'

'O'Hanlon is a sinister figure.'

'Yes, I agree. I found I was a bit put off by his attitude over the stud business in Wicklow recently.'

'I read about that.'

'He showed a ruthless streak.' Fitzsimmonds smiled. 'I know, we investment bankers are all tarred with that brush, but O'Hanlon went very tough about it. Then he suddenly became all charming and showed great interest in the art fund.'

'His own efforts in that direction had become kind of a *fracaso*.'

'Indeed. If Justin Harrington had still been involved, I don't think his interest would have been with us, but Justin was gone. O'Hanlon had a remarkable amount of cash in his coffers. He thought the Chippendale thing was great. Liked the investment, the publicity we'd arranged, the works.'

'Then I turned up.'

'Then you turned up. And turned him off. Right off, at any price.'

'You were keen.'

'We were. I'd heard rumours about O'Hanlon but every check we made came back positive. Good ratings all over. And all the time the FBI were closing in. It would have been a major disaster for us.' He looked straight at me. 'You saved us from that.'

'By accident and obstinacy, thanks to a book Lionel found. I have to tell you I thought you were using Professor Patrick Gardene as a rubber stamp.'

'No, not me. That man's a bloody fool. Jim, who introduced him, was really upset. He's still sore.' He paused, seeming to think with the same deliberation before he spoke. 'I'm aware that in my excitement to get the Fund launched with a spectacular acquisition I implied that I didn't want you to dig any deeper. I owe you an unreserved apology for putting that pressure on you at the time.'

Pressure, I thought, pressure? It seemed more like a threat to me.

'No problem,' I said. 'No offence taken.'

'I regret my misjudgement. I thought you should know that we've shelved the art investment fund.'

'What about Kippax?'

'He turned down our much reduced offer. Says he's going to auction.'

'I'm not surprised. He knew all along. He and Justin must have had an agreement.'

'The bastards.' He finished his drink and looked into the empty glass. 'Can I take up your offer of a refresher?'

'Of course.'

I took his glass, went to the kitchen and refilled us both. He took a swallow and looked at me reflectively.

'Justin really was a crook, wasn't he?'

'More or less.'

'I thought so. An attractive crook, but a crook.'

'That why you asked me in?'

'You knew him. But I heard you didn't get on with him. I thought you wouldn't join in any scam he had going.'

'Very accurate.'

'It was personal, was it? The animosity, I mean.'

'Mostly. Did you get all this from Celia at the same book launch you mentioned? Or later?'

He smiled wryly. 'Later.'

'I see.' I had to pause to think about that, and my misjudgement of Celia, for a moment. 'There was a book deal he reneged on, too. I don't think badly of him, though. Life won't be the same without him.'

'To have friends one need only be good-natured; but when a man has no enemy left there must be something mean about him.'

'That sounds like Wilde.'

'Oscar himself. Justin was fond of quoting him. The thing that gets me is that he ran a TV programme that looked askance at antiques, ever the insightful journalist, whilst all the time he was deep in deception himself.'

'He got so close to the pit, he fell in.'

'Something like that. But his presentation was so convincing.'

'A mask tells us more than a face? That's Oscar too.'

He grinned. 'Bravo. So it is.' He downed his drink and stood up. 'I must go. The Art Investment Fund is shelved for the moment – there are going to be too many of them for honesty or predictable profit – but I'd like to think I can call on you again some time when the position is clearer?'

'Yes, you can.'

He held out his hand. 'Thank you, Bill. I'm very grateful. You've got a credit balance at Leggatt's. Call on it any time you need it.'

The shop doorbell rang and Spikey came stamping in like a man on hot bricks. He checked, and stood in the sitting room door staring at us.

Fitzsimmonds smiled a knowing smile. 'Enter the cavalry,' he said, 'late as usual. See you, Bill. Take care, now.'

'See you,' I answered. 'You too.'

He left and Spikey put on a perplexed expression. 'I saw the Bentley outside and I thought Christ, I thought—'

'Bless you, Lionel. I know what you thought. But I'm OK. They don't shoot you from Bentleys. Come and have a drink and I'll tell you all about supping with the Devil.'

The expression went curious. 'Are you a bit drunk?'

'Not yet. But with any luck I soon will be.'

Chapter Thirty-Eight

After Spikey left I sat down in an armchair in the sitting room and pondered for a bit. The idea occurred to me of going upstairs to the back bedroom and opening up the trunk full of photographs in some sort of atavistic reprise. The images drifted across my mind in a way that made it unnecessary to look at the originals, though. There we would all be, frozen for ever in time, in that bleak School House garden, paraded in rows. Henry Oliver, Baz Stevens and Harris were gone. Tertius, who would now be immured in mushroom darkness rather than squished books, or rather books with bread and margarine squashed in them, would still be squinting at the camera. My father would still be standing by the cactus, clad in an uncharacteristic poncho, and my mother on the promenade at Pocitos. My friends would still be lounging nonchalantly in front of the British School. Mixed images of married life and others waited for some sort of coherence to be imposed. What was the point?

Yesterday's gone.

Unwilling to induce the detachment that disconcerts me, the sense of thinking about myself in the third person, I stayed where I was. The gap where the Eastlake-Blomfield cabinet had stood reminded me that I must soon get going again, looking for replacements of suitable quality for Chuck Vance. Then there was Steve to set up properly, once his college course ended. He and Ellen and I would always know about Elizabeth, or think that we knew, speculation riding over unestablished fact.

Better forgotten.

I must have dropped off for a bit because the next thing was that I heard the shop doorbell ring. I didn't move. The time was too late for customers. After a pause, steps sounded through the hallway and Ellen came into the room. She was neat and spruce. I noticed her small feet again, and how she still swelled in the right places.

'Steve has gone to a party,' she said.

Her eye went from me to the empty glass beside me.

'You need some coffee,' she said.

She went into my kitchen and bustled about. For the first time, I felt content to sit and let her do it. After a while she came back with two mugs of strong coffee and I drank a good deal of mine before speaking.

'Harris had a real shedful of forgery kit,' I said, after a while. 'Poor bugger.'

Then I told her about Fitzsimmonds, and O'Hanlon, and Spikey's arrival. And how Detective Sergeant Walters and his boss would probably never get to O'Hanlon in America or get the bikers to cough up the truth. Everything was more or less over.

'Life leaves a lot of loose ends,' she said.

'Who said that?'

'Me.'

'Elizabeth will be one of them.'

'Only in one sense, I hope,' she said.

And looked at me.

'Only in one sense, that is what she really did up there at Ousedon.'

'I shan't be meeting her again. Nor Celia.'

'That sounds pretty final.'

'It is.'

'Me too, then.'

She got up, went outside and came back carrying a small, soft, canvas holdall, printed with a sort of carpet pattern.

'What's that?' I asked.

'My overnight bag,' she said.